JAYNE FAITH

Stone Blood Legacy

First published by Andara Publishers 2020

First edition

ISBN: 978-1-952156-03-8

Editing by Mary Novak
Proofreading by Tia Silverthorne Bach of Indie Books Gone Wild
Cover art by Deranged Doctor Design

This book was professionally typeset on Reedsy.
Find out more at reedsy.com

Contents

Chapter 1

WITH ONE FIST tucked against the small of my back and the other wrapped around the grip of a practice foil, I took the classic fencing stance.

Facing me from several feet away, my twin sister Nicole imitated my posture. She'd only been in Faerie for a couple of weeks, and it wasn't long before then I'd learned of her existence. I was pretty sure she'd asked me to teach her some swordplay more out of boredom than actual interest.

We stepped through some light drills. Her sword work was average for a beginner, but her years as a professional ballerina gave her impressive agility on her feet.

"Good!" I called to her, my voice automatically taking on the gruff edge my instructors had always used with me. "Hold your body angle. Don't give me any more of a target than necessary."

As a changeling newly introduced to her Fae roots, Nicole was bound to stay here for a period known as the homecoming before she would be allowed to choose whether to stay or renounce Faerie forever and return to her life on the other side of the hedge. Usually that was how it worked. There was a good chance Nicole wasn't going to have quite the same freedom in her options.

She managed to block one of my attacks with a flick of her wrist.

I nodded. "Now summon your stone armor."

I squinted at her in the sunlight of perpetual Faerie summer. Ever since Oberon had taken power as the High King of Faerie, the Fae had enjoyed centuries of bright sunshine by day and pleasant starlit nights. It was hard to imagine any other season in Faerie.

Nicole's movements faltered as she tried to keep up the swordplay while calling upon her newfound magic. Sweat beaded on her forehead, and her eyes narrowed in concentration. Then she lowered her foil and let out a frustrated groan.

"I can't do it," she said. "It takes all my focus to form the armor. I can't even walk and form armor at the same time, let alone swing a sword."

I hid a smile and said a few encouraging words. She cared about trying to do it right, and she got frustrated when she couldn't—yet another sign that she was tipping toward making Faerie her permanent home. Personally, I wouldn't blame her if she wanted to leave—it would have been hypocritical of me because I was working toward reestablishing my own independence away from Faerie. And at twenty-seven, Nicole was one of the oldest changelings ever to be brought home to Faerie, which made the transition much more difficult. But if she decided to stay, I knew it would win me favor with Marisol, the monarch of the New Gargoyle Stone Order, to which I was sworn.

Until recently, I'd managed to mostly steer clear of Order business and Faerie politics in general, but that had all changed when my father, Oliver, had asked me to save Nicole from the Duergar King Periclase.

By that act of taking Nicole out from under Periclase's nose, I'd unwittingly set off a shit storm of events that had ended with me being knighted as the Stone Order's champion and then fighting Periclase's brother Darion. I'd refrained from killing him, but only barely.

My victory had been enough to get the Duergar off our backs momentarily, but the peace didn't last long. And in the time I'd been wrapped up in Fae business, I'd lost my apartment and gotten suspended from my job at the Mercenary Guild in the Earthly realm. I had no choice but to move into the stone fortress, the stronghold of the New Gargoyle Stone Order, which pleased Marisol to no end. She'd been wanting to pull me back in for years.

"I think we've done enough for today," I said to Nicole. "Let's pick it up again tomorrow."

She went to the side of the training field to sit on the grass and do some of her ballet dancer stretches.

As I went to turn in my foil and retrieve Mort, my magic-imbued broadsword, I noticed Marisol's son Maxen strolling over to chat with Nicole. She smiled up at him, and his sunny laughter floated across the training field. It wasn't the first time I'd seen them bat eyelashes at each other. Maxen wasn't particularly manipulative by nature, but I couldn't help wondering if his interest was genuine or if Marisol had sent him to help charm Nicole into staying.

In any case, it wasn't really my business. And besides, I wasn't speaking to Maxen much these days. We'd exchanged some harsh words after my battle with Darion.

Sharp shouts drew my attention away from Maxen and Nicole. I looked around but didn't see anything amiss. Probably just some students getting rowdy in one of the training yards that was out of sight. Still, I scanned for threats. After the recent servitor attacks, I was always wary of the sudden appearance of intruders.

Just as I'd decided my paranoia might be on overdrive, a young man stumbled out with a bloodied face and panicked eyes. I drew Mort and ran toward him, tossing my scabbard aside as I went.

I slowed long enough to shout a question. "What is it?"

"Intruders," he said. "A bunch of them appeared out of nowhere."

Damn. Only servitors could materialize out of thin air.

"Tell Maxen," I said over my shoulder. "Get everyone out here armed."

I darted into the hallway, following the shouts and forming full stone armor as I went. Magic licked my skin, quickly replaced by nearly impenetrable plates from my neck to my ankles. Rock armor had the inexplicable quality of rigidity that still allowed body movement. It was one of the things that made New Gargoyles like me some of the best fighters in Faerie.

I emerged in an open area where several hallways met. The scene was chaos. New Gargs were battling stocky enemies dressed in identical dark green clothing. The shirts had hoods, and the attackers wore masks that covered everything but their eyes.

I jumped into the fray, pushing power into Mort as I swung at the nearest attacker, whose back was turned to me. My broadsword lit with violet flames of magic that sliced like razors if they licked flesh.

The blade sliced through the enemy's torso as if it were water, and the figure dissolved into a puff of mist that smelled of copper and ashes.

Definitely servitors. They were beings that seemed real but were conjured by their master to carry out specific tasks. We'd had a similar attack a few weeks ago. Those servitors had been smaller in stature and came wielding throwing knives. These ones carried heavy bludgeons.

One of them charged me, swinging his short-handled bludgeon around on a cord until it blurred with motion.

I sidestepped and ducked under the bludgeon, letting his momentum carry him past me. Before he could recover, I pivoted, gripped Mort with both hands, and stabbed down into his shoulder. He dissolved into mist.

The creatures were incredibly strong to be able to wield such a weapon that way, despite how they dissipated to nothing when touched by Mort.

I cut through three more servitors as I pushed into the center of the room. Maxen had joined the fight not far away. The attackers' numbers were dwindling, but not without taking some casualties on our side. The servitors weren't real, but the injuries they inflicted sure as hell were. Out of the corners of my eyes I saw the still forms of three New Gargs on the floor. A wide pool of dark blood had already formed around the head of one.

My father, Oliver, was battling at the mouth of one of the hallways. More fighters from the New Garg battle ranks poured in, and within a few minutes, all the servitors were gone.

Oliver and I locked eyes across the room for a second, our chests heaving. We'd fought off the first servitor attack on the fortress. That one hadn't claimed any casualties. In fact, we'd mowed through the intruders before anyone else had even noticed they were there.

I went to the nearest injured, a young man I didn't recognize who'd fallen and lay face-down. One ear and the scalp above it were torn and bleeding, but his skull looked intact. I touched the side of his neck and found a pulse.

"Thank Oberon," I muttered, grasping his shoulder to gingerly turn him over.

His eyes opened as he rolled to his back. He looked dazed, but at least he was alive. A healer rushed in with a first-aid kit and fell to her knees next to him, nudging me out of the way.

I rose, looking over at the other fallen. Oliver had knelt next to the one with the most blood, who was also face-down. My father pulled off his shirt and placed it over the person's head and upper body. When Oliver's eyes lifted and caught mine, his mouth pressed into a grim line, and he gave a slight shake of his head.

I pounded the side of my fist into my thigh. "*Damn* it."

I looked across the room at a woman I'd feared dead, but others were helping her up. I let out a breath of gratitude.

But a death, and right here on fortress ground.

Oliver rose and we met in the middle of the room. Once I was really seeing him, I realized one of his shoulders was bleeding and a nasty bruise had already started to form on one of his forearms. He didn't seem to notice. The attacks seemed to be getting more violent in terms of brute force, but at least the bludgeons hadn't been poisoned.

"Who was it?" I asked.

He sighed. "I don't recall his name. First year battle ranks, by the patch on his shirt."

Maxen and one of the legion captains were organizing people to help the injured—there were other injuries aside from the ones who'd ended up unconscious on the floor—and cordoning off the area. Oliver got called away, and Maxen beckoned me over.

"You okay?" he asked stiffly. We'd barely exchanged two words since he'd figuratively backed me into a corner, all but blackmailing me into staying at the fortress after I defeated Darion in the arena. It was a manipulative move that seemed uncharacteristic. But perhaps his mother's ways were finally rubbing off.

I focused my attention on my broadsword rather than looking at him. "Yeah. You?"

He shrugged irritably. "I barely caught the tail end of the fight."

We both surveyed the wreckage of the room. There was a good amount of blood, and everything that was breakable lay in pieces—furniture, and what had been a vase but was now scattered shards of crystal.

"What can I do?" I asked. I skirted a sidelong look over at him.

"Help us figure out who the hell is sending them," he said, his face pale and his eyes haunted.

Normally, Maxen was atypically warm and easy-going for a New Gargoyle. But at that moment, he looked dazed and angry, and I caught the briefest flicker of fear in his sapphire-blue eyes.

My stomach hollowed as I recalled a piece of information. Jasper Glasgow, illegitimate son of the Duergar King Periclase, had told me something about the servitors. He'd said the threat was bigger than just the obvious violence or supposed assassination attempts. He'd said

6

the servitors were breaching Fae kingdoms in a systematic way that allowed them to come back again with larger creatures that wielded more force, which certainly appeared to be the case here. The same fear I saw on Maxen's face had shone in Jasper's gold eyes when he'd spoken of it. At the time, his words hadn't made much sense, and I'd been trying to escape capture, so I hadn't a chance to follow up. But I could no longer brush off what he'd said.

"I may know something," I said to Maxen.

His brows twitched upward in curiosity. "Then you need to tell Marisol," he said.

He said a few words to the captain in charge, and then we walked silently side-by-side away from the scene of the fight. The hallways of the stone fortress were abuzz, and pairs of men and women from the battle ranks jogged by every which way. The fortress was going into full lockdown, which meant Marisol was being kept in a safe place away from where the attacks had taken place.

It took us a little time to get past the layers of security. When we finally did, we were escorted into a section of Marisol's quarters that I'd never seen before. It was a windowless, spare set of small adjoining rooms that had a vault-like feel to them. They were set up with all the basic necessities—bed, kitchenette, bathroom—like a sort of bunker.

The leader of the Stone Order was regal and poised as always, but she looked pale, her eyes strained.

"What is this information you have?" she asked me.

I glanced at the four guards who stood in the room with us, quiet and tense, with their hands resting lightly on the swords at their hips. Two of Marisol's assistants also stood nearby. Then I looked pointedly at Maxen.

"This is sensitive," he said to his mother.

She waved her minions over to the door where we'd come in—the only door that I could see—and then the three of us moved near the fireplace.

"The Duergar may know why the servitors have been sent," I said. "Jasper Glasgow, bastard son of Periclase, told me that with each breach the servitors pick up magic that not only allows them to get back in but also gives them more power. But that wasn't the most disturbing thing he told me. He said the Tuatha De Danann have returned, and they're riding with the Dullahan. Which, of course, has to be wrong, but I thought it worth mentioning." I shook my head and snorted a humorless laugh.

Her face became pinched and gave when I mentioned the Tuatha De Danann. The Tuatha were the gods who'd created Faerie eons ago, but they'd disappeared many generations before I was born, and many considered them to have died out. But she didn't protest. She didn't even call me crazy when I spoke of the Dullahan, the Bone Warriors who, as the myths said, would detach their own heads and carry them under their arms as they rode into battle, creating a horror spectacle to rattle their enemies and even hurling their heads as weapons. At least, I always thought the stories of the Bone Warriors were just myths. But as I watched the way Marisol absorbed the information I gave her, my stomach twisted.

"And how did this Jasper Glasgow learn this information?" she asked, her voice heavy.

"He didn't really say," I said.

"Do you think he would speak to you again, if you were able to contact him?"

Jasper had wanted my help. He'd seemed convinced that the two of us could somehow avert a war between the Duergar and the Stone Order. I seriously doubted that and had said so, but his plea meant he probably would be open to a conversation.

"I believe so," I said.

She went to the door and called in one of her assistants.

8

"We must send a message to Jasper Glasgow at the Duergar palace," she said. "Tell him Petra Maguire wishes to speak with him."

Remembering the intensity in Jasper's golden eyes, I wondered how he'd react to the message. And how he'd respond when he discovered that the matriarch of the Stone Order didn't think his claims were crazy at all.

With a slightly queasy feeling in my stomach, I realized I was most likely getting myself even more embroiled in Faerie politics. Possibly starting down a path of doing exactly what Jasper desired—helping to form a bridge between our two realms, to try to unite us to face a larger, more dangerous enemy. One that I'd thought only existed in legend.

Chapter 2

THERE WERE NO wires that connected the Fae kingdoms and territories. Distances and locations in Faerie didn't operate in a way that made it possible to string phone lines through this side of the hedge. Most palaces and strongholds, like our fortress, had been modernized with local networks and devices that could be plugged into them, but without things like Wi-Fi, cell towers, or the ability to hardwire phone lines over distances, we had to resort to archaic methods of long-distance communication.

That meant relying heavily on messenger ravens. Not Great Ravens, like the giant bird I'd ridden to escape the Duergar palace for the second time in as many days, but regular-sized ravens similar to the ones that lived on the Earthly side of the hedge. They were incredibly intelligent birds who had a system of doorways of their own, portals they used to pass from one realm into the next, which made them very swift messengers.

If relations had been better between the New Gargoyles and the Duergar, I was sure Marisol would have sent me in person. She might have even tried to summon Jasper to the fortress. But in the past couple of weeks, I'd stolen Nicole from the Duergar, put King Periclase's bastard daughter Bryna in the fortress jail, and nearly killed the Duergar king's brother. If I dared step foot in the Duergar realm, I likely would have been met with a bouquet of swords pointed at my throat. If anything, there were probably Most Wanted posters with my face plastered all over Periclase's kingdom.

Marisol's assistant dispatched a raven immediately with a message to Jasper, and I expected the Stone Order's monarch to dismiss me while we waited for a response. But she seemed to have other ideas. She sent another assistant over to the kitchenette to prepare tea and then gestured at me and Maxen to sit down with her by the fireplace.

I stifled an impatient sigh. Tea with Marisol. Oh, goody. Well, I might as well try to get something useful out of it.

"My mention of the Dullahan didn't seem to faze you much," I said quietly to Marisol. "Neither did the return of the Tuatha. I'd like to know why."

Her eyes unfocused for a long moment.

"I've heard whispers," she said, matching my low tone.

She waited for her assistant to serve tea and then move away before continuing. I held my crystal saucer and teacup with my still-bloody hands. Marisol, to her credit, didn't bat an eye at the dried blood on my skin and clothes, not to mention the fact that I probably smelled absolutely delightful after working out in the training yard with Nicole and then battling the servitors.

I glanced at Maxen. He hadn't seemed too shocked at what I'd said, either.

"I know the Tuatha are real, or once were, anyway. But I thought the Dullahan were just scary characters in stories," I said.

"When something has been gone long enough, it fades into legend," Marisol said. "But that doesn't mean the legends didn't begin as truth."

A shiver passed over my scalp and down my spine.

"But why would the Tuatha come back only to sic the Bone Warriors on us?" I asked. "What the hell did we do?"

She shook her head. "Oberon only knows." Over the rim of her tea cup, she let out a short, humorless laugh. "Actually, Oberon himself may not even know."

Oberon was one of the Old Ones, a Fae so long in the world many considered him god-like. But he wasn't a god. The Tuatha were actual gods, preceding even Oberon, Titania, and the other Old Ones. The Tuatha De Danann had left the Old Ones in charge of Faerie, so the tales went.

"Even if Oberon did know, it wouldn't do us much good," Maxen muttered with uncharacteristic irritability.

He was right. Oberon had disappeared before my battle with Darion. It was pretty clear from Titania's foul temper that they'd had one of their epic quarrels. If anyone knew where Oberon had gone, they weren't talking.

"Could there be a connection between the servitors and this rumor about the Tuatha and the Dullahan?" I asked.

I sipped from the cup for the sake of appearance. The tea was surprisingly good—full-bodied and very earthy. Probably a cup of the expensive mushroom stuff Marisol loved.

"I don't know," Marisol said. She stared at a point on the floor, her gaze again losing focus for a moment.

My hand paused, my cup halfway between my lips and the saucer. I didn't like that, Marisol not knowing. The stone monarch always had answers, even if she didn't share the exact details. I flicked a glance at Maxen. He was watching his mother, too, and his face reflected my own unease.

"What are we going to do?" he asked, his voice low.

She inhaled through her nose. Her gaze sharpened and swung first to him and then to me.

"We'll see what this Jasper Glasgow has to say," she said. "And I'll reach out to my contacts in other kingdoms to see what they know."

She stood, went to one of her assistants, and began dictating instructions for more ravens to carry messages.

I looked around the room, suddenly feeling just how small the Stone Order was. My people, the New Gargoyles, had carved out only this space in the stone fortress for our territory. We were a new Fae race and hadn't yet had the time or wealth to establish ourselves deeply in Faerie. Or rather, Marisol hadn't yet done so—saying "we" was presumptuous of me, seeing as how I usually tried to give Stone Order affairs and Faerie politics a very wide berth. That had been easy when I'd had an apartment and a job on the Earthly side of the hedge. Since I was back inside the fortress, not so much.

"You've got to ply Jasper for more," Maxen said to me. "He likes you, so just be friendly with him. But don't make any promises."

I slanted my gaze away from him and lifted my cup to my mouth.

"Petra?" Maxen said, drawing out my name in a warning tone.

I looked across the room, as if the conversation between Marisol and her assistant were so fascinating it absorbed all of my attention.

"*Petra.*"

"What?" I asked innocently.

"Did you already enter into a binding agreement with him?" he asked, and it almost felt like old times between us. Our mutual freeze-out seemed to have lifted, at least temporarily.

"I didn't really have a choice. He helped me escape the Duergar palace. Twice, actually. I was there to rescue one of our changelings, remember?" I asked pointedly, trying not to sound defensive but not really succeeding. "I was doing a service to the Stone Order. At the cost of my Guild job, I might add."

"Yeah, the first time," Maxen said. "The second time was all your doing."

Okay, so maybe things weren't warming up all that much between me and Maxen.

Suddenly, he snorted a laugh that he quickly tried to muffle against the back of his hand.

"*What?*" I said again.

"Only you would end up in a binding agreement with the Duergar king's bastard son. The very king who was calling for your head." He peered at me. His words were probably meant to be teasing, but his expression and tone weren't particularly lighthearted. "He obviously kept the agreement from his father. Jasper really must have an interest you. More so than I realized."

I lifted my gaze upward, annoyed at what he was implying. "Let's just drink our damn tea," I muttered.

I didn't like the look on his face. It wasn't jealousy, but he certainly seemed to be thinking hard about something. A few seconds of awkward silence passed, which only heightened my irritation.

"You seem to have an interest in Nicole," I said evenly, purposely repeating his phrasing.

He blinked rapidly a couple of times. Ha, I'd caught him off guard.

"What do you mean?" he asked, his tone mild.

"You're making a point to interact with her. Is that really you, or did the Queen Mother order you to make nice?"

His face clouded, and he clinked his cup a little harder than necessary onto his saucer. He seemed on the verge of a response when Marisol rejoined us.

She looked at me. "You're dismissed. The concierge has a message for you. Not from Jasper Glasgow yet, obviously, but you might as well see who it's from."

I inclined my head, and ignoring Maxen completely, I set down my cup and saucer on the tea service tray and left Marisol's quarters.

It was a relief to get out of the small, windowless rooms—and away from Maxen's scowl. He and I had known each other since we were kids, and over the years he'd more than hinted about his interest in a deeper relationship. But we both knew we weren't on the same path. He was destined to bend to Marisol's will in a strategic arranged marriage.

And he knew I had zero interest in such a future, even if she would have approved me as a match. Which she wouldn't. I'd never taken his overtures too seriously, and we'd managed to remain friendly. Until recently.

The flurry of activity throughout the fortress had calmed somewhat, but men and women from the battle ranks seemed to be stationed at every turn, and pairs of them patrolled the corridors.

When I reached the marbled lobby area, I turned to a window off to the side, the sort you'd stand at to buy movie tickets on the Earthly side of the hedge. The concierge desk was a hub of information and assistance in the fortress. It was also the place where messages from outside the fortress were held for distribution. The man behind the counter went to a row of small boxes at the back wall, retrieved an envelope, and passed it to me through the window.

I turned it over, and noticing it was sealed—both in the regular sense and with a wax seal and an additional application of a wisp of magic—but not with Fae magic. This message was sealed with human magic from the Earthly realm.

Magic seals allowed a message to be opened only by the intended recipient. I slipped my finger under the chunk of wax and popped it open.

Inside was a note written in an unfamiliar scrawl. The first line caught my interest immediately.

Today's your lucky day. You've been assigned to help a human merc track down her mark in Faerie, and you'll earn half the bounty. More important, this will be your only route to reinstatement with the Guild. Contact Gretchen within the hour. Don't screw this up.

There was a phone number written at the bottom, and the note was signed by my Mercenary Guild boss, Gus.

I perked up at the possibility of earning some side cash. I was saving for when Marisol released me from my obligations to the Stone Order so I could reestablish myself on the other side of the hedge. Cash flow problems had been part of what landed me in the fortress, but I planned to get back to my life as a vamp hunter for the Mercenary Guild as soon as I could.

I wracked my brain for a moment, trying to put a face to the name Gretchen. Then I remembered—she was a Guild merc about my age or a little older. Decent level of magical ability.

This happened sometimes—a mark would find a way to take refuge in Faerie, and if the merc assigned to the bounty wasn't Fae, the merc was shit out of luck on the assignment. Or, the merc could find a Fae to help.

The cash would be good, but I wasn't sure how the hell I'd fit in a merc job around everything going on in Faerie. I was at Marisol's mercy, especially since I lived in the fortress full-time.

I went to the main fortress entrance, intending to go out and cross over to the other side of the hedge where my cell phone would work, but a couple of guards blocked my way.

I recognized both of them from my graduating class.

"Guys, come on," I said. "I just need to make a call. It'll only take a minute."

"We're on lockdown, Petra," one of them, a muscular woman, said. "You know what that means."

I was just about to try to pull rank as the Stone Fortress Champion, which I was still, if anybody cared to remember, when someone called my name.

I turned to see Emmaline, a young Order page, hurrying toward me. She'd served as my attendant during a trip into the Duergar realm and my squire when I battled Darion. Still a student in her last year of school and battle training, she had dreams of buying a sword like Mort and working for the Guild. In some ways she was a younger version of me, but infinitely more refined than I'd been at her age. Or than I was now,

16

for that matter.

Her lavender eyes were wide. "Lady Lothlorien sent me. She said to tell you that a response has arrived and asked you to come right away."

I cast a look at the fortress exit and tried not to curse. I was under a deadline to get in touch with Gretchen. Once again, Marisol was thwarting my efforts at independence, and she probably didn't even know she was doing it.

I sighed and tucked Gus's note into the pouch on my scabbard that held my phone, which was just a useless hunk of plastic and metal on the Faerie side of the hedge.

"Wouldn't want to keep her waiting. Let's go see what the Duergar bastard son has to say," I said and gestured for Emmaline to lead the way.

Chapter 3

EMMALINE PEERED AT me with an expression similar to Maxen's earlier when Jasper's name had come up.

"The message is from Jasper Glasgow?" she asked, dropping her voice to a whisper at the end.

I glanced around, belatedly wondering if anyone had heard me mention the Duergar man. I really needed to take Emmaline's example and use greater discretion while I was in the fortress.

"Yeah, but you don't repeat that to anyone, understand? Not a soul," I said sternly. I waited for her to nod emphatically. "Good."

I waited until we'd turned a few corners before asking, "Why did you look at me that way?"

"What way?" Her gaze shifted away.

"Like you were about to see a preview for the next episode of your favorite soap opera."

Her lips twitched, but she managed to hold back a smile. "I apologize, Lady Maguire—I mean, Petra. I didn't mean to infer anything."

"Like hell you didn't," I groused.

She pulled her lips in and bit down on them, clearly trying to restrain a smile or snicker.

This was just grand. Did everyone in Faerie know there was a spark of something between me and Jasper Glasgow?

"The note isn't personal. I contacted him on Marisol's order," I said.

I slid her a side-eye. "Just so you know."

She nodded. "Oh, sure. I understand. Official business."

We'd arrived at Marisol's regular office. Apparently, things had calmed down enough that she'd been freed from her bunker. Emmaline stayed outside while I went into the inner chamber of Marisol's office. As soon as she saw me, she plucked a scroll from her desk and rose.

I unfurled the curled paper, its seal already broken. It had been addressed to Marisol, not to me.

I'll meet with Petra Maguire alone. The Golden Gate doorway at dusk.

I turned it over, for some reason expecting more.

"Short and sweet," I remarked.

"You'll go, of course," she said. "And come directly back here after. If you're not back by ten, I'll take it as a sign you ran into trouble."

Her ordering tone irked me, but I had to force myself not to do a little fist pump at the prospect of getting out of Faerie. I could contact Gretchen about her runaway mark, and maybe, just maybe, it would lead to a nice little addition to my nest egg. If Gus hadn't decided by then that I'd missed the deadline. Well, not much I could do about it. I'd just have to hope he'd let the delay slide.

"Of course, my lady," I said formally, not wanting to give her any reason to change her mind.

She narrowed her eyes at me, and I held what I hoped was a neutral, innocent expression. She gave a slight nod and shifted her attention to a tablet on her desk, and I turned and hightailed it out of her office.

By the time evening came, I was nearly itching with anticipation to be free of the fortress. I could have used an internal fortress doorway to get to the meeting point. Faerie doorways were portals that allowed us to travel great distances in a matter of seconds by stepping into the void of the netherwhere. Instead, I exited through the front and jumped on my vintage Vespa I'd named Vincenzo, eager to feel the freedom of zipping the scooter down Bay Area streets. The evening was overcast, but at least it was dry.

When I stopped to gas up, I dialed the number Gretchen had given me. She answered on the second ring.

"This is Petra Maguire," I said. "Is the job still available?"

There was an exasperated sigh. "Yes. But only because I saved your ass. Gus was ready to give it to someone else after an hour went by and you didn't call. I had to stall him."

"Thanks for that," I said. I decided to go for bravado. "You won't be sorry. I'm the best there is."

She gave a short, lilting laugh. It was more sharpness than amusement. "Your humbleness is overwhelming."

"What's the payout?"

She quoted the price on her mark's head. It was a decent bounty.

"And the Guild is really offering half?" I asked.

"Yep, if you help me apprehend the mark in Faerie. If it turns out she's not on the Faerie side of the hedge, then the deal's off, and I go after her alone and retain the full amount."

"Sounds reasonable," I said. "What's the deadline on the bounty?"

"Midnight two days from now."

I sucked in air through my teeth. "Cutting it a little close, aren't you?"

"It took me a while to figure out where she'd gone," Gretchen said. "You know how that goes."

I was pretty sure that was a reference to my last mark, a vampire named Van Zant. He'd given me quite the runaround in Faerie. And I'd mistakenly turned in a box of ashes to the Guild, believing they were his remains. Not the easiest job I'd ever had, but in the end it had been a live capture and the reward had been substantial.

"Where was she seen last?" I asked.

"Nuh-uh," Gretchen said. "I need our agreement in writing before I tell you who or where."

"Hey, I'm no mark swiper!" I protested. It was horrible form, but there were a few unscrupulous mercs who poached jobs. I'd never been one of them.

"Sorry, but I've been burned before. I'll write up the contract and text it to you. Sign it and send it back to me, and then we'll talk again."

She hung up, and I grumbled at the dead line. Humans and their need for written contracts. In Faerie, we had our fair share of paperwork in the modern era, but when it came to promises, there was no need for paper or signatures. We could magically bind each other to such agreements.

I paid for the gas, started up my scooter and continued on to the Golden Gate doorway. The deepening colors of twilight were giving way to darker shades of dusk. I steered through the Presidio toward Fort Point, where the doorway was located. I'd arrived a bit early, so I steered to a spot on the curb and then went to the edge of the pier. There was some trash scattered around, and the water below didn't smell great, but there was a sweeping view of the San Francisco Bay and the Golden Gate Bridge.

"Great spot to watch sunsets," came a voice behind me, one I recognized immediately as Jasper's.

He'd startled me, but I managed to resist the urge to spin around with Mort flaming in my hand. Instead, I turned casually and then leaned my hip against the concrete partition that helped keep people from sliding down the short rocky cliff to the cold ocean below.

I crossed my arms. "We missed the sunset, so we might as well get down to business," I said.

The last fading light in the sky seemed to intensify the gold in his eyes as he strode closer, matching my casual movement.

"Why so frosty?" he asked, the hint of a smile dancing around his eyes. "You summoned me. And you're indebted to me. You haven't forgotten, have you?"

"You're right." I gave him a wry smile. "And of course I haven't forgotten."

Maxen and Emmaline be damned, I had to admit to myself I was happy to see him again.

"I heard of the servitor attack on the fortress," he said, growing grave. "I'm sorry for your loss."

I inclined my head slightly. "I'll pass your condolences to Lady Lothlorien. It's a tragedy, but we're fortunate it wasn't worse. These servitors were much stronger and deadlier than the knife-tossing ninjas you and I battled."

Jasper and I had fought off a servitor attack while I'd been in the Duergar palace. In retrospect, I wondered if that might have been what prompted him to help me escape later. Perhaps he'd felt he owed me something for helping him defend the palace. No—that was how a human would have taken the situation. Fae were much more stingy and careful with favors. I'd spent so much of the past many years on the Earthly side of the hedge, it had clearly started to skew my thinking.

"Why did you help me escape?" I asked, suddenly realizing how much the question had been gnawing at my mind.

The twinkle in his eyes returned. "Which time?"

I cracked a very small smile. "Either one. Both."

He came to sit on the cement partition I was leaning against, planting himself about an arm's length away from me. The wind shifted, and I caught the faint scent of his soap. His slightly shaggy hair had comb marks in it, and it was darkened a bit, still wet from a recent shower.

"It seemed like the right thing to do," he said.

I snorted. "Are you not loyal to your liege? Your father?" I gave slight emphasis to the last word.

"My father is a king. It doesn't mean he's always right," Jasper said, his faint brogue more apparent as the intensity of his tone increased. "Only a fool would blindly let another man dictate his own set of values.

I judge each situation on its own merits, and I make my own decisions."

I considered that for a couple of seconds. "Does he know you're here?"

"No." Jasper had been looking off to the distance, but he turned his golden gaze on me. His eyes were the brightest thing in the immediate vicinity, almost reflective like a cat's irises. It was hard not to stare at them.

"Why not?"

"Because of what I spoke about before," he said. "I want you to help me smooth things between the Duergar and the Stone Order. We shouldn't be wasting our time or resources fighting with each other."

"You could call in your favor and compel me to do it," I said.

He gave me an imploring look, his mouth pressed into an unhappy line. "What good would that do? I need you to believe in the importance of it, Petra. Compelling you to work with me wouldn't truly achieve what needs to be done."

I squinted at him in the fading light of dusk. "You really believe in the larger danger that's looming?"

"I do."

"I told Maris—uh, Lady Lothlorien—what you told me. She wasn't nearly as surprised as I would have expected."

He tilted his head. "It was her idea to contact me, wasn't it?"

"Yeah." I peered at him. "That disappoints you, doesn't it?"

"Like I said, I want you to be genuinely behind my cause. *You*, Petra. Not the monarch ruling the Stone Order."

It was the second time he'd said my name in the past minute or two. There was a warmth, almost an intimacy in how he pronounced it, despite the fact that I was causing him some amount of frustration. I never would have admitted it out loud, but there was some part of me that wanted to hear him say my name again.

I mentally flicked myself in the head for such an asinine passing thought. Thank Oberon, neither Emmaline nor Maxen would ever know it had passed through my brain. I blinked hard and forced my focus to the matters at hand.

"But why me?" I asked. "Why not go to Maxen, or even Lady Lothlorien herself? Or anyone in the fortress with political pull?" Or anyone who actually gave a shit about inter-realm scuffles and Faerie politics.

"You're the champion of the Stone Order now. You've got plenty of influence."

I wagged my finger at him. "Ah, but I wasn't champion when you first tried to persuade me on this."

He chuckled. "True enough. Still, I'm confident in my choice. I was terribly pleased Uncle Darion didn't kill you in the arena, by the way."

"Gee, thanks," I said with mild sarcasm.

He pushed off the barrier and leaned against it, partially imitating my posture.

"So," he said. "What did the lady of the Stone Order hope you would get from me?"

"She'd like to know how you came about the information you gave me. How you found out the Tuatha are coming with a Dullahan army. And why they're coming, if you happen to know that. I'd like to know, too."

"To the second query, I have to say I don't know, though I sorely wish I did."

"And the first?" My stomach tightened a little in anticipation.

"I can't say," he said. "To do so would betray the confidence of someone very important to me."

Someone more important than his father, I took it. Interesting.

"Can you at least tell me what proof there is?"

"The Great Ravens have seen the Dullahan riding."

That shut me up for a good long moment. The Great Ravens weren't capable of lying. And I knew of Jasper's connection to the legendary birds because the last time I'd escaped from the Duergar realm, Jasper had bailed me out by revealing himself to be a Grand Raven Master by summoning one of the great birds. I'd ridden away on its back as the Duergar guards cursed me from the roof of the palace. Jasper had told me that they wouldn't suspect him of helping me because they didn't know he was a Grand Raven Master.

Not breaking the silence, he pushed away from the barrier and started toward the walking path that meandered near the water. I followed and fell in step beside him, and we kept a strolling pace.

I shook my head. "I still don't understand why the Tuatha would be coming at us with the Bone Warriors. How do we even know they're threatening *us*? They could be coming for some other reason. We're the people of the land of Faerie they abandoned. What the hell did we do to piss them off so badly? Maybe they're coming to fight some other foe we haven't considered."

"They're not," he said shortly, his face turning grim. "The Ravens know. The Tuatha De Danann are sending the Dullahan against us."

"But *why?*"

I felt suddenly affronted by the idea that the Tuatha planned to attack us. Faerie had gone on for generations after they'd faded into the mist of legend. Why were they angry with us? What had we done?

"Only the gods know," Jasper said.

I looked up at him sharply and then turned my gaze to the distance. Up until then, most Fae would have said "only Oberon knows." But if the gods were coming back to Faerie, they'd stand above the Old Ones like Oberon. My insides twisted at the thought.

"It's like the God of the Christian Old Testament returning," I mumbled.

Jasper looked down at me. "That's an apt analogy. The Old Ones who have been ruling us for many generations have left us to our own devices to a great extent. There's plenty of brutality in their roots, but they've treated us as somewhat distant parents. But the Tuatha . . ." he trailed off.

"They're old-school brutal, and they're pissed at us," I supplied, shivering. "What else do you know?"

He ran a hand through his hair. "Not much. I'm trying to find out more."

"The Great Ravens?"

"They're one source of information."

"Who else is delving into this the way you are?" I asked. "What's the actual state of knowledge across Faerie?"

"There are others trying to understand what's coming, but many are in denial." He sighed heavily. "Or they're simply distracted by more immediate issues and aren't ready to try to deal with a threat that seems vague and far-off right now."

"But all of the Faerie rulers know?"

"I believe they've all at least heard murmurs."

"How much time do we have before the Dullahan strike?" I asked.

His boots scuffed to a halt on the walkway. "You believe me?"

I raised a palm. "Say I do. When will it happen?"

"We don't know. But not immediately. According to the Ravens, the Tuatha are still gathering themselves. They're growing their army. They're gods, so to them time is different than it is to us. It could be months. It could be decades."

A chill spilled over my scalp and down my spine at the mention of the Dullahan increasing their ranks. According to legend, there was one way to grow the Dullahan army: by taking humans or Fae living in the Earthly realm. It was one of the stories Fae mothers used to keep their children inside of Faerie: don't stray to the other side of the hedge or the Dullahan will take you and cut off your head, and you'll ride forever with the Bone Warriors. According to the story, Fae made the most fearsome Dullahan fighters because after they were transformed into Bone Warriors they still had Fae magic.

I shook my head, looking past Jasper to the dark water of the San Francisco Bay. "I don't see how we can stand against the gods and an army of Bone Warriors."

"If we're divided, distracted, and fragmented into separate interests, we don't stand a chance."

I wanted to reject all of it, to brush it off as stories or mistaken information. But my mind kept snagging on the part about the Great Ravens witnessing the Tuatha and the Dullahan preparing to descend on Faerie. The legendary birds couldn't lie.

I peered up at Jasper. Was he bending the truth? I didn't think he was.

"If I were to agree to go along with your plan to smooth things between the New Gargs and the Duergar, what would that entail?" I asked.

"First, we'd want to eliminate the points of friction. One being the lineage of the changeling, Nicole."

My pulse bumped. Nicole's lineage was *my* lineage. The Duergar King Periclase was absolutely convinced he was Nicole's blood father and insisted she belonged in his kingdom. No one but Nicole, our father Oliver, and my best friend Lochlyn knew that Nicole and I were twins. At Oliver's insistence, we'd kept it secret. Our mother, who died when I was a baby, had been terrified when Nicole and I were born because of one of Marisol's prophecies. In her vision, she formed a New Gargoyle kingdom on the bloody corpses of twin New Garg girls. Marisol's singular goal in life was to bring the Stone Order into kingdomhood. Apparently, our mother had been so sure that Nicole and I were the ones in the prophecy, our mother had insisted on hiding one of us in the Earthly realm.

"And how would we address that?" I asked.

"By obtaining proof."

My eyes widened. "You mean go to Melusine?"

He shrugged. "Do you know of any other way to definitively prove Fae parentage?"

He was right. Human DNA tests didn't work on Fae. Melusine was one of the Old Ones, and the only one alive who could divine Fae parentage. Like many of the Old Ones, she could be terribly foul-tempered, violent, and difficult to locate.

"It doesn't matter, though," I said. "Nicole summoned stone armor, proving she's at least part New Gargoyle. She has a right to stay with the Stone Order even if King Periclase is her father. Which he's not, I'm positive of that. Periclase can't insist that she return to the Duergar kingdom."

Our father was Oliver, the full New Gargoyle man who'd raised me.

"Yes, she's New Garg, but that doesn't matter to Periclase," Jasper said. "He's convinced that Nicole is his daughter, and as long as he believes that, he's going to try to get her back. Children are rare in Faerie—you know that. Princesses are even more precious, and they're valuable commodities to their ruler parents."

I thought of Maxen, Marisol's only son. Everyone in Faerie knew that she would dictate who he married because of the strategic nature of high-level Fae unions and her goal of raising the Stone Order a proper Faerie court.

"Just seems like a hell of a lot of trouble to get him to drop that bone," I muttered.

"Agreed. But he's obsessed. Trust me, the rift between our two realms will not be repaired until this matter is settled."

"Prolly didn't help that I nearly killed his brother in the battle of champions over this," I said, trying not to sound smug. I'd had to fight in the battle because Periclase had been so enraged that I'd taken Nicole out from under his nose.

28

"No, but that was a battle you won fair and square. Periclase can't argue with that."

I pushed my fingers into my hair and yanked. "It just seems so damned stupid."

He chuckled. "That may be. But Fae wars have erupted over less than this."

"I suppose you want me to go to Melusine with you, as a witness to her findings."

"Yes. Marisol would insist on an Order witness, you know that."

I blew out a loud breath. I couldn't believe I was agreeing to this. "Okay. If you can locate Melusine, then I'll get a vial of Nicole's blood and accompany you to verify her lineage once and for all."

It wasn't quite a binding agreement, but I'd keep my word. After all, I had a very personal interest in the results. I already knew Oliver was my father, but he'd always refused to tell me who my mother was. I could finally get the answer. Maybe. Melusine wasn't likely to make it easy on us.

"Actually, I know where to find Melusine," Jasper said.

Of course he did. I let my head fall back. I'd figured I had at least a few days, maybe much more, before Jasper found the Fae witch. It would have allowed me time to try to capture Gretchen's mark and collect half the bounty.

He gave me a broad grin. "We can set out first thing in the morning."

I stifled a groan, and he chuckled gleefully.

Chapter 4

I RETURNED TO the stone fortress and reported to Marisol with the information Jasper had given me. Her face gripped with tension when I told her the Great Ravens had observed the coming threat.

"Jasper Glasgow has a connection to the Ravens?" she asked.

"Uh, presumably so," I said.

Damn. I hadn't meant to allude to his secret but didn't see how I could convince Marisol the info was good without the detail of the Ravens. Everyone in Faerie respected them and knew they spoke only truth.

I dug my nails into my palms as a reminder to keep my responses minimal, and I hoped she wouldn't probe further.

"Is he a Raven Master?" she asked.

Double damn. I couldn't lie. Fae can't lie to each other, not outright, but we can get clever with words.

"I don't know if he's a Raven Master," I said carefully.

I *did* know he was a Grand Raven Master, but that wasn't the same thing. A regular Raven Master was a trained keeper of the smaller messenger ravens. The Great Ravens were a different species. Splitting hairs by human standards, maybe, but that was how we Fae liked to roll.

"Is he a *Grand* Raven Master?" she asked pointedly.

Shit.

"Yes."

"That's good," she said. "That means he's close to the information that's coming in."

"Please don't repeat that to anyone," I said. I hated pleading. "He revealed himself as a Grand Raven Master to help me escape the Duergar palace. But King Periclase doesn't know. I'm not sure any Duergar know."

Her brows shot up. For Marisol, that was the equivalent of screeching with surprise.

"Interesting," was all she said.

"Will you keep his secret?" I pressed.

"I will."

I could have asked for a binding agreement, but it would have pissed her off, and I didn't need more Marisol ire piled on me. I was still bent on saving up my pennies and getting the hell out of Faerie and back to my job at the Guild as soon as she'd let me go. It wasn't that I didn't care about the fate of my people. I'd pledged my life to hunting criminal vamps because one of them had killed my mother. Working as a vamp hunter for the Guild was the best way I could think to honor the mother I'd never known. She'd been troubled and vulnerable, and there was a certain ilk of vamp who liked to prey on others like her. I wanted to save innocents from her fate, if I could.

But for the moment I was in the fortress, and I also had to tell Marisol about the little errand to Melusine. She seemed skeptical at first, until I explained to her just how deeply Jasper believed King Periclase was digging in on this issue.

"Jasper is sure that his father will never let Nicole go," I said. "And I have no reason to doubt what he says."

"I don't like being backed into a corner like this," she said. "Nicole is here, she chooses to be here instead of with Periclase, and she's proven she's one of us. Not to mention that you defeated Periclase's brother in the arena to atone for your so-called sin of rescuing Nicole from the

Duergar."

"Yes, and I said all of that to Jasper, more or less."

"But if Periclase refuses to let it go, then I suppose we have no choice."

Marisol was in a tough spot. King Periclase was vying to absorb the New Gargoyle Stone Order into his court. He wasn't the only one. We New Gargs didn't have huge numbers, but we were born fighters and trained to be some of the best in combat in all of Faerie, as I'd demonstrated against his brother. That was one of the main reasons we'd remained independent up to this point. But it also made us a desirable addition to a kingdom. Periclase had submitted a formal appeal to Oberon to claim the Order as part of his kingdom.

To make matters even more complicated for Marisol, King Periclase actually had some New Garg blood. The New Gargoyle Fae race had formed spontaneously at the Cataclysm, which was a break in the magical universe that happened before I was born. At that time, some Fae, like Marisol and my father, spontaneously became full New Garg. Other Fae spontaneously became part New Garg. Periclase was one of them.

So, Marisol had been pitted against King Periclase in the political arena for the past several months. At first, she'd tried diplomacy tactics. In fact, when I'd rescued Nicole from the Duergar, I'd been part of a diplomatic envoy from the Stone Order. Maxen had led the trip, and then I'd royally screwed up his efforts by stealing Nicole. Not that it probably would have made much difference in the end. Periclase was a real asshole, and I seriously doubted he would have allowed himself to be talked out of his bid to absorb the Stone Order. I might, however, have forced the conflict to develop more quickly by escaping his clutches twice and then kicking Darion's ass when Periclase tried to make me pay for it.

Eh, too late to do much about any of that. Except that perhaps we could settle the question of Nicole's bloodline, and thereby possibly get Periclase to back the hell off that, at least.

If not for Periclase's threat of ruining her plans for a proper court, I doubted Marisol would have given two shits about getting Melusine to verify Nicole's lineage. It was an extreme thing to do in Faerie. Fae generally didn't have the level of human-ish obsession with knowing who our biological parents were. Only when there was something significant at stake, and the average Fae wasn't important enough for that.

"Very well," Marisol said, suddenly looking tired and older than I remembered. "You'll go with Jasper in the morning to seek out Melusine. I'll get someone to draw a sample of Nicole's blood for you to take with you."

I inclined my head in a small bow and then about-faced and left. I was ready to turn in for the night, knowing it would be an early morning, but a page stopped me in the hallway outside Marisol's office.

"There's a message waiting for you up front," he said.

I went to retrieve it. Another envelope like before, and this one was from Gretchen as well.

I've been trying to reach you. We need to move on my mark. Contact me tonight, or I'll assume you're out.

I glanced at the guards on either side of the main doorway. The fortress was still in lockdown. I'd only gotten out to speak to Jasper on Marisol's order. If I couldn't step outside of Faerie to call Gretchen, I'd be out a chunk of change. I wasn't ready to give it up, even though I didn't quite know how I could go after Gretchen's mark and accompany Jasper to visit Melusine.

Well, *someone* was going in and out of the fortress in order to retrieve messages from the Earthly realm like the one I held, so the lockdown wasn't a perfect seal. I went to one of the house phones on the lobby wall and asked to be connected to Marisol.

"I know we're on high alert and comings and goings are restricted, but I need permission to step out of the fortress to contact someone at the Guild," I said when she answered. "I just received a message from outside, and it's rather urgent."

"Guild business is no longer your priority, Petra," she said. She only sounded vaguely irritated. Mostly, she sounded distracted.

"I understand, my lady, but I promise it'll only take a moment. I'll take a couple of guards with me if it would make you feel better about it."

"No, you're capable of defending yourself," she said brusquely. "Don't go beyond the front door. You have five minutes to do your business. A second longer, and I'll send a battalion out there to physically drag you back in. Wait in the lobby until I can get an officer down there to tell the guards you can pass."

I clenched my fist in a little gesture of victory. Sometimes, if you asked for what you wanted, you actually got it.

While I was waiting for Marisol's order to make it down the chain of command, my father strode into the lobby. He spotted me and turned my way.

If Marisol was stoic, Oliver was downright stone-hewn. Large, muscled, and broad-shouldered even for a New Garg, he was one of the most powerful fighters in Faerie. He'd been close to Marisol since before I was born, defending her decisions and forwarding her mission of forming an official kingdom of the Stone Order as if they were his own personal obsessions. Until recently, I never would have guessed he'd kept any secrets from her.

"Did you come to reclaim the title of champion?" I asked wryly when he approached.

Oliver had been the Stone Order's champion up until I'd taken his place. It wasn't because I was better, but because King Periclase had called me out and I had to assume the title in order to battle in the arena.

"Nah, you can keep it," he said. Then he leaned in menacingly. "For

34

now."

For a split second, I thought he was serious, but then saw a brief little glimmer in his eye. That was about as far as Oliver went in terms of a sense of humor. I cracked a small grin.

"Marisol told me you'll be going with Jasper to Melusine," he said.

I peered up at him, suddenly realizing what the implication of the quest might mean to him.

"Yes," I said quietly.

"We need to speak before you go," he said. His tone foreshadowed something that made me suddenly uneasy.

"Sounds serious," I said.

"Everything is serious these days." He gestured at the guards. "I'll let them know you can pass."

Sometimes I forgot that Oliver was a high-ranking officer in the Stone Order's legion. I thought of him more as Marisol's right hand than a military man, but in reality, he was both. Probably more. I'd long suspected that he'd shared Marisol's bed at least occasionally over the years. He wasn't Maxen's father, though. Marisol had been married to a man who'd died around the time my mother passed away. Except for Maxen's eyes, which were the same sapphire blue as Marisol's, he was a spitting image of his deceased father, so his parentage was never in question.

The guards let me out of the fortress, and I stepped through the invisible barrier that marked the line between Faerie and not-Faerie—the hedge. The barest whisper of magic passed over my skin like a silent breeze, pulling slightly at me as if it had some viscosity to it. Then I was across the hedge and standing in the Earthly realm.

My phone lit up and made a series of blips as messages and missed calls downloaded. I didn't bother looking at them, and instead called Gretchen directly.

"How soon can you go?" she asked, not bothering with niceties.

"First thing in the morning," I said.

I'd have to figure out how to juggle Gretchen and Jasper at the same time. My mind whirled, trying to work out logistics.

"We need to go tonight," she countered.

I suppressed a groan. If there was any way I could pass this assignment, I would have, even in spite of the money on the line. I just didn't have the bandwidth to attend to Faerie business and try to complete a Guild capture.

"Where are you?" I asked.

"Boise, near the Guild."

Boise was my adopted hometown, where I'd shared an apartment with my best friend Lochlyn up until recently.

"I'm not able to go there," I said, thinking fast. "You'll have to come to San Francisco. We'll pass through one of the local doorways here."

"Why?" she demanded, clearly annoyed.

"I, uh, can't leave the fortress tonight. Faerie business." It was true. There was no way I could disappear into Faerie with Gretchen right then. "Catch the six-a.m. flight out in the morning and meet me at Fort Point near the Golden Gate Bridge."

"Petra, we need to go *now*. Plus, I need you to come and get me so we can travel by doorway. The Guild isn't going to cover a flight."

"You can take the cost of travel out of my half," I said, my words clipped with impatience. She seemed to be hemming and sawing, and my five minutes were almost up. "Look, do you want an escort into Faerie or not?"

"Well, that's where my mark is," she said irritably. "But it's *your* job on the line."

"I know, I know," I said, my words rushed. "But I can't come and get you right now, and I can't help you tonight. Get on that flight, and I'll see you in the morning."

I hung up and scooted back into the fortress just under the buzzer. I grinned at the guards, who'd obviously been on the verge of coming out after me.

"Carry on," I said, and gave them a little salute.

I'd been abrupt with Gretchen but didn't know her well enough to guess whether she might complain to Gus. I put it out of my mind and headed for Oliver's quarters.

Outside his door, I stifled a yawn against the back of my wrist. It was getting late. So much for turning in early in preparation for what promised to be a very busy day.

I knocked, and Oliver let me into his bare apartment. There was one easy chair and very little else in the way of furniture. He took the chair, and I removed my scabbard and sprawled on the floor. It was either that or stand.

He leaned forward, propping his elbows on his knees and pressing his fingertips together. My insides tensed as the silence stretched out. He was generally a man of few words, but his demeanor put me on edge. Whatever he had to say, it was either very difficult, very awkward, or something he knew I wouldn't like.

"I want you to be prepared for what you may learn from Melusine," he said finally.

My chest tightened. "Okay?"

"I'm not a hundred percent sure I'm your blood father."

Chapter 5

I BLINKED. "BUT I thought you and my mother were a couple. At least for a short time?"

Oliver leaned back, drawing a long, labored breath, and looked off to the side before meeting my eyes. "You know the period around your conception and birth was a very tumultuous time, right?"

I gave a little nod. "The Cataclysm happened not long before and basically turned Faerie and the supernatural world upside-down for a while."

"Your mother was troubled. It was a chaotic time. We were apart for long stretches."

My brows pulled down. I sat up out of my relaxed posture and pulled my knees into my chest. "She cheated on you?"

"No," he said quickly. "Not exactly. I got the idea she may have been abducted, but she was in a state that made it hard to tell what was truth. I never really knew if it was against her will or not. Our relationship wasn't, ah, strictly defined."

He let out a long breath and ran his hand over the top of his cropped hair.

Something unpleasant began to take root deep in my gut. "Wait . . . she was abducted by, or with, or whatever, the Duergar? She was with *Periclase*?"

His gaze met mine, and I knew the answer by the haunted look in his eyes.

I squeezed my eyes closed, shaking my head. "You're saying the fucking Duergar King Periclase might actually be my father?"

When he didn't respond, I opened my eyes.

"It's a possibility," he said.

"Wow," I said lamely. I couldn't seem to form a more coherent response.

"I just wanted you to be prepared," he said.

"Gee, thanks."

I pushed to my feet and reached down for Mort.

Oliver rose and took a step toward me. "Petra . . ."

I raised a hand. "No, don't say anything. It's fine. I'm sure you had a really good reason for keeping this from me. Just like you had a good reason to not tell me I had a twin sister out there. And to refuse to tell me who my mother is. I guess all the secrets are coming out into the open, now, huh?"

I turned and left.

Some part of me knew I shouldn't be so angry with him, that he likely did have very good reasons to keep my lineage hidden. But in that moment, I felt betrayed, and I didn't care about Oliver's reasons.

I stalked into my own quarters, only to be startled by Nicole's presence there.

Her eyes widened when she took in my expression, and I tried to settle my face into something less pissy.

"Everything okay?" she asked cautiously.

We'd been roommates for the past couple of weeks but had hadn't seen much of each other as we'd gone our separate ways for most of each day. I usually didn't return to crash until late at night, after she'd already turned in. It was only in the past few days that we'd started doing things like practicing in the training yard together. We were still strangers, for the most part. She even looked like a stranger—we barely resembled each other, except in a few vague ways like skin tone and eye color.

"Eh, it'll be fine," I said.

I took off my scabbard and propped it against the wall near the door and watched her for a moment as she went about making a sandwich in the kitchenette.

I moved over to the counter and leaned a hip against it.

"Actually, there is something," I said. "This may not mean a ton to you, all things considered, but Oliver just told me he's not completely certain he's our blood father."

She paused with a mayo-covered knife in her hand and looked up at me. "Who else would it be?"

"You're going to love this," I said drily. "King Periclase."

The corners of her mouth pulled down, and she gave me a look like I'd just told her I wanted to serve her chocolate-covered dog shit for dessert.

"Yeah," I said. "My thoughts exactly."

She slowly went back to her sandwich-making, and I gave her a few seconds to digest the information.

"Did someone already ask you for some blood?" I asked.

She nodded. "And they told me it was to verify my parentage, but I had no idea . . . *that* was a possibility."

"I didn't either, until a few minutes ago."

She looked up at me, her forehead lined with worry. "What are the implications?"

"Well, if it turns out to be true, Periclase will try damn hard to get you to come back. He might try to do it by force."

"Even if I've sworn to the Stone Order?"

I lifted a shoulder and let it drop. "I don't think he'll give up easily. Apparently, he's really dug in on the idea that you're his daughter, and if you are, that makes you a Duergar princess."

She huffed. "But wait. Isn't that one girl also his daughter? The one who gave you the vamp ashes, what's her name?"

"Bryna," I supplied. "Yeah, you're right. He fathered her. But that's the screwed-up thing about Faerie courts—well, one of many screwy things. Some children of royals are never officially recognized."

She leaned on the counter, her sandwich forgotten. "That makes no sense. You told me Fae fertility is really low, so children are prized. Children of royals are especially valuable because they can make strategic marriages or do diplomatic work like Maxen does. So why would Periclase deny Bryna?"

"I don't know the exact reason in her case, but it could be a number of things. King Periclase's wife might have some special grudge against Bryna's blood mother, and may have forbidden him from accepting Bryna as his."

"Periclase doesn't seem like a man who'd let his wife tell him what to do."

"You never know, but you're probably right. It likely has something to do with the status of Bryna's mother. Could even be political. Like, recognizing Bryna would give power to someone in a different kingdom or something. Who knows."

"Well, *someone* knows. I bet Bryna does. And the way Unseelie love to gossip and backstab, I bet at least a few Fae know."

"Ah, you're becoming versed in the nastiness of the Unseelie." I gave her a slow smile. "Has Maxen been tutoring you on the ways of Faerie?"

Suddenly she became very re-interested in her sandwich. "He's told me a little. I've learned from others who've been helping me with magic and the homecoming process." She took a bite and chewed and then looked up at me. "Hey, Jasper Glasgow is Unseelie. He's not so bad, is he?" She raised a brow at me.

I rolled my eyes. "Maxen said something to you about Jasper, didn't he? That turd."

41

I had a sudden stab of longing for my best friend Lochlyn. She'd been my roommate on the other side of the hedge, before she'd lost her job and I'd gotten sucked back here to the fortress. She and I had often gone days without seeing each other, due to our weird schedules, but when we'd finally cross paths at the apartment, we'd sit around and bullshit like this. I really missed it.

"What is it?" Nicole asked, peering at me.

I shook my head. "I was just thinking of my friend Lochlyn. She and I had a place together before I moved back here. You'll have to meet her sometime."

"Is she Fae, too?"

"Yep, half Cait Sidhe and half Baen Sidhe."

She tilted her head.

"Half cat, half banshee," I explained. "Goodness to Maeve, you do *not* want to be in the next room when she's having sex."

Nicole snorted. "I can only imagine."

I pushed away from the counter. "I'm going to hit the shower and then turn in."

She nodded, and her posture seemed to contract a little as she hunched over her sandwich. I glanced back at her again from the bathroom doorway, observing the worry lines forming across her forehead.

"Don't worry about the dad stuff," I said. "It'll all be okay. Worst case, you swear to the Order, and technically Periclase can't touch you if you do that."

Her frown eased a little.

I just hoped Maxen wasn't leading her on too much, with all his attention and sparkly sapphire gazes.

I crashed on the pullout bed on the sofa, having more or less turned over the bedroom to Nicole. I tossed for a while, thinking about King Periclase. That bastard couldn't be my father. No fricking way.

Morning came too soon after a restless night. I left the lights off and got dressed and then pulled on my scabbard over my cropped leather jacket and slipped out.

Emmaline met me in the lobby to deliver a small leather pouch.

"There's a glass vial wrapped in gauze," she said. "The Fae witch should only need a smear of blood. That's what Marisol said, anyway."

I tucked the drawstring bag into the pocket of my jacket and zipped it closed.

This time, instead of taking Vincenzo to the Golden Gate Bridge, I used one of the fortress's internal doorways. Two guards stood there, but they must have gotten word that I was allowed to leave because they didn't try to interfere.

Standing before a carved marble arch in a rock garden that was fashioned after a Japanese Zen design, I traced the sigils in the air with my finger that would tell the doorway where I wanted to go and whispered the magic words that would give me passage through the doorways. Then I stepped into the arch and lost all sense of time, space, and form. The only sensation in the netherwhere was cold, but without a body, I wasn't even sure how I sensed it. It was like that for everyone—the chill and the nothingness were the only features of the space between doorways.

I emerged through a doorway at Fort Point, where I'd met Jasper the previous night. To the untrained eye the doorway looked like nothing more than a craggy tree. I had a few minutes before Jasper was due to meet me, so I headed toward a park bench and dialed Gretchen.

I still didn't know how I was going to explain Gretchen and Jasper to each other, but I'd worry about that when the time came. Which was probably in the next fifteen minutes.

Gretchen picked up.

"I don't know where I'm supposed to go," she said. "I've already circled the place once."

I looked for the nearest street sign and told her where I was. A minute later, headlights appeared. A gray compact rental pulled to the curb, and the driver killed the engine.

A woman stepped out, and I realized with surprise just how petite she was—five feet two inches was probably being generous. She didn't look like a typical merc. Even from many feet away I could tell she was softer and prettier, somehow. I imagined she'd look right at home in a nice three-bed, two-bath family house in one of the developments outside Boise, baking chocolate chip cookies with a couple of kids running around.

"You're right on time!" I called cheerfully.

She strode toward me, an attractive woman with long strawberry-blonde hair pulled back in a thick French braid that draped over one shoulder. She had no visible weapons, though I suspected she had at least a few knives hidden in the pockets of her cargo-style pants and perhaps under the corduroy vest she wore. The vest hadn't always been a vest—the ragged edges where the sleeves had been ripped off betrayed the modification.

The corners of her mouth were drawn down slightly in irritation, her brow furrowed over blue eyes as she came to a stop in front of me. I decided to chalk up her cloudy mood to the Bay Area traffic. It was enough to make even natives frazzled, and coming from much smaller and quieter Boise, Idaho, she wouldn't be used to battling the morning commute.

"If the delay cost me my mark . . ." she started with a warning tone.

Okay, maybe her cranky demeanor had less to do with traffic.

The vague threat sent a prickle of annoyance through me.

"Relax," I said. "You agreed to it, so don't get hung up on what's already past. We'll get your mark."

She crossed her arms and looked around. "Where's the doorway?"

I pointed to a group of seemingly random trees not far away. "That way. Let's head over."

I looked at her sidelong out of the corners of my eyes as we walked.

"Nobody else in Boise could help you out?" I asked. I wasn't trying to rub it in. I was genuinely curious why she was willing to come all the way here to work with me.

"Like I said, I've been burned before when I've tried to partner with Fae. That was one reason I was willing to go along with Gus assigning this to you." Actually, she'd said she'd been burned, but not specifically by Fae. She flipped a glance my way, her eyes not quite meeting mine. "I hear you're some kind of fighting champion in Faerie, so I figured you'd give me a good shot at bringing in the mark. I know you're on probation and got evicted from your apartment, so I knew you'd be hard-up for cash and would be especially motivated."

It was an honest answer, and I appreciated it. She'd been okay with giving up half the bounty, too, which was generous. Surliness aside, I decided Gretchen wasn't so bad.

Suddenly she stiffened and stopped short. The tingle of human magic burst into the air around me as she drew power.

I reached for Mort before I realized Jasper had arrived and had obviously spooked her.

"He's no danger," I said, pushing my broadsword back into its sheath.

She didn't release her magic, keeping pace with me when I sped up to meet him.

"Who's this?" Jasper demanded with a flick of a glance at Gretchen. He drilled me with a look that was nearly a glare. "Why did you bring a human?"

Great, two cranky travel companions.

"She needs to go into Faerie," I said. "I'm going to escort her."

He shook his head vehemently. "No. I didn't agree to this. We can't have a human tagalong."

I grabbed Jasper's forearm, towed him a dozen feet away from

Gretchen, and then faced him.

"Look," I said in a low voice. "She won't interfere. I'm under contract to help her capture a mark for a Guild job, and she's on a deadline. I didn't have a choice in the matter."

He jammed his hands on his hips, and his golden eyes flashed with annoyance. "Why didn't you say something?"

"I'm sorry I didn't mention it. I didn't know for sure until late last night that she'd be joining us."

"I thought you were fired from the Guild."

I huffed indignantly. "I wasn't *fired*. I'm on probation."

He ran a hand through his hair and looked over my shoulder toward where Gretchen stood. "I haven't even told you where Melusine is. How do you know our errand will take us in the same direction as the human's?"

"Uh, I don't," I admitted. "But that's the magic of Faerie doorways, right? You can jump between realms and cover great distances."

I spread my arms as if I'd just revealed something miraculous and looked up at him with an exaggerated, huge grin.

After a couple of seconds, his stern expression cracked, and he made a noise deep in his throat that was half-growl, half-laugh. "I have a feeling you're going to be the end of me, Petra Maguire."

"See? I knew you'd get that it's not a big deal." I gave his arm a little punch, and he rolled his eyes.

His face grew serious again. "Fine, the human can come into Faerie. But our errand takes priority, and she will not under any circumstances accompany us to see Melusine. Not that the Fae witch would allow it, anyway. Agreed?"

I nodded. "Agreed. Where will we find Melusine?"

"Spriggan kingdom, in the Old World," he said. His light brogue seemed to thicken a bit at the mention of Scotland.

He described the doorway he wanted to emerge from, one that was on the edge of the town that surrounded the Spriggan stronghold. Old World meant we'd be going into a part of Faerie that was anchored in Scotland. All the kingdoms had territory anchored to Earthly locations in the Old World, usually Scotland, but sometimes also Ireland or England. I double-checked with him that I knew the sigils to trace to get there.

We rejoined Gretchen, who was standing with her weight shifted into one hip and her arms crossed.

She pierced me with a squinty glare. "What's going on, here? Who's this guy?"

"This is Jasper, a Fae prince," I said. I held up a hand when he started to say something, and I plowed on. "It turns out I've got Faerie business with him today, too, so we're all going together."

Her head whipped back and forth between us, and then her blue eyes flashed anger at me. "No way! I want your full focus on this assignment. This is a breach of our contract!"

I brushed past her, heading toward the stand of trees. "There's nothing about this particular situation in our contract," I said over my shoulder.

Gretchen started stalking after me, which was exactly what I'd hoped she'd do.

"Oh, I'm pretty sure I can find something," she hollered at my back.

I went to the tree that hid the doorway and turned. "Really? Could you show me?"

She whipped out her phone and angrily swiped at it as she continued stomping to where I stood.

She held out the device. "See, this part could be interpreted as an agreement to—"

Her words cut off with a squeak as I grabbed her wrist with one hand, traced the sigils with the other, and then yanked her through the doorway with me.

We emerged from the cold void into the middle of a circle of huge stones reminiscent of a miniature Stonehenge.

Gretchen fell to her hands and knees in the dirt, and her phone skittered away. She stayed there, hyperventilating, while Jasper materialized through the arched stone behind her.

When she raised her head, her blue eyes were equally frightened and furious.

"Welcome to Faerie," I said and made a flourish with one hand as I bowed.

Then I turned my attention elsewhere, taking in the surroundings. Everyone panicked on their first trip through the netherwhere, and I wanted to give her a moment to recover.

Jasper came to stand beside me.

"Been here before?" he asked.

I shook my head. "Not this doorway. The stone circle is a nice touch."

The sun was only just up, and the sky was filled with pale-pink and orange tones. To our left began the thick Spriggan woods. To our right, across a small field of wild grass, was a dirt road, and beyond that the town that butted up against the Spriggan stronghold. As with most things in this realm, the castle was made of wood. But not just any old wood, because that would have left it vulnerable to attack. It was so-called ironwood. Impervious to fire, and almost as hard as stone. There was no iron in it, of course, as iron was harmful to Fae.

Gretchen came to stand at my other side, and I gave her an appraising glance. "Okay?" I asked.

She nodded and swallowed hard.

"You never did tell me where your mark was," I said. "I don't suppose she's in the Spriggan realm. That would be too convenient."

Gretchen lifted her phone, started swiping the screen, and then frowned.

"No cell service in Faerie," I said.

48

"Damn, that's right," she muttered. She frowned, thinking for a moment. "She's in the, uh Dug . . . Derg . . ."

I suppressed a groan. "Duergar kingdom?" I supplied.

"Yeah." She took in my expression. "That's bad, I take it?"

"Well, it's not good for my sake, at least," I said. "But Jasper happens to be a native of that realm."

She glanced at him. "Oh. It should work in my favor to have a prince of that realm with me, though, right?"

"In theory," I said drily and then turned to Jasper. "Which way to Melusine?"

I thought he would point at the town. Instead, he swung around to face the thick woods. "She's somewhere in there."

Chapter 6

"*SOMEWHERE* IN THERE?" I asked. "Can you maybe be a bit more specific?"

"You don't even have an exact location?" Gretchen demanded.

"Do *you* for your mark?" Jasper shot back at her.

She crossed her arms again and muttered under her breath, sending an irritated look off into the distance.

"Okay, kids, one thing at a time," I said. "Jasper. What's the intel on Melusine?"

"She's taken up residence in a cabin somewhere in the woods," he said.

I swiveled and faced the forest doubtfully.

"It kinda goes on forever," I pointed out. "We can't spend the next year hunting through the trees for a cranky old Fae witch who doesn't want to be found in the first place."

He'd recovered his composure, now giving me that look of vague amusement I remembered from our time in the Duergar palace. He'd been nearly unflappable, even when there were knives flying at us.

"The dryads will help us," he said in that mild tone I'd come to know.

I frowned, shaking my head. "I don't know. Dryads aren't known to be the most reliable bunch. Plus, they're shy."

All of a sudden, a flock of dark birds appeared in the air above us, seemingly from out of thin air. They circled overhead in a dizzying vortex of black wings.

I looked at Jasper, and his gold eyes twinkled. "The ravens are going to help, too."

"Ah, now you're sounding like a man with a plan," I said.

Jasper raised his arm straight in the air and made a fist, and the flock descended and then the vortex unfurled as the birds fanned out over the tree tops. One by one, they dropped down into the trees. He lowered his arm and began walking toward the tree line, to a spot that looked like the head of a trail.

"We'll follow the path for a while," he said over his shoulder to me. "If it becomes clear that we have a long distance to cover to get to Melusine, we'll find a doorway. The two of you can go after the mark while I continue the search for Melusine, and then you can rejoin me."

Gretchen and I traded glances.

"This is going to waste too much time," she said. "A wild goose chase on the side was *not* part of our deal. The delay could very likely cost me the assignment."

"It won't," I said. "We'll find your mark."

She crossed her arms and gave me an angry glare.

"Fine, I'll take a pay cut for the delay."

"Your share gets cut by a third," she said.

"Deal."

She wagged a finger at me. "And don't think you can worm your way out of this adjustment to our contract just because I don't have cell service to update it."

I held up my right hand. "With this Duergar prince as our witness, I solemnly swear that I will abide by this oral revision to our original agreement," I said, my voice tight.

She jabbed her index finger toward Jasper. "You heard her. You're my witness."

Then she stalked past me to follow him.

My pulse bumped in anticipation as we crossed over from open space into the realm of trees. The air seemed to soften, becoming cooler, moister, and earthier. Once we were about fifty feet in, the sky was almost totally blocked out overhead. We moved single-file, Jasper in the lead and me at the back.

When one of the ravens swooped over us and landed on Jasper's shoulder, Gretchen let out a little shriek. The black bird softly clucked and chirped in his ear for a moment and then pushed off and took flight.

"What'd it say?" I asked.

"She said we're good to stay on this trail for now," he said.

The light grew more filtered and dim as we walked deeper in. Croaks, chirps, and rustlings surrounded us, giving the distinct feeling that we were in the domain of small creatures. We were the intruders, there.

There was a soft sound of rustling behind me, and Gretchen yelped. I whirled around, drawing Mort and sending magic into the blade. She'd pulled her own power, and it seemed to crackle in the air.

"Something grazed my arm," she said, her voice high and tight.

There was nothing there. Jasper moved off the path, looking into the woods off to the side. I happened to tip my gaze up, and on a branch about five feet overhead, a pair of solid green eyes with no pupils or whites met mine.

"Hello, there," I called softly to the enchanting little creature.

She hugged the branch with her arms and legs, swinging upside-down and peering at us. There was a deep scar along one of her arms. It looked like a scratch in the thin bark of a very young tree.

"What is it?" Gretchen whispered.

I sheathed Mort. "A dryad. They're creatures of Faerie, but they're not like us. They're part plant. Release your magic so you don't scare her."

Gretchen did as I asked but remained tense by my side.

"We mean no harm," Jasper said, his voice pitched much higher than usual. "We're looking for Melusine."

The dryad's green eyes went large and round at the Old One's name. She swung herself back up to the branch and scuttled higher in the tree until she was out of sight.

"That was helpful," I muttered.

Gretchen was running her hands up and down her upper arms as if she had a sudden chill. "Mind if I stay in the middle?" she asked. She had the decency to look a little embarrassed by her skittishness.

I gestured for her to walk in front of me, and I took one last look up in the tree. Not seeing any sign of the little woodland Fae, I fell into step behind Gretchen.

"Who is this Melusine, anyway?" Gretchen asked.

"She's a Fae witch, and she's been around longer than these trees," I said.

"Why are you seeking her?"

"We need her to verify someone's lineage."

Gretchen shook her head. "Isn't there an easier way?"

Jasper glanced over his shoulder, meeting my eyes for a brief second. "No, not in Faerie."

We walked in silence for a minute, and I swore the forest grew even darker. It suddenly occurred to me that we might not finish our quest in daylight. There was nothing particularly foreboding about the woods, but I didn't relish the idea of being out here all night.

"What brought you to the Mercenary Guild?" I asked Gretchen, hoping to keep her distracted from the fact that we were probably going to be tramping through the forest for a while. "Lots of other things a mid-level witch could be doing."

"When I was a girl, I dreamed of fighting great battles," she said, her tone bemused. "I suppose when I got older the Mercenary Guild was the closest thing I could find to that."

It was an interesting thing for a human with magical aptitude to say.

"Are you trained with weapons?" I asked.

"Not really," she said. "It was the influence of my godmother when I was a child. She's kind of a legend back in my world."

"What's her name?" Jasper asked idly.

"Ella Grey."

My mouth fell open in surprise, and my shoes scuffed to a halt. "Your godmother is Ella Grey?" the words came out much louder than I'd intended.

Gretchen stopped and turned, her mouth quirking in a smile. "You've heard of her?"

"Trust me, Ella Grey is a legend on *both* sides of the hedge."

Ella Grey was the human who'd prevented the Cataclysm from becoming the annihilation of the entire world of magic. We hadn't escaped unharmed, and there'd been a period of chaos afterward that still echoed through Faerie and the Earthly realm alike. But if not for Ella Grey, it would have been so much worse.

If not for the Cataclysm, I probably wouldn't exist. New Gargoyles certainly wouldn't exist.

I glanced ahead at Gretchen with new respect.

"She's still around," Gretchen said. "But I don't see her much. She likes her solitude. She usually spends the holidays with us. Me, my parents, and my siblings, that is."

"What about Loki?" Jasper asked.

"Her hellhound-labradoodle is still around, too," Gretchen said.

We continued on for a while, and after a steep climb up to a ridge, we stopped for a moment to catch our breath.

Gretchen paced a little and then heaved an impatient sigh. "This is obviously going to take a while," she said. "We need to switch over to my job. I'm on a deadline, but you might need a week to find this Melusine, for all you seem to know about her."

"We'll do your thing soon," I said, not willing to offer anything specific. I was getting a little antsy, though. It was really going to cost me if I failed this job.

Gretchen looked ready to press me, but Jasper cut her off by putting two fingers to his lips and blowing to make an ear-splitting, two-toned call.

A moment later, a raven swooped down to his shoulder and made soft bird sounds in his ear. He gave a little nod, and the bird took flight.

"Gretchen's right. The raven says there's a doorway past this ridge," he said. "If you want, you can take it into the Duergar realm. I don't know the sigils for this doorway, so you won't be able to return to it, but you can go to the one we used to enter this kingdom. I'll send one of the Great Ravens to get you and bring you to where I am."

Gretchen frowned at him. "Wait, you're not coming with us into the Duergar place?"

He shook his head. "One of us needs to keep on the path to Melusine. Petra is the one who's bound to help you with your assignment, so that leaves me to continue on."

"Just seems like it would help if we had a prince with us," she said, obviously apprehensive.

"Yeah, but he's not part of the contract," I said wryly.

She shot me a glare.

"I'll go as far as the doorway," Jasper said. "I need to angle off in that general direction, anyway."

We all turned the way he indicated, which was off the trail we'd been following. We had to weave around trees to keep our direction true, but there wasn't much underbrush to get in our way.

"Did the raven happen to say how far to Melusine, by chance?" I asked, trying to keep a neutral tone. I didn't want to sound like a whiner, but Melusine hunting was turning out to be a lot more tedious than I'd hoped. "Or maybe they could scout ahead more, or . . . something?"

Jasper's eyes sparked with amusement at my impatience. It was hard not to stare at them. Blue rings demarcated his outer irises, the blue bleeding into gold that transitioned into grass-green around the pupil. Even back in the dim light of the ravine, the colors had been so clearly visible, glowing as if lit from within.

"It doesn't work that way," he said. "The exact location of Melusine's hideout changes. We'll keep getting closer with the help of the ravens, but we won't actually reach it unless she wants us to."

"Awesome," I grumbled. "So, we could spend days in this forest inching closer and closer but may never catch up with her."

"That's about right," Jasper said. He seemed unconcerned, but I couldn't put any stock in it because he was naturally mild-mannered.

"How do you get Melusine to agree to see you?" Gretchen asked.

Jasper quirked one brow. "Hope she's in a good mood and likes the look of us."

Gretchen gave a little laugh, a light, lilting sound that seemed at odds with her sometimes dour mood.

"Seriously, it's a good question," I said. "What can we do to up our odds?"

"I wish I knew," he said.

This entire venture was a good illustration of why Faerie drove me batshit crazy at times. Things were often so changeable, unclear, and reliant on the whims of moody old Fae.

All of a sudden, there was a flurry of ravens above and the air filled with the sound of their calls. Even I could tell they were trying to warn us of something. Before I could ask Jasper, something sharp jabbed into the back of my hand. I flicked at it, thinking it was a bug trying to take a bite, but instead came away with a miniature barbed arrow in my fingers. A drop of blood leaked from where it had pierced my skin.

"Ow!" Gretchen hollered, pulling arrows from her shoulder and thigh. "What the hell?"

"Use your magic to form a shield," I barked at her.

56

I drew my own magic and sent it out over my skin, and a moment later I was covered by thin plates of stone armor. Calling on his own stone blood, Jasper had done the same.

Little arrows stuck in my clothes but stopped at my armor.

"Sprites," Jasper said grimly. "Head toward the doorway!"

"What the hell are sprites doing here?" I yelled as I followed his advice. Gretchen was right on my heels. "This isn't sprite habitat!"

"Probably Melusine," he said.

If she was sending creatures to attack us, it didn't bode well for our chances at an audience with her.

Unseen creatures with their nasty little bows sent a hail of needle-like arrows at us, seemingly from every angle. Sprites were counterparts to dryads, except part-bird instead of part-plant. They lived in the English Faerie territories, often near the coast where the winds were constant. They were crack shots with bows and arrows, and they were going to take us down by way of a thousand tiny pricks if we didn't find cover. My armor protected me from neck to wrists and ankles, but my head was exposed except for a few decorative tendrils of armor over my face, and the sprites were trying to turn my scalp into a pincushion.

I winced every time an arrow hit me in the head, my eyes tensed in a squint as I ran. If one of them hit my eyeball, I'd really be screwed.

Up ahead I spotted a tree shorter than the rest, with a bifurcation in its trunk that formed a natural arch. It had to be the doorway. Arches were always a dead giveaway.

I pointed at it. "That's where we're going," I called to Gretchen.

She'd stopped yipping since she'd formed a shield of magic to protect herself. It was barely visible to me as I glanced at her, appearing as a rainbow soap bubble that moved with her. As we ran, she broadened the shield to surround me and Jasper, too.

Thank Oberon, it was such sweet relief.

We reached the tree and stopped, all of us breathing hard.

"We can't just leave you here unprotected," I said to Jasper. "Those little shits will toothpick you to death."

"I can handle it," he said. "The two of you should go. Be back at the doorway in the stone circle two hours from now. I don't want to keep Melusine waiting if I happen to find her and she wants to receive us."

I reached into one of my scabbard pockets and pulled out the pouch containing the glass vial of blood. I held it out to Jasper.

"On the off chance she does want to see you and I'm not back, this is Nicole's blood," I said.

He blinked at the pouch, and then his eyes met mine. "But you need to be there to witness her proclamation of lineage."

"It's okay. I trust you," I said.

His hand slowly closed around the pouch, his fingers touching the back of my hand.

His gaze seemed to intensify, and for some stupid reason, my eyes flicked down to his lips. The lower one was slightly fuller than the upper, and he had a perfectly formed cupid's bow. I'd have bet he was a phenomenal kisser.

I cleared my throat and tore my eyes away from his mouth.

"I'll be back," I said and then turned to Gretchen. "Hold onto me while we step into the doorway."

She held the shield intact, giving Jasper a few more seconds of protection, while I drew the sigils and whispered the words that would take us into the Duergar kingdom. I only knew the sigils for three doorways there, and two of them were much too close to the palace and King Periclase. The one I chose was located in a very old pub, the Aberdeen Inn, owned by a Ghillie Dubh named Morven. He was a Fae almost as old as the Old Ones, and a rare solitary one, independent of any court. I'd gone to him a handful of times when I really needed information. He was a man who knew things, but he always demanded a price, and it wasn't a price everyone could pay.

Gretchen had moved even with me, with her hand resting on my upper arm, ready to step through the doorway. She dropped her shield. Just as the netherwhere beckoned with its chilly fingers, something slammed into us from the back with such violent force I flew clear off my feet, toppling forward at an awkward angle.

Gretchen grappled at my arm, jerking it forward into the doorway and nearly out of the socket, but then she pitched into the arch. At the same time, my forehead conked against the edge of the arch with a sickening crack. The last thing I sensed was Gretchen's hand breaking contact with my arm. She'd gone through the doorway without me.

Chapter 7

WHEN I AWOKE, I was lying down, and Jasper's remarkable eyes filled my field of vision. His face was pinched with worry.

I jerked up to sitting, nearly crashing my forehead into his nose. My pulse jumped and then sped.

I blinked rapidly, looking around what looked like a tiny room with walls of woven branches. "Where's Gretchen?"

"She went through the doorway," Jasper said. "I tossed you over my shoulder and tried to go in after her, but it wouldn't accept us."

I reached up to touch the middle of my forehead and gritted my teeth when my fingers brushed a fresh goose egg.

"Why wouldn't it let us through? It doesn't matter. We have to go after her," I said. "We've got to find another doorway. She's a human. She can't wander around in Faerie alone."

I shifted over to my hip, and that was when I saw the dryad. By the scar on her arm, it was the same one we'd scared earlier.

My gaze swung over to Jasper. "What happened to the sprites?"

"The dryads drove them off."

I looked over at the dryad again, my brows raised. "You did that?"

She was tucked into a corner of the room, knees pulled up against her chest and her solid-green eyes wide. She nodded.

"That was very brave," I said.

"They are one with the trees, whereas the sprites were invaders,"

Jasper said.

I crouched, balancing on my toes. The roof of the little room was too low for me to stand.

My head was pounding nauseatingly. "We need to go." I started duck-walking over to the rough-woven burlap flap.

"We do," Jasper agreed. He didn't seem to be in much of a hurry, though.

I pushed the flap aside and bit back a squeak. We were about thirty feet up, well into the tree canopy. The little room was a sort of treehouse. Or maybe it was the actual house of the dryad.

It was going to take us a half hour to get down.

"How the hell did you manage to get me all the way up here?" I asked. A sprite attack here would be inconvenient. The woods seemed peaceful, now, though. I was poised to lower myself down to a branch just below.

"A Great Raven dropped us on top of the canopy, and then I climbed down with you," he said. I looked up, and his lips quirked in a small grin. "Wrong way. We need to get to the top." He pointed up.

It was a little easier going than I'd expected. Before long, we breached the canopy. We clung to the thin upper branches as Jasper took out a little whistle and blew into it. It seemed to send a ripple outward, and a moment later a couple of huge, dark birds appeared on the horizon.

Jasper's gaze was glued to their approach.

"They can't land up here," he said. "They're going to grab us in their talons. Just keep still, and you probably won't get dropped."

I looked at him dubiously. "Probably?"

"Well, they've never dropped me, but there are no guarantees," he said mildly. "You'll be taken back to the circle of stones so you can go after Gretchen, and I'll continue on after Melusine. Two hours from now, I'll send a bird to pick you up, and you'll join me wherever I am. Hold your arms out straight from your sides."

I didn't have time to reply, as a bird with an almost impossibly huge wingspan swooped down. I stuck my arms out, my legs tensing to keep me on my branch. The beating of the Great Raven's wings stirred up leaves like a small tornado, and powerful talons wrapped around my upper arms and shoulders and squeezed.

I dangled from the bird's grasp and tried to hold still, not daring to turn my head to look back at Jasper. Last time I'd hitched a ride on a Great Raven, I'd been on the bird's back. This felt markedly more precarious, and in a matter of seconds, I determined that it wasn't my preference to dangle in the air.

When the bird dropped me near the stone ring, I landed in a crouch and let out a relieved breath at touching solid ground again. Not even waiting for the Great Raven to take flight, I sprinted to the doorway, traced the sigils, and sprang through.

I emerged back into the world in a corner of the Aberdeen Inn not far from the bar in an area roped off to keep patrons from standing too close to the doorway. I stepped around the barrier and scanned for Gretchen.

When I spotted her sitting on a stool at the bar with a mug of ale near one hand, I nearly went limp with relief. But then she turned, and I caught the glassy look in her eyes. My heart dropped a few inches in my chest.

I strode forward and grabbed her arm just as she picked up her glass. A bit of beer foam sloshed onto the ancient wood bar top.

"Petra, you made it," she said and gave a little lilting laugh.

I glared across the bar at Morven, the Ghillie Dubh who owned the place. He looked like Santa Claus, with his ruddy cheeks and white beard down to his chest, if Saint Nick were a part-time body-builder. Then I swung my glare to Gretchen.

"You let him take your power," I said accusingly to her.

A part of me knew it wasn't really fair. There was no way she could have known to be careful with Morven, and he had a way of making offers that were hard to resist. Most Fae knew how to steer clear of him, except in the cases where his services were needed, but a human in Faerie for the first time was completely vulnerable.

"Well, he didn't take *all* of it," she said, slurring slightly. "No need to be such a sour apple."

She was clearly feeling the after-effects of allowing Morven to suck away some of her magic. That, mixed with the very strong Fae beer was making her glazed and silly.

Morven was slowly wiping a rag over the wet rings left by frosty mugs.

"Hello, Petra Maguire," he said in his deep voice. "Don't worry, I left her plenty for herself."

Ignoring Morven, I drew magic and probed around her, trying to discern how much Morven had sucked away. Her power didn't seem diminished by too noticeable an amount. I just had to hope she hadn't given away any special skills. But if she had, it was too late anyway.

Gretchen wiggled out of my grasp. "He told me where my mark is! How great is that? I was just waiting for you to show up."

She tried to push her stool back from the bar, but it tipped onto two legs, and she nearly toppled backward. I caught the seat with one hand and righted her before she fell. She managed to get her feet on the floor without falling on her face. I took her shoulder and steered her toward the exit. She flicked little waves to the Fae we passed on the way, as if she and they were old friends. I swiped a glass of water off one of the tables and carried it outside. As soon as we were clear of the door, I tossed the water at Gretchen's face.

She shrieked and pushed her fingers into her closed eyelids, swiping the water away.

"Sober up," I commanded.

She just stared at me, her mouth hanging open. Then she blinked a few times and wiped her face with her sleeve.

"Sorry," I said, setting the glass to one side of the door. "We don't have time to dick around. We've got to find your mark and get back to Jasper."

Giving her head a shake, she widened her eyes and looked suitably more lucid.

"No, it's okay," she said. She looked at me deadpan. "I think I needed that."

I cracked a small grin. "Where's the mark?"

"In a hotel in the direction of the Dugger—Derger . . . the castle in this realm." She looked at me helplessly. "I can't say it right."

"It's Duergar. Know the name of the establishment?" I asked.

She raised her arm, turning it so she could look at the pen scrawls on the inside of her wrist. "Blue Boar Tavern and Inn."

I nodded. Good. I knew the place, about a mile from the Duergar palace. If I kept my head down, I should be able to get in and out before anyone had time to spot me and report to King Periclase. "It's a hike from here, but it'll give you time to sober up some more."

I angled down a street that was designated horse-and-cart only. Most of the streets in the Old World Faerie territories weren't wide enough to accommodate modern cars. Some territories didn't allow autos at all, which always made me feel like I was on the set of some new section of Disneyland. But it was all authentic. Many of the buildings and cobblestone walkways were almost as old as the Fae. If Oberon ever decided to open Faerie to human tourists, the kingdoms would make a killing.

I kept a swift pace as we walked through the Duergar streets and faced away any time we encountered anyone. I didn't have to worry about the people who'd seen me at the Aberdeen—Morven might not be completely trustworthy, but his regulars weren't snitches. He was picky about who he allowed to patronize his pub, and no one who had Morven's favor wanted to lose it.

"What did I do?" Gretchen asked after about ten minutes of walking.

Her head had been on a swivel, but it appeared the novelty and her buzz were starting to wear off. "Back there. What did I do when I agreed to pay the price for the information Morven gave me?"

"You let him siphon some of your magic," I said bluntly.

She pressed a palm into her chest and rounded her shoulders forward, as if she could still feel the sensation of paying Morven's price.

"Oh, God," she said, looking a little sick.

"You'll be okay," I said. "But you have to be very careful with such things in Faerie. *Very* careful. Some Fae know how to use the right turns of phrase to get you to promise your life away without much effort."

"That's just creepy," she said. "I can't believe he took some of my magic. I can't believe I let him."

We were on a busier road, and every time I passed someone I tucked my head down into the collar of my jacket or turned my face into one side of my hood.

"Don't feel too bad about it. You got something you needed in return, and you're none the worse as far as I can tell." I peered at her sidelong for a second. "Feels pretty damn awful when it's happening, though, doesn't it?"

"You've made deals with Morven?"

I dipped my chin in a nod. "More than once. But he won't make deals with just anyone. You must have a special kind of magic. Something he covets."

She shuddered. "What does he do with the magic he collects?"

I shook my head. "I don't know. As far as I can tell, he never leaves the Aberdeen, and I've never seen him use magic, except to collect it from others. I've never even heard a story about him wielding magic."

"He must be saving it all up for something," she said quietly, and shivered again.

I frowned, considering the possibilities. "If he actually has the ability to save and then wield all that he's collected over his lifetime, that would make him one of the most powerful Fae ever."

She made a little groaning noise low in her throat. "If that ever happens, I hope we're on the same side."

"Me too," I said. I gestured ahead. "Just another couple of blocks."

Just as the words left my lips, there was a series of booms like small thunder claps that seemed to come from all directions. I stopped short, whipping around to find the source of the noises. Others on the street looked equally confused.

A couple of seconds later, hulking, tusked ogres began pouring in from the side streets.

My pulse kicked as I caught sight of the huge battle axes they wielded.

"Oh, shit," I breathed.

I grabbed Gretchen's arm and wheeled around, already springing into a run and drawing Mort. But ogres were closing in from the rear, too. There had to be at least fifty already on our block, and they were stampeding, swinging their axes. One of them sliced through the neck of a part-Spriggan woman who was too slow to react.

I summoned my stone armor and pushed magic into my sword. Violet flames erupted along the blade.

"Your magic!" I shouted at Gretchen.

But then I glimpsed her panicked face and remembered she'd just "donated" to Morven. She was too weak to protect herself.

The ogres were closing in. I backed up against the nearest storefront, shoved Gretchen behind me, and lifted Mort.

Chapter 8

THE OGRES WERE easily twice my breadth shoulder to shoulder and towered two feet taller than me. They were fearsome brutes, with tiny, beady eyes and horns laid back on their heads as if they'd been slicked over their skulls.

I summoned my stone armor and sent a stronger surge of magic into my sword. I wasn't going to be able to hold the armor for long. I'd pulled it a couple of times in the past day, and I'd need some regenerative magic soon before my ability started to sputter out. Purple flames of power flared out from the blade. I swung at the ogre charging me. The magic reached beyond Mort and slashed like razor blades where it touched the ogre. Face, torso, down to his left thigh, my magic hit home. The other ogres stopped short, hesitant to come within the blade's reach.

The one I'd cut let out a roar, dropping his axe and grabbing at the eye I'd sliced. I lunged and drove Mort into his torso. Smoke began to rise from the ogre's fingertips and ears, and in the next second he dissipated in a cloud of sooty residue. His axe vanished with him.

Instead of scaring the other ogres, the disappearance of their comrade just seemed to piss them off. Three of them charged me at once with their axes raised, bearing almost identical snarls.

Mort whipped through the air, deflecting axes and opening wounds, but I was barely holding them off. More crowded in trying to get at us, and in the press of bodies a few of them began fighting with each other.

The blade of a battle axe slammed my forearm hard enough to make my entire body ring. My armor kept it from breaking skin, but there would be a nasty bruise. Grinding my teeth against the pain, I refocused my defense.

Behind me, Gretchen had drawn a wisp of magic, and was using it to help deflect the hits. She didn't have enough power to form a true shield, but changing the angle of the axes that got close enough to threaten me was enough to make the blows glance off my armor instead of slam edge-on into me. My clothes were going to be sliced to shreds. That beat having my body carved up. But she was weak from paying Morven, and I could tell she was running out of steam.

"See any escape?" I grunted at her through gritted teeth.

"We're up against a wall, and the nearest door is twenty feet to the right," she said.

Shit.

Bugle calls suddenly blasted through the air loud enough to make me wince. Some of the ogres looked around in alarm. Then the explosions began. Right away, I recognized the neon yellow sparks of spitfire. It was an innocuous-sounding name for an extremely volatile gravel-like substance mined from deep in the ground of Faerie that the Duergar had weaponized.

I took advantage of the confusion.

"Come on," I said over my shoulder. "Let's go."

We side-stepped along the wall to the door she'd spoken of. The ogres had paused their fighting, which opened up some space. It seemed they'd forgotten about us, their attention turned to the spitfire.

We made it into the alcove but found the door locked. I swung Mort at the handle, but the blade just clinked and slid off, not even leaving a divot in the metal. Trying to break the pane of glass in the door also proved fruitless. It must have been magically sealed against intruders.

I growled in frustration and faced the street. "Okay, next move." Before I had a chance to locate other escape options, there was a piercing, hot sizzle and a streak of yellow through the air.

"Get down!" I hollered at Gretchen a fraction of a second before the explosive hit the street.

I turned my back and tucked my head, shielding her with my body and trying to protect my face.

The spitfire explosion was so close we were blasted with air a split second before the heat and magic washed over us. I screamed out when the burn hit my exposed skin. It even seemed to seep through my armor, and it was agonizing, like pins dancing over every nerve.

When it dissipated, I straightened and turned to survey the damage. The street was clear of ogres—live ones, anyway—and the face of one of the buildings across the street was completely gone. The interior was exposed, and the whole thing smoked from several singe points. If we hadn't made it to the alcove, we probably wouldn't have survived the blast.

One by one, the ogre corpses shriveled and disappeared.

My eardrums still numb and ringing from the blast, I turned to see how Gretchen had fared. She looked up at me with stunned eyes. She'd gotten scraped up, but I couldn't see any spitfire burns.

She stood slowly and swallowed hard when she saw the wreckage. "You saved my life," she said, blinking dazedly.

"We can get all misty about that later," I said. "We need to get out of here before the Duergar military shows up and someone recognizes—"

"Too late," she cut in and pointed.

I twisted around. Duergar soldiers were already filling the street, and about half a dozen of them broke off, heading straight for us. There was nowhere for us to go. Once again, we were trapped.

When I caught sight of the magi-zappers the guards brandished, I sheathed Mort. The last thing I needed was to get knocked out and carried off to Periclase's palace. I wasn't sure how I was going to get out of this, but I wouldn't be able to do anything if I were unconscious. I couldn't antagonize them.

The six guards formed a semi-circle, enclosing us in the alcove. But they didn't make a move. Then another figure appeared behind them.

My chest clutched. It was King Periclase. He was in full battle gear, with one of his signature capes cascading over his broad shoulders and down his back.

Damn it. Someone had managed to spot me and report my presence to the palace in the short time we'd been on the streets.

"Stall them for a minute," Gretchen whispered. "I'm going to make us disappear. Just hang on."

I flicked a questioning glance at her but didn't have a chance to respond.

The guards shifted so Periclase could stride within the arc they'd formed. The Cataclysm had left Periclase with a face that was stone across the temple next to his left eye, over the cheekbone, and along the jawline on that side. He also had one hand that was curled into a permanent stone fist. The Cataclysm had given him New Gargoyle blood, but in a way that was almost useless. He had those permanent areas of rock armor and lacked the ability to summon more armor on the rest of his body. Still, the permanent stone on his face made an already intimidating figure that much more fearsome.

He moved closer and closer, clearly meaning to rattle me by invading my personal space. My hand itched to reach for Mort, but I kept my arms at my sides. Drawing my sword against a king wouldn't end well for me. I stood my ground as he stopped almost toe-to-toe with me.

He peered down, locking my eyes with his steely gaze.

"You shouldn't have returned to my realm," he said very softly, bending over until his face was nearly level with mine. "Daughter."

I stiffened, and my breath died in my throat.

Periclase raised one hand, and it was obviously a signal. His men began closing in. "It's a good thing Darion didn't kill you in the battle of champions," he continued, keeping his voice low, his words meant only for me. "Now that I know you're mine, you're valuable."

I started to shake my head, but before he could say another word, the world went blurry and distorted as if I were looking through a glass of water.

"Stay low and *move*," Gretchen hissed at me. "Keep right next to me."

It took me a second to react, but when I saw Periclase's head whipping around in confusion and the guards muttering and shifting, I realized what Gretchen had done.

She'd actually made us disappear. Or at least become invisible to the men.

I couldn't imagine how she'd managed it, still weak from having her magic siphoned. She was either an incredibly fast healer, a hell of a lot more powerful than I'd realized, or both. At that moment, I didn't really care what the explanation was. We slipped in between two of the guards, and then she took off running with me hot on her heels.

She flipped me a reproachful look over her shoulder. "You should have told me it was so dangerous for you to be here. I'd have used this spell from the start."

"If I'd known you could make us invisible, I would have," I said. "And how the hell did you recover so fast?"

"I've always been quick to bounce back," she said, quirking a little smile.

"How long can you hide us?"

"I can hold it another ten minutes. If I can turn it off for a couple of breaks, I've probably got a half hour in me."

"Damn," I said with true admiration, suddenly wishing I had human magic.

Much of Faerie magic was traditionally for helping Fae deceive humans. Glamour, mesmerization, and similar powers, most of which didn't work on other Fae. Useful when I was on the Earthly side of the hedge, but not so much in Faerie. I was exceptionally strong in magic for a New Garg but had a fairly short list of skills—stone armor, a handful of different spells related to my shadowsteel spellblade, and a few other minor tricks. Human magic, on the other hand, was incredibly versatile.

I glanced up at a clock tower as we passed a quaint little town square.

"We've only got a half hour before we need to get back to the Spriggan realm," I said. "It would be good if you can hold out that long so we actually make it out."

"Which way to the Blue Boar?" she asked.

Right, the mark. In the confusion of the attack and the shock of Periclase's words, I'd nearly forgotten.

"No time," I said with a pang of regret. "It'll take us twenty minutes to get back to the doorway in the Aberdeen."

"That rock-faced guy knows you're here now," she said, referring to Periclase. "We can't use that doorway anyway because that's where we came in. I can't hold the invisibility spell all the way back there."

We'd slowed to a side-by-side jog. At the mention of the Duergar king, Periclase's words came back to me again, and I shivered. He'd called me "daughter." If he knew I was Nicole's sister, that meant he'd discovered a secret that only a handful of people in the world knew. And one of them, my mother, was dead. But that was just conjecture. I wasn't certain he knew Nicole was my twin. The main question in my mind was whether he truly was my blood father, as he clearly believed. I was starting to think the possibility wasn't as remote as I'd assumed.

"Petra? Still here?"

I gave my head a shake, forcing my mind back to the conversation. "The only other two doorways I know are too close to the Duergar palace," I said. Then I brightened. "But that won't matter if we're invisible whenever we pass someone, and we'll be away from the roads, so you won't have to hold the spell the whole way."

She grinned at me.

"We're still going to have to haul ass, though," I said.

I took the lead, weaving us through the streets to the Blue Boar Tavern and Inn.

Periclase's words played through my head again and again like background music in my mind.

I ducked into a narrow alley.

"We're almost there," I said. "Take a quick break."

She dropped her magic, and the world sharpened around us. We stood with our backs against the wall, inhaling the faint aroma of trash from the bins farther down.

"Did Stone Face call you 'daughter'?" Gretchen asked.

My head swiveled, and I peered at her sharply. "You heard that?"

"Well, yeah, I was right there."

I'd thought he'd spoken too softly for anyone to hear.

"He did," I said.

"He's the king of this place?"

"Yeah," I said reluctantly.

"That would make you a Fae princess."

"No," I said quickly. "Well, there's a possibility. Shit, I don't know."

I closed my eyelids and pushed the heels of my hands into my eyes, suddenly wanting to get the hell out of there. A pang of longing for my former life outside Faerie cut through me. I took a slow breath, somewhat consoled by the thought of the money that would come from this mark, which would help me reestablish myself on the other side of the hedge.

"We need to push on," I said brusquely. "Ready?"

I felt human magic wash through the air, and then everything grew rippled and distorted again.

We ran the rest of the way to the Blue Boar. When the front entrance came into view, a vamp woman and a Fae man were just emerging.

"Holy shit, that's her!" Gretchen pointed. "The woman, that's my mark."

The two of them turned right and began walking away from the Blue Boar. Gretchen and I went to the corner where we could intercept them. She let the invisibility spell drop. They were so surprised when we appeared suddenly in front of them they didn't have time to react.

Gretchen held up the bounty card, shoving it under the woman's nose. There was a flash of yellow-orange magic, which expanded in a cloud to surround her. Her fangs popped out, but it was too late.

I gave the Fae man a hard stare. "You'd better run if you know what's good for you."

He backpedaled a few steps and then turned and hightailed it away.

The magic from the bounty certificate had positively identified the woman as the mark, and the cloud coalesced around her wrists. It forced them together behind her back. She was young and had that gaunt, malnourished look of someone who'd gotten too deep in the underbelly of society. She struggled, trying to free her arms, but it was useless. When she realized she was done for, she pushed her face out, bared her fangs, and spit at Gretchen, who hopped back to dodge the glob of saliva.

"The spell," I muttered at her, eyeing the Fae around us.

In a blink, the world turned watery again. The mark gasped, her eyes popping wide.

"We've gotta go," I said.

Gretchen and I took off at a run with Gretchen gripping a fistful of the vamp's sleeve and trying to hurry her along, but it was quickly apparent that the emaciated girl wasn't going to be able to keep up for the mile-long trek to the nearest doorway.

"Stop a second," I said.

I went up to the girl, squatted, and wrapped my arms around her upper thighs. I flexed my legs and quickly straightened to lift her over my shoulder. It wasn't magic, but physical strength was one of the things my New Garg blood had graced me with.

"Bite me, and I'll cut your head off," I growled. I drew magic to form stone armor just in case my threat wasn't sufficient.

We sped up, flying through the streets. There was a doorway in the woods behind the Duergar palace that I'd used once before.

"I'm going to have to take you through to the other side of the hedge," I said to Gretchen, my words jarring each time one of my boots hit the ground. "You can't order a Guild transport for a capture from within Faerie."

"Damn, that's right," Gretchen said.

"Yeah, that detail slipped my mind, too."

But it would be better this way. I could rejoin Jasper and put this capture behind me, knowing that a nice chunk of cash would soon be warming my bank account.

We stopped once within the cover of a ruin of an old barn so Gretchen could release the spell for a minute. I set the mark on her feet. She still seemed dazed.

"What'd she do, anyway?" I asked Gretchen.

"Dealing VAMP3 blood," she said.

My brows rose. "That was my last mark's crime, too. Coincidence, or is it becoming a bigger problem?"

Gretchen stared at me. "You haven't heard? There were two dozen slaughtered at a Vegas club last week. A bachelor party came in hopped up on VAMP3, and several of them went feral."

My chest clutched as I contemplated so many dead. I let out a low whistle. "I've been in Faerie the past few weeks. Not much news filters through from the other side of the hedge into the fortress."

Type 3 vamps, like New Gargoyles, were a product of the Cataclysm. A new form of the vampire virus had spread through the population, infecting people at random. VAMP3s were charming to the point of being almost impossible to resist, if you were a human with no defenses against glamour. They were able to walk in sunlight and could keep their violent sides under control. Unlike VAMP2s, who were required by law to have an implant that controlled their raging bloodlust.

VAMP3s were naturally less dangerous than VAMP2s in terms of bloodlust, but apparently VAMP3 blood was growing in popularity. It gave a soaring high, as well as imparting the VAMP3 powers of charm on the user. But after a few highs, it turned some users into mindless, murderous maniacs.

I went to the mark and slung her over my shoulder again, and this time she didn't even bother trying to resist. I nodded at Gretchen. "Let's ride."

We hoofed it to the doorway under cover of Gretchen's spell. When she released it again, she looked pale, her blue eyes bloodshot and strained.

"You going to make it?" I asked her, setting the mark on her feet.

Gretchen pressed her lips into a hard line and nodded.

I linked my arm though the mark's, since her hands were cuffed behind her back, and Gretchen placed her hand on my other shoulder. The doorway was in a huge, old oak. I traced the sigils, whispered the words, and then dragged the mark forward. The three of us passed into the oak and tipped into the void of the netherwhere.

We emerged in the misty late-afternoon light of the San Francisco Bay, at the doorway Jasper, Gretchen, and I had used to go into Faerie earlier that day.

I powered on my phone just to check the time. It vibrated and chimed as it connected with a tower and messages downloaded. I didn't have time to read them. I only had five minutes to get back to Faerie.

"Thanks for the job," I said to Gretchen. "Maybe we'll work together again at some point."

"Thanks for helping me," she said.

She gave me a little wave, already pulling out her phone to call the Guild for a transport.

I went back into the doorway, and a moment later stood in the circle of stones in the Spriggan kingdom. I took a slow breath, trying to shake off the events of the past couple of hours. I couldn't seem to wipe Periclase's face from my mind's eye as he loomed over me and called me "daughter." My skin crawled at the memory.

Shading my eyes against the low-angled sun, I spotted a large, dark shape among the trees nearby. The Great Raven, my ride back to Jasper. It had been waiting for me.

The huge bird hopped forward, cawing and turning its sleek head to peer at me with one black eye. It seemed agitated, though I knew I wasn't late. It hunkered down and flicked me a glance, indicating I should get on. I jumped onto the creature's back, quickly settling myself low on its neck between its wings. I held on tight with fistfuls of shining black feathers, my thighs gripping the bird's back as it pumped its powerful wings.

It flew hard, and tears streamed from my eyes in the blasting wind of its motion. When it began to slow, I scanned the woods. The forest floor was too shadowed this late in the day for me to see much below the treetops, but there was a clearing on top of a ridge ahead, and the bird seemed to be aiming for that spot. I didn't have a good sense of how much progress Jasper had made, as I didn't know the terrain well enough to recognize where we'd left off.

I spotted him down below and almost lifted my hand in a wave, but then thought better of letting go of my hold when the Great Raven dipped a wing and began to spiral downward. As we descended, I could see better through the late-afternoon gloom.

One side of Jasper's face was covered in blood.

The Great Raven landed, and I nearly sprawled flat on my face in my haste to dismount and rush to Jasper.

"What happened?" I demanded.

I reached up and grabbed his cheeks, turning his face to look for the source of the blood. It looked like it was seeping from a gash over his ear and temple. There was a smaller cut over his eye.

He winced, but he didn't pull back out of my grasp.

"It's nothing, really," he said, looking sheepish. "Stupid. The sprites chased me down a hill, and I tripped and tumbled about twenty feet. My stone armor protected me from breaking any bones, but the exposed areas of my head took a few hits."

I let out a breath and stepped back to survey the rest of him just to make sure he wasn't trying to hide any other injuries. Finally convinced that the cuts, if bloody, weren't too serious, I nodded.

"Looks like you'll live, but we at least needed to try to bandage your head," I said.

"Where's Gretchen?"

"I left her and her mark in San Francisco."

"Ah, good." His golden eyes shone with mild amusement as he scanned me up and down. "And what happened to you?"

I looked down, suddenly remembering my clothes were in shreds from the fight. My jacket had absorbed most of the abuse. But some of the rips in my t-shirt were gaping, revealing bare skin and glimpses of my pale-blue sports bra. Since I'd turned my attention to my clothing, I realized I felt a draft at my back. I turned so Jasper could see.

He let out a sound that was half laugh, half horrified exhalation.

"The top half is completely burned away," he said.

I faced him again and caught his gaze roaming over the rips in my jeans left by glancing axe strikes. Instead of trying to pretend he hadn't been looking, his gold eyes rose to mine and the corners of his lips widened slightly. I held his gaze, and something that had only been hinted at before seemed to burn more intensely.

"There was a servitor attack while we were in the Duergar realm," I said, finally breaking the thick silence between us. I drew magic and formed armor over my upper back so it wouldn't be completely exposed, just in case we met more sprites, or worse. "Ogres this time, huge and wielding battle axes. The royal army came through with spitfire." I raised my arm and pointed at my back. "That's what burned the clothes."

Jasper's brow furrowed.

I reached down to rip a long piece from the bottom hem of my ragged t-shirt. I didn't mention the run-in with Periclase, preferring to avoid the topic altogether for the moment.

"Here, bend down," I said, holding up the scrap of fabric.

Jasper went onto one knee so I could better reach his injuries, the worry lines smoothing from his forehead as I began to wind the makeshift bandage around his head. I secured the fabric with a knot, tucking in the ends.

He rose before I could move out of the way and stood so near I could see the faint pulse at the side of his neck. His lips parted slightly, and for once it seemed like his usual mild calm had dropped away. In its place was an unexpected intensity.

My breath stilled, and time seemed to slow. For a moment, I was mesmerized by his eyes, and everything in me was calling out for me to lean just a little bit closer. That was all it would take, I could see it in his face. Just the slightest movement from me, and his mouth would lower to mine. That pouty-full lower lip would be between my teeth, and—

I jerked my head back and swallowed hard, suddenly remembering King Periclase's face looming over me, and what it would mean if his words were true. Periclase was Jasper's father. If what the Duergar king had said was true, then that meant . . . yeah, that meant Jasper and I were related.

I cleared my throat and took a step back. A flash of disappointment shaded Jasper's face for a split second.

We needed to find Melusine. I wanted answers.

"We should get moving," I said. "Are we any closer to Melusine's hideout?"

Carefully avoiding my eyes, he pulled his raven whistle from a pocket and began turning it in his fingers, focusing on it more intently than necessary.

"The ravens say that way," he said, pointing. His gaze briefly swung my way but didn't quite meet mine.

Something had been on the verge of happening between us a moment ago, but I'd cut it off, and he was clearly still mulling that over.

"Let's go," he said, his face closed off.

We hiked in silence as the sun lowered in the sky and the air began to cool. Every so often, a raven came to update Jasper. The minutes stretched on, and neither of us tried to make conversation.

Some small part of me wanted to explain myself, why I'd pulled back. But the larger part of me wanted to sink into my mood and let the implications of my possible Duergar bloodline swirl darkly around in my head. Mostly, I just wanted to know the truth.

Yet another raven alighted and perched on Jasper's shoulder. After a few seconds, he halted.

I stopped, too. "What is it? Are we close?"

He turned to me, his eyes finally meeting mine. "She knows we're coming. She's invited us in."

Chapter 9

"IS THIS A trick?" I asked, remembering the sting of the sprites' arrows and Jasper's suspicion that Melusine had sent them to mess with us.

"I think the invitation is sincere," Jasper said. "But she may not make it straightforward. You know how the Old Ones have their games and moods."

"Sun's going down," I said. "It'd be good to have a place to shelter, in any case."

He nodded his agreement and lifted his arm to point down the small slope we stood on. The trees were thinner in that direction, and I could see some of the landscape beyond. The ridges gave way to a meadow filled with tall grass below, and then the woods began again.

"Across there," Jasper said.

I squinted in the failing daylight and thought I saw faint lights blinking on and off over the meadow.

"Lantern bugs," I said under my breath. The flashing insects meant there was water nearby.

Jasper was already moving down the slope and didn't hear me. I caught up with him, and we picked our way through the meadow, around ancient stumps and dry rivulets. About halfway across we did meet up with a winding stream, just as I'd expected. We followed it until we were blocked by a wide pond at the far edge of the meadow. We hadn't been able to see it from above because of the deep shadows of evening and the tall grass growing up through the water. The lantern bugs had moved back into the trees on the other side.

I leaned over to look in. "It's not deep here. Only a few inches. Maybe it's shallow enough to walk across."

"The mud might suck us right in, though." Jasper picked up a stick and poked it into the water. It easily sank over a foot. "I don't like the look of this."

I swung my gaze left and right. The pond went on as far as I could see in either direction. "Guess we should go around. Pick a side."

"Let's go left," he said. "The meadow is shorter that direction. Perhaps the pond is, as well."

We jogged along the squishy edge of the pond for about fifteen minutes, and I zoned out a little in the rhythm of our boots hitting the ground. When I refocused and really looked around, something wasn't right. I slowed and then stopped. Jasper went on a few feet and then turned and came back to where I stood with my hands planted on my hips.

"We're not any closer than we were," I said, turning a slow circle.

"What?"

"Look." I pointed across the pond at a gnarled formation that had once been a tree but was now dead wood. "See that crag? It was right across from us when we reached the pond. *Before* we ran along the edge for a quarter of an hour."

He cocked his head as he peered across the water and then sent long looks left and right. "Damn," he said softly.

"I think Melusine wants us to go across," I said. "I think we're supposed to follow those lantern bugs."

As if in response to my words, the insects began to blink on and off more rapidly and move in more agitated patterns.

The sun had set, and the light around us was failing. I was really regretting wasting the last few minutes of visibility on a fruitless jog through some kind of magical illusion.

"I'll call a Great Raven to ferry us across," he said and pulled out the whistle.

He blew into it, several short puffs. We both turned, looking for a great bird approaching. A couple of minutes ticked by and no Great Ravens appeared. I frowned, suddenly realizing that the smaller ravens hadn't come to chatter at Jasper since we'd entered the meadow. He whistled again.

"What does it mean if they don't come?" I asked.

"Either they're all occupied or they can't hear my call."

We waited another few minutes, but the sky remained empty.

"We could try going back the other way. Perhaps we simply chose incorrectly," Jasper said.

"We should be able to find out pretty quick."

I began running back the way we'd come, and he fell into an easy lope beside me. After about five minutes, it was obvious we would fare no better in this direction. The crag was still opposite us across the water.

We stopped, and Jasper muttered a few choice curses under his breath. We stood side-by-side at the edge of the water, the soles of our boots sinking an inch into the soft ground.

"No point in wasting more time," I said and took a long step into the murky pond.

Jasper followed, and within half a dozen steps, I was in deep enough for the water to come up and over the tops of my boots. I grimaced as they flooded and suddenly weighed about ten more pounds apiece.

We sloshed along, and when we'd nearly reached the halfway point to the other shore, I began to think that waterlogged boots might be the worst thing we'd take away from our slog.

Then something caught my eye. Movement under the dark surface. Unease stirred deep in my gut, and I quickened my pace.

Again, I thought I caught a flicker of something in the water.

"Did you see that?" I asked, my voice low.

"Aye," was all Jasper said.

We both drew magic and summoned our stone armor. I felt the wash of his magic in the air—it had a distractingly refreshing sense to it, like a very fine spray of mist on my exposed skin.

Something broke the surface of the water, just skimming it, but I didn't get a good enough look to see what it was. I drew Mort and extended magic into the blade. Violet flame surrounded the sword, reflecting on the rippling surface of the pond.

About ten feet away, something breached. Jasper and I froze as a huge ridged back rose from the water. The highest ridge was taller than me, which meant the creature it was connected to must have been enormous. Impossibly large for this pond, considering we weren't even waist deep. My brain tried to make sense of it as the ridges rose and then disappeared.

"What in the name of Maeve was that?" I asked shakily, my eyes wide and scanning the water for movement. "There must be a deep trench out there."

I could hear Jasper's rapid breath next to me but didn't dare look away from the water to read his reaction.

"I don't think so," he said, his voice admirably calm.

"Another illusion of some sort?"

"Possibly."

A second later, the illusion, or whatever the hell it was, sprang out of the water. There was just enough light left in the late-twilight sky to see the creature looked like a giant koi. A koi the size of a fricking whale. It rose into the air above us. Impossible, but there it was.

Seeing what was coming, I started to backpedal and then turned and started hauling ass back toward the shore. But my boots were too heavy and the mud too deep. It was like one of those slow-motion nightmares where the monster is behind you and suddenly your feet feel like two anvils.

I twisted to look over my shoulder as the creature reached the apex of its impossibly high jump. Its mouth was stretching wider and wider into an O that seemed big enough to swallow the entire pond.

I planted my feet, wrapped both hands around Mort's hilt, and braced my shoulders like a batter at the plate. Out of the corner of my eye I saw Jasper do the same a few feet away. As the creature descended upon us, the space inside of it seemed to go on forever. I wasn't sure there would even be anything within reach for me to slash at.

I swung anyway as the darkness of the fish's insides came down around me. My boots lost contact with the ground, and I pitched forward, tumbling ass over tea kettle in sloshing water. The shock and jolt interrupted my magic, and Mort's flame extinguished. I flailed in darkness so complete I lost all sense of direction. I desperately fought to keep a grip on my broadsword and prayed to Oberon that Jasper and I didn't run each other through with our swords.

After another few seconds of tumbling around in watery darkness, I was floating.

No, not floating.

I'd passed over into the cold void of the netherwhere.

Panic began to grip me in its chilly, strong hands. I hadn't purposely entered a doorway. How would it know where to spit me out? What if there *wasn't* a way out?

I floated in the nothing, powerless.

Then all of a sudden, I went sprawling onto the ground. Mort flew from my hand. I lay there for a moment, dirt sticking to my lips and tasting the grit of it, just grateful to be back out into the physical world. My clothes and hair were soaked, and I could swear to Oberon that I smelled a faint fishy odor in the air.

There was a groan from a few feet away. I raised my head and looked around, but I was back among the trees, and the moon's light didn't penetrate to the forest floor.

"Jasper?"

Another groan. I reached for Mort and then crawled toward the noise, not feeling steady enough to try to walk over unfamiliar terrain in the dark. While I was moving, the lantern bugs meandered down from above, providing enough light to see that Jasper was lying on his back, his own sword tossed nearby.

"Is anything broken?' I asked.

He sat up and dropped his head into his hands for a moment. The bandage I'd fashioned around his forehead was gone. He stretched his arms out in front of him and then brushed his hands down his sleeves.

"Nah, nothing important."

The swarm of lantern bugs was descending on us, and they buzzed and blinked around our heads.

I dumped water out of each boot, and he did the same. Then I stood and offered him my arm. We linked elbows, and I heaved back to pull him up. My hip bumped his upper thigh as he righted himself on his feet, and the memory of his lips hovering inches from mine not long ago flashed through my mind.

"Where do you think we are?" I asked.

He pointed into the trees. "Other side of the pond."

I followed his gaze, and sure enough, there through the trees was the pond and the meadow, lit with pearly moonlight. As we watched, something rippled along the surface, and a creature's ridged back breached momentarily before disappearing into the water again.

We both turned away from the pond to where the cloud of glowing lantern bugs hung. They seemed to know they had our attention and began moving away in a thick winding ribbon to the head of a path.

"Guess that's our cue," I said.

We set off toward the trail and followed the bugs deeper into the forest. Jasper let me walk first.

"If that was Melusine's idea of a warm welcome, I don't think we're going to get along too well," I said over my shoulder.

He snorted a wry laugh. "It was pretty rotten. But you have to go along with their whims. You know how it is with Old Ones."

"Actually, no," I said. "Having not grown up in a proper Faerie court with all the courtly pomp and nonsense, I have very little personal experience with Old Ones. Unlike you, Prince Jasper."

"Nah, it wasn't like that. I'm a bastard," he said.

"But Periclase claimed you as his. He seems to respect you. You grew up in the Duergar court, right?"

"I didn't come to the palace until later. I spent most of my childhood with my mother."

I glanced back at him. "So that was when you became a Grand Raven Master?"

"Aye, 'twas," he said, his brogue thickening momentarily.

"Where's your mother now?"

"She's in a small town in the Duergar realm, still in my childhood home."

"Was she a courtier?" I asked, figuring she must have spent time in the palace to have had a liaison with King Periclase.

"Nope."

I thought of pressing him, but there was something up ahead—lights. I slowed, but the lantern bugs sped up, darting ahead of us.

"There's a cottage," I said. I squinted into the darkness, trying to make out the contours of the structure.

Smoke puffed lazily from the chimney, tracing a line up and away into the night. The smell of logs in a fireplace wafted past, the homey welcoming aroma at odds with the tightening in my gut.

We crept up to the edge of the weak light cast from the windows of the quaint little house.

"A lone cottage in the middle of the woods," I whispered. "These stories always end happily for the ones who wander in, right?"

Jasper muffled a chuckle against the back of his hand.

"Well, this is what we came for." He stepped out of the protective shadow of the trees.

I drew a deep breath and followed him.

Lunar moths flitted around the moon garden to the left of the cottage. The lantern bugs rose above the roof, tracing a loose spiral up through the trees. The hoots of owls and soft calls of night birds formed a pleasant audial backdrop to the scene.

The little house itself seemed drawn straight from a fairy tale. The windows were round, and the roof steep and dormered, and it had a vaguely Swiss-chalet look about it. A stream meandered to the right, fed by the larger pond we'd gotten all too well acquainted with. I eyed the water warily as we approached the front door.

Jasper and I exchanged a glance, and then he gave a little shrug, reached up, and rapped his knuckles on the door.

I could just make out soft sounds of movement inside, and something darkened a window off to the side—there and gone too quickly for me to catch more than a pale face.

The wooden door opened inward with a gentle creak.

There stood Melusine, her face in shadow as she was backlit by the crackling fire in the hearth behind her.

"You made it, I see," she said. "I suppose I must invite you in. Enter at your own risk, little ones."

She swung the door wider and let out a soft, dry cackle, a fitting laugh for the witch she was.

I swallowed hard and stepped inside.

Chapter 10

THE COTTAGE WAS much larger inside than it appeared. So much so, I felt vaguely dizzy as my brain tried to reconcile it. Another trick of Fae magic, no doubt, like the shallowness of the pond and the enormous size of the koi in it.

Melusine had the same stately and ethereal look as Oberon and Titania, the only other Old Ones I'd seen in person. Her skin was like white porcelain, her hair black and glossy as the feathers of Jasper's birds. Her eyes were haunting, the irises the rosy color a ripe peach's skin. Her coloring would have looked gothic and overly-dramatic on a normal Fae, but on her it was mysterious. And like the other Old Ones, her beauty was so exquisite it was almost painful to look straight at her.

"The walk didn't do much to dry you off, did it?" she said, her mouth twisting a little in distaste as she surveyed our wet clothes.

I suppressed a frown. It was her fault we got soaked in the first place.

She fluttered the fingers of one hand, and the air around me seemed to compress. The pressure grew uncomfortable, but then it was gone, and with it the water was drawn from my clothes, hair, and boots. A fine, thick mist formed around me and Jasper and then began to dissipate into the room.

"What did you think of my doorway?" she asked and cackled again, louder than before.

I blinked. "You formed a doorway in a fish?"

"Pretty trick, isn't it?"

I wasn't sure how to respond. It seemed cruel to insert a Faerie portal in a live creature, but perhaps the fish was only an illusion. In any case, we needed her help, and it wasn't going to further our cause if I criticized her method of bringing us here. For once, I managed to keep my trap shut.

She turned and went to a carved, high-backed chair set up near the fire and sat down, propping her feet on a tiny footstool with miniature carved legs that matched the chair's. As she settled herself, she pierced first Jasper and then me with uncomfortably long, unblinking stares.

Something moved over the top of the chair's back. My eyes widened as a spider larger than my hand paused on a carved flower and then began to descend toward Melusine's shoulder. I started to raise a hand to warn her, but then she reached up and stroked the spider's furry back as it perched just above her collarbone.

I cringed and tried not to shudder too visibly.

"I don't like fish much. They eat insects," Melusine said. Her gaze settled on Jasper. "That's why I couldn't allow your birds in my realm. They'd prey on my lunar butterflies and other pets." She looked down at the creature on her shoulder with an affectionate little smile.

I was pretty sure ravens weren't stupid enough to try to take on a huge, hairy spider, but she was probably right about the moths.

"You know why we've come, my lady?" Jasper asked.

"Hmm, yes," she said, still gazing at her pet. "You need Melusine to tell you who your mommies and daddies are."

She said it as if speaking to small children. Which, to her, we probably were in some ways. When you'd lived for many centuries, what was a twenty-seven-year-old Fae? A mere baby. But there was also a mocking note in her voice, indicating she didn't think much of us. Or maybe just young Fae in general. Or perhaps she didn't really like anyone. She did, after all, tend to live in places that made her impossible to find unless she wanted to be found.

I glanced at Jasper as something she'd just said tickled at my mind. "We only need to discern the parentage of one individual," I said. "We brought a sample of her blood."

"No," she said sharply.

My heart dropped. She was going to refuse Nicole's blood?

Melusine narrowed her eyes at us and again fixed on Jasper. "He wants to know, too."

I swung my gaze around at him. "I thought you knew who your parents were?"

He flicked a glance at me but didn't respond.

Melusine cackled at me. "You thought wrong."

"Petra's right in that we've come primarily for another." He reached under his breastplate and drew out the little drawstring bag I'd given him before I'd left with Gretchen. When he took out the wad of gauze, I heard a faint crunch.

I winced. *Shit.* The vial had broken.

He unraveled the gauze to reveal glass shards.

"Oh no, did your little swim wash away all the changeling's blood?" Melusine asked in a high-pitched, mocking voice. She pulled an exaggerated sad face, her eyes wide and the corners of her mouth pulled down.

Jasper shook his head at the broken vial and then looked up at me. "I'm so sorry, Petra. It's gone, completely gone. There's not even a blood stain. Our trip has been in vain."

Melusine began to chuckle, her lips closed and the sound coming from deep in her throat. It sent chills spilling down my spine.

"Not in vain," she finally said. She raised one graceful arm and extended it, pointing at me. "You've got a walking skin bag of blood right there."

He flicked a glance at her and then squinted at me.

"Are you going to tell him, or am I?" the Fae witch asked me in an admonishing tone of a parent who'd caught her child in a lie. "This is your only chance to discover the truth. I will not be granting you audience again."

I fought back a scowl. She was clearly enjoying all of this, and I hated being toyed with. I couldn't help wondering who else knew my secret, if Melusine was aware of it. In any case, she wasn't going to allow me to get another sample of Nicole's blood.

"You have three seconds," Melusine said irritably. "Or I'll tell him."

It was now or never.

I met Jasper's gaze. "Nicole is my twin sister," I finally said. I had to. If I didn't, Melusine obviously would. She let out a pleased titter.

His eyes widened momentarily. His lips moved as if he wanted to say something, but no words came.

Melusine brought her hands up under her chin and gave a couple of delighted little claps.

"The two of you could be half-siblings!" She crowed. She looked at Jasper. "That's what you're thinking, right?"

Jasper's brows drew low, but he smoothed his expression before it became a full-on frown. He reached down to his belt and withdrew a small folding knife, which he passed to me.

I flipped it open, and with a quick flick, I nicked the blade across the back of my wrist. I didn't want to damage my hands, in case I needed them later in a fight. Blood swelled from the cut, and I looked up at Melusine.

Her eerie pale-orange eyes were fixed on the cut.

"Come closer," she whispered, beckoning.

It was literally the last thing in the world I wanted to do, the way she was looking at my blood with a greedy glint in her eyes. But I did it anyway. When I reached the side of her chair, her hand darted out and her cold fingers wrapped around my arm, just above the cut, squeezing hard enough to make me want to pull back. Then she jerked my arm up and ran her tongue over the bead of blood.

Bile rose in my throat as I realized what she'd done. The swell of revulsion was quickly drowned out by a new sensation that began at the cut and seemed to worm its way through me. It was as if a horde of scuttling beetles had been poured into my bloodstream.

I squeezed my eyes closed and gritted my teeth, trying with everything in me not to scream and writhe. When the sensation spread up my neck and into my head, seeming to beat at the backs of my eyeballs, I couldn't hold back a low moan.

When she finally released my arm, the invasive, crawling sensation began to recede. In its wake was a horrible exposed emptiness. The depth of it stilled my breath. It was like standing naked in front of every living person on Earth and in Faerie while everything I'd ever done or thought rolled across a screen for all to view.

I opened my eyes and met her orange gaze, and somehow I knew she'd seen into everything that made me who I was, that nothing was private anymore or ever could be again.

I'd wondered what the price would be, what I would owe Melusine for her information. This was it. She knew my every thought, wish, and fantasy. I couldn't imagine what she'd do with such knowledge, but I felt as if I'd been turned inside out and spread on a table for her perusal.

I swallowed hard, fighting the urge to vomit in her lap.

Her lids lowered partway, and the tip of her tongue flicked out to her lips, as if she were still tasting my blood. My stomach tumbled as I waited for her to speak.

Chapter 11

"OLIVER MAGUIRE IS not your blood father," Melusine said. "The Duergar King Periclase is."

My entire body went stiff, and I reeled a little, desperately pushing back at the tidal wave of thoughts that tried to crash through me.

"And my mother?" I managed to grind out through clenched teeth.

"Carmen MacPharlain, deceased."

The name was completely unfamiliar to me. I filed it away for later examination.

I drew a shaky breath, and another. Then I turned and stumbled away from Melusine and nearly plowed into Jasper. He caught me by the upper arms and held me steady.

"What did she say?" he asked.

I looked up into his golden eyes. "You didn't hear?"

He shook his head.

"Periclase is my father."

His eyes tensed, his golden gaze holding mine.

I still had Jasper's knife clenched in my fist. I pushed it into his hand. He glanced past me at Melusine, clearly hesitant.

"We're here," I whispered. "If you have any doubt, you might as well do it."

As the blood on my wrist dried, I watched Jasper play out the same scene I just had. Melusine tasted his blood, but when she spoke to him,

I heard only a grating hum. Her lips seemed obscured somehow, so I couldn't even try to lip-read.

When Jasper finally turned to face me, he was pale, but his eyes were intent with a faint spark of something that seemed . . . heightened. Surprised, and maybe awed. I was still too stricken to try to understand it.

"Let's go," he mumbled in my ear. "She took what she takes. We don't owe her anything more."

I glanced back at Melusine. She leaned forward and pushed her hands down on the armrests. The spider scuttled back over the chair right before she rose, and when she stood she somehow appeared taller than before. She seemed to be stretching upward, elongating until her head brushed the ceiling. Her face darkened, distorting with anger. I blinked, trying to make sense of it, but it was like trying to find the logic in a fever dream.

And she was getting pissed.

"That's right, go," she said, clenching her fists at her sides. "You only came to use me!"

Jasper was pulling me toward the door, but something in the plaintive tone of her voice made me pause. I stopped in the doorway and turned.

"We don't have to leave," I said calmly.

She blinked at me.

"We don't mean to be rude," I said. "Would it please you if we stayed for a bit, my lady?"

She shrank down to her normal size and flopped back into her chair, slamming an elbow onto the chair's arm and slumping to rest her face in her hand.

"I guess you could warm up by the fire," she finally said, her voice low and sulky. "And bed down in the barn. If you want."

I flicked a glance a Jasper. He didn't look happy about it, but he gave a tiny nod.

Something about Melusine reminded me of Morven. They were both dangerous in their own ways and both lived to take from others, but the difference was that Morven was always surrounded by people. He had his pub and his regulars, people who enjoyed being at the Aberdeen and weren't only there for the other services he offered. In contrast, Melusine seemed very much alone. Perhaps she truly preferred it that way, but something in her childish outburst told me she didn't necessarily relish her never-ending isolation. And I'd learned with Morven that it paid to show a bit of kindness, even if he wasn't someone to trust and was happy to steal whatever you were willing to give.

Kindness can be carefully offered. It can make a dangerous person, if not into an ally, possibly into someone slightly less dangerous.

Melusine gestured to the high table in the small kitchen area. "Pull those stools over."

Jasper and I each carried a stool and set them near the hearth. I wondered if she ever had a guest at her little dining table with only the two seats, or if the other stool was always empty.

My stomach grumbled noisily, and I pressed a hand into my midsection, casting a glance at the Fae witch.

"There's stew on the stove," she said.

I started to rise, but Jasper put his hand on my arm, gently pushing me back down. The look in his eyes said he preferred to get away from Melusine, so I let him go to the kitchen and rummage for dishes for our dinner.

With Jasper across the room, the Fae witch leaned forward with her lips pursed and her pale-orange eyes gleaming.

"He's terribly good-looking," she whispered. "Don't you think?"

My brows jumped up at her sudden change in demeanor. I tossed a glance at Jasper, but he was still busy in the kitchen. Either he hadn't heard, or he was pretending for the sake of manners. Either way, the ancient Fae witch was looking at me expectantly, obviously wanting my opinion.

"Yes," I said. "He is a handsome man."

Her huge spider peeked over the top of her chair and then tentatively moved to perch on her shoulder again. "Mm, yes, look at his backside."

I didn't.

"You fancy him," she said, narrowing her eyes at me and reaching up to pet her spider's back with one finger. "I know you do. I felt it."

I shifted uncomfortably, and not just because of the reappearance of the enormous crawly thing. "I might, if, you know, we weren't *related*."

She leaned back, laughed, and waved a hand. "Oh, that."

I thought she was going to say that being half-siblings shouldn't stop us. Old Ones had different ideas of taboos, and it wouldn't have surprised me if she thought it silly to be concerned about incest. After all, most of the Old Ones were related to each other in some way, if distantly.

Instead, she leaned forward again.

"You're not related." She raised her hand to her mouth and let out a little conspiratorial giggle muffled by her fingers.

My eyes popped wide and my mouth dropped open, but before I could say anything, Jasper was there next to me holding out a steaming bowl. It smelled like heaven.

Our gazes met, and I let mine linger longer than I meant to. Blinking hard, I looked down into the bowl.

"Do you enjoy it here in the woods?" I asked Melusine. The question was awkward, but I wanted to get her talking about something else before she brought up Jasper's ass again.

"Well, why wouldn't I?" she said, her former irritability returning. "I can live wherever I want to, and I chose this place."

I stuck a spoonful of stew into my mouth, as there was no good way to respond to her sulky words. The stew was fragrant, hot, and the only food I'd had in many hours. I was willing to put up with Melusine's moodiness for a warm meal and a roof over my head for the night. I sorely needed a salt soak, having pulled armor so many times in the past couple of days. Being in Faerie full-time gave me a lot more stamina, but still, there were limits to my magic.

"Do people come to you often seeking your expertise?" Jasper asked.

I slid him a glance, surprised that he wanted to engage with her.

A sly smile spread over Melusine's face. "Oh, they try, but I rarely deign to speak to them."

"Why us?" I asked.

For a moment her brows lowered, and I thought she would respond with another temperamental outburst. But then her expression turned considering.

"The truth of your blood carries importance," she said, looking at each of us in turn. "Equally so for both of you. As individuals and as a pair."

I shifted on my stool. A *pair*?

"Can you tell us why?" Jasper asked quietly. "Or at least tell me why for my own situation?"

I wondered what he meant by "situation," but I didn't even have a wild guess. There was clearly a lot more to him than just working as a high-level soldier in his father's ranks. Scratch that—in King Periclase's ranks. Not his father's. I peered at him side-long, trying to guess whether his lineage was different than what I'd assumed. He had stone armor, so clearly there was New Gargoyle blood. He easily passed for part-Duergar, too, based on the square line of his jaw, his straight brows, pale skin tone, and wide shoulders. His mother lived in the Duergar realm, which meant she had at least some Duergar blood, so he could have gotten those features from her. New Garg, Duergar . . . and something else? If he'd ever had his blood divined—different than what Melusine did—he'd know his racial mix.

Melusine snorted. "I'm not a fortune teller," she said with a condescending twist of her lips. "I'm not here to tell you the future or what to do with yourselves after you leave."

"That's not what I meant, my lady," Jasper said with his signature mild tone. "Why do you believe the truth of our blood is important?"

She drew in a slow breath and turned her gaze to the flames in the hearth. Several seconds of silence ticked by.

"Because believing falsely about your respective lineages would lead you to take a . . . less desirable path," she said finally. She seemed far away, almost as if she'd forgotten we were there.

She'd said she wasn't a fortune teller, but her response suggested she knew something of our futures, or at the very least had some opinion on the directions we took in our lives.

Jasper and I exchanged a long look, the fire creating miniature dancing flames over his gold eyes.

When my gaze returned to Melusine, I saw that she'd been watching us intently. For a moment, only a split second, her eyes were soft and vulnerable. Her face seemed to reflect regret and longing. But her expression quickly hardened.

"The barn is out back," she said. She flicked her hand dismissively and turned to stare into the fire again. "The moths will show you the way."

The Fae witch was clearly finished with us, so we silently rose, left our dishes in the kitchen, and moved our stools back to the little table.

Once we were outside, I let out a long exhale. At the end of the breath, the truth that Melusine had revealed to me came crashing down like a ton of rocks. My feet slowed and then stopped. About a dozen lunar moths flitted in a moving cloud of pale wings and then peeled off to form a line. We were obviously supposed to follow, but my feet wouldn't budge. A fatigue deeper than any I'd ever felt had taken hold, with invisible hands grasping my ankles and preventing me from taking a step.

Jasper turned when he realized I wasn't coming with him.

"Petra?" He came back to where I stood.

I pulled my palms down my face, as if that would wash away the weariness.

"I think my mother was raped," I said, my voice barely a whisper. "She was Periclase's captive. That's what Oliver told me."

I shouldn't have been saying such personal things, and it wasn't like me to do so, but the echoing aftershocks of Melusine's revelation had beat down some of my usual barriers. Oliver had prepared me somewhat, but the reality of it was still buffeting me from different directions. The more dangerous problem was that Jasper, who Periclase believed was his, knew I was Nicole's sister. He knew that both of us were Periclase's blood. That wasn't good. Not at all.

Jasper didn't say anything. He only watched me with his golden eyes and a patient expression.

"It doesn't really matter," I said, my tone too flippant to be convincing.

I gave my head a shake and forced my feet to move. I brushed past him, following the moths.

He caught up and walked beside me around the cottage to a trail leading away into the trees. I could just make out the roofline of what must have been the barn Melusine had given us use of.

"It's perfectly understandable to be upset," Jasper said. "This is a shock. Periclase is an asshole. I thought so even when I believed he was my father, but I honestly don't think he's a rapist."

He was trying to be understanding, comforting even, but I wasn't in the mood for heartfelt discussions about my newfound daddy issues and what might or might not have gone on between my blood parents.

"No one can know about me, that I'm Nicole's sister," I said, my voice hard-edged. "That knowledge wasn't part of our deal, Jasper. The broken vial and Melusine compelled me to reveal it. I trusted you to carry the vial, but it broke and forced my hand."

If I could get a binding promise out of him to keep my secret, it would be ideal, but I doubted he would agree to it. After all, he was sworn to the Duergar king. He was here as a representative of Periclase, to witness the information Melusine had given us.

"I have no reason to tell," he said.

"Right now, maybe, but what if that information becomes useful at some point?" I pressed.

"You want me to enter into a binding agreement," he said.

"Of course I do," I burst out. "It was none of your business in the first place, and it's—well, it could be dangerous. For me. On top of that, the last thing I need is for Periclase to start hounding me to swear to him, because that sure as hell isn't going to happen." My outburst trailed off into a string of cursing under my breath.

He stopped and gripped my upper arm, forcing me to halt and face him.

"Take a breath, Petra," he said in that annoyingly calm tone of his. "I'm not out to destroy your life. I won't tell."

"Swear to it?"

He shook his head. "No binding agreements."

Anger shot through me. "Why?" I demanded.

"I want you to trust me," he said. "How about a secret for a secret, instead?"

"Fine." I peered up at him in the darkness. "Who's *your* pops?"

"Pick something else."

I folded my arms. "Not happening. Come on, Dad for Dad. It's only fair."

He took in a breath and held it. I couldn't really see his face in the dark, but I got a strong sense of his trepidation.

He let out a long exhale. "Finvarra."

I blinked a couple of times. "*King* Finvarra? The ruler of legend? The

High King of the Unseelie court?"

"You think there are other Finvarras in Faerie?"

"Okay." I scoffed. "You're trying to be funny. Who is it, really?"

"You know I couldn't lie," he said quietly. "It was a direct question. I gave you the answer. It's the truth."

I knew that, of course, but . . . the only response that would have surprised me more was if Jasper had said Oberon himself was his blood father. King Periclase was powerful and imposing, but he ruled only one court. King Finvarra was above Periclase, the unifying ruler of all Unseelie courts. And he'd been around for *centuries*. He wasn't Oberon and Melusine old, but he was a living legend, much like Morven. Finvarra and his deceased wife Maeve had been responsible for the rise of the Unseelie courts to become on par with Oberon's Seelie courts. Before that, the Unseelie had been inferior in every way—fewer numbers, courts that were constantly disrupted by coups and assassinations, and too much backstabbing and animal hedonism to ever change their position in Faerie.

Finvarra and Maeve had organized the Unseelie, brought structure and some semblance of discipline to their courts, and created something that previously no one had thought possible—a High Court to rival Oberon's. A Winter court to oppose the Summer court.

But I couldn't recall anyone speaking of an actual sighting of the Unseelie High King in my lifetime. At least, not when I'd been growing up and living full-time in Faerie. After I moved to the other side of the hedge, I only kept track of what Faerie news might help me in my job as a Guild mercenary.

"How?" I asked, still dumbfounded. "How could Finvarra be your father?"

"I believe you're old enough to know how babies are made," he said mildly. He seemed to be taking the news about his blood father with remarkable ease. I'd have been freaking the hell out if I'd just found out I'd been sired by a legend.

I shot him a withering look. "You know what I mean."

He shrugged. "No idea. This was news to me."

"Do you think your mother knew it wasn't Periclase?"

He was silent for a long moment.

"Yes," he said finally. "She did tell me once that it was better to allow the Duergar king to believe what he believed. That it would be better for me, for my station in life. I'm not a Duergar prince, though. I've always been treated with only the bare minimum acceptance. In the context of Duergar royalty, I am formally recognized as his, but I'm still a bastard."

"That's better for your station in life than being Finvarra's son?" I asked doubtfully.

He gave me a sharp look. "Well, yes, if my mother was trying to keep my life somewhat normal. With Finvarra as my father, I'm in line to inherit the Winter Court. He's not immortal. And he's very old."

My lips parted as a new truth dawned on me. "Finvarra has no known living children. Until now."

I looked at Jasper with fresh amazement. The moonlight glinted off the planes of his forehead and cheekbones. He went quiet, suddenly seeming a bit shaken.

"If Finvarra dies, every Unseelie ruler would go for your throat. Hell, they'd do it *before* he dies, just to have you out of the way when the time comes to fill Finvarra's position."

"Now you know," he said at a near whisper. "You must keep my secret too."

"I will."

We continued on in silence for a few steps, and I sank into thought, alternately considering what I'd discovered about my own bloodline and what Jasper had learned of his.

"I tend to forget you're Unseelie," I said suddenly.

He gave a quiet laugh, seemingly relieved to change the subject. "What's that supposed to mean?"

"You seem like a decent person," I said. "I know you're trying to persuade me to help you bridge the rift between Duergar and the Stone Order, but you're doing it . . . honorably."

That seemed to have shocked him into silence for a second or two.

"That means more than you know," he said, his voice pitched low.

I pulled my jacket tighter around my torso, already regretting I'd spoken so freely. I was getting way too candid around Jasper. Maybe it was the fact that we'd been thrown together in so many strange ways over the past few weeks. Or perhaps it was having discovered unexpected truths about our bloodlines at the same time. It didn't matter. I needed to be more careful.

Yes, Jasper *seemed* like a decent man, but he suddenly had information he could use to hurt me. Not to mention the binding favor in his hip pocket that I was bound to pay him at some point.

I felt agitated all of a sudden. My brain itched, and my muscles wanted to beat up something. I half-wished some of those servitors might find us here just so I'd have an excuse to draw Mort and slice off a head or two.

We reached the clearing with the promised barn, and the lunar moths turned and headed back to Melusine's cottage. As we approached the dark building, a small flame suddenly lit, and I nearly reached for my sword. But it was just a lantern hanging on the side of the barn. We must have tripped one of Melusine's wards. Possessing human witch magic, she probably had them set up all over her property.

Jasper took the lantern from its hook. The structure was small and probably more for the quaint look of it than for actually housing any livestock, also betrayed by the absence of the smell of manure or any nearby corral. He opened the door, and I followed him. Inside, there were stalls, one of them stuffed with hay, and a loft. It smelled clean and earthy. On one wall there was a long basin with a faucet. There weren't any horses, but all the gear was there—saddles, all manner of miscellaneous tack, and blankets.

"Hope you're not allergic to hay," I said, gesturing to the stall. "Because that looks like the only decent place to sleep."

Jasper shot me a quick, assessing look.

"I'm not proposing we *roll around* in it," I said, a bit more harshly than I intended.

His face eased into a faint smile, but there was a new intensity to his gaze. He straightened. "That's right, you did just call me honorable."

I snorted and went to work bench that held the pile of blankets. "You're not going to let me forget about that, are you?" I pulled off a few and turned with the stack in my arms.

I hadn't heard Jasper move up behind me, and when I turned around, my hands bumped into his chest. His face was tipped down, that mild smile still playing over his lips.

With deliberate movements, he set the lantern on the bench and then lifted the blankets from my arms and dropped the pile next to the lantern.

He stepped into me, his hand coming up to rest on my cheek, and the gold in his eyes seemed to flare. Everything slowed and then stopped, even the beat of my own heart. Then he lowered his mouth to mine just as I reached up for him. When our lips touched, my pulse bucked and galloped. His lips were firm, and there was no hesitation. In spite of his often mild manner, his kiss was strong and hot with passion.

My body responded with its own heat. Our kiss deepened, and the flame in my core grew to a blaze.

Just as Jasper's other hand moved around to firmly press into my lower back, drawing me tighter against him, there was a loud crash at the far end of the barn.

Chapter 12

I SUCKED IN a startled breath, and Jasper and I both whipped around in the direction of the noise just as a white horse came galloping through the big double doors. They'd smacked into the walls as they'd burst open, and they were still swinging on their hinges.

As the beast came toward us, I saw it wasn't a white horse. It had a slender spiraled horn growing from its forehead.

I swallowed hard as the unicorn slowed but continued to approach. Unicorns were vicious killers and very difficult to take down. I suddenly regretted my earlier wish for something to swing my sword at. She stopped opposite us, turning her head to stare at us with one eye across the work bench.

Jasper and I had edged away from each other, and both of us were tensed, ready to draw our weapons. Then the beast's mouth opened, her lips pulled back, and she let out a laugh. Not a horsey whinny, but a human cackle—*Melusine's* laugh.

I relaxed slightly. "Another one of her illusions, like the koi," I said.

Jasper stared at the unicorn for another second and then shook his head and breathed an amused chuckle.

He cocked his head at the beast. "I believe she's sent a chaperone," he said, and the unicorn bucked her head in what almost looked like a nod of agreement. "Do you think she was trying to send us a message, what with unicorns' obsessions with virgins?"

I snorted a laugh and I pushed my hair back from my face. My lips still throbbed slightly from the pressure of his mouth. I was no virgin, but I was suddenly sure the unicorn wasn't a random choice.

"Well." I planted my hands on my hips, regarding the conjured unicorn. "I guess it's time for lights-out, then."

He quirked a grin at me, the flame of the lantern dancing in his eyes as he held my gaze for a long moment. I pulled in my lower lip and bit down on it as I let out a disappointed sigh, which made his mouth stretch wider.

"Guess so," he said, with a hint of regret in his voice. More than a hint, actually, but his expression was good-natured.

The unicorn followed us over to the stall of hay, and she watched as we mounded piles of it and then spread the blankets over the top of the makeshift beds. Jasper and I traded a glance, and then both of us looked at the unicorn. She moved past us to the stall, stood right in the middle of the blankets, and proceeded to lower herself to the floor, curling up in a way that clearly said she had no intention of moving.

Jasper and I had no choice but to take spots on either side of the beast.

As I settled on my side facing the white beast with my scabbard alongside me, I chuckled a soft laugh. I couldn't even see Jasper past the creature. Cock-blocked by a unicorn. Clearly Melusine had a strong opinion about what transpired—or not—between me and Jasper that night.

Fatigue cooled the heat created by Jasper's kiss, weighing down my limbs and thickening in my brain. Sleep claimed me.

When I awoke, the unicorn was gone and so was Jasper. I sat up and picked pieces of straw off my skin and clothes and then found the outhouse outside the barn. A quaint touch by Melusine.

When I emerged, Jasper was sauntering up the trail leading from Melusine's cottage with half a loaf of bread in his hand. He split it and handed one piece to me.

"Morning," he said, his golden eyes bright as the dawning sun.

"The two of you had breakfast together without me?" I asked with mock accusation.

"Aye, and talked about you the whole time."

I gave him a side-eye, unsure if he actually had shared a meal with the Fae witch.

He shook his head. "I just wanted to make sure we were clear to leave. And also find out whether we'd be obliged to go by way of fish belly."

"Oberon's balls, I hope there's an easier way out of here," I said.

"There is," he said. His face grew serious. "I also wanted to ask her about the Tuatha's return."

I stopped chewing.

"She confirmed what the Great Ravens saw. Not that she'd seen it with her own eyes, but that she's heard whispers from sources she trusts."

"The Dullahan, too?"

He nodded.

"Was she concerned?"

His face became even more grim, his brows lowering over tense eyes. "She seemed a bit afraid."

I swallowed a bite of bread, forcing it down my suddenly dry throat. I didn't like the thought of moody, powerful, lone-wolf Melusine afraid.

"Did she have anything to say about why the Tuatha would turn against us?" I asked.

"She only said that when the gods are displeased, it's because the world they created has gone astray of their vision. She was speaking philosophically, mind you, not from direct knowledge of state of mind of the Tuatha."

"It's hard to believe the Tuatha would rise against even the Old Ones," I said, shaking my head slightly.

The Old Ones like Oberon, Titania, and Melusine were almost gods to us. Nearly immortal. Practically infallible. Almost . . . nearly . . . practically. The fact was, the Old Ones weren't gods. They never had been. The true gods were returning, and apparently they were pissed.

I finished the last bite of bread and looked around Melusine's woods as I chewed. I couldn't help a small sigh as I realized this place felt like a bit of a haven, in some strange way. A break from Marisol's rule, Faerie politics, and money concerns. It had even been a respite from the animosity between the New Gargoyles and the Duergar, for soon Jasper and I would part ways, each of us going back to our respective leaders to report what Melusine had told us about Nicole's blood father.

"So, if we're not traveling by fish, where's our exit?" I asked.

He lifted his chin at the trail winding away from the barn and leading off in the opposite direction of Melusine's cottage.

"Is it strange that I'm not eager to leave?" Jasper asked as we began walking.

I crooked a small smile up at him, managing to keep my eyes on his rather than letting my gaze dip to his lips. "Not so strange."

The trail ended at a stone arch. It was an unnatural place for such a structure, and I wondered whether Melusine had conjured it, too, just for our benefit.

I opened my mouth. "It's been—"

"Until we—" Jasper started talking at the same time. He inclined his head. "You first."

"It's been . . . enlightening," I said. I honestly hadn't been certain how I was going to end the sentence. My word choice seemed to disappoint him a bit. I gave him a pointed look. "As we part, we both have secrets to keep."

"I have no intention of betraying your confidence," he said. "And I still believe that you and I will be the ones to repair relations between our respective kingdoms."

The corners of my mouth twitched. "Not letting that bone go?"

"You shall hear from me soon." He swept out one arm in a gallant gesture toward the arch. "Until we meet again, Petra Maguire."

I stepped up to the stone structure, traced the sigils, and whispered the words. The netherwhere took me into its chilly embrace and then spilled me out through the doorway just outside the stone fortress. I'd purposely come back to an exterior doorway to give myself a moment.

I leaned against the solidity of the former prison, tipping the side of my head to the rough stone and closing my eyes. Periclase was my father. Jasper, the son of a legend, had kissed me. And the gods were coming with the Bone Warriors.

I pushed away from the wall, inhaled a sharp breath through my nose, and squared my shoulders. I passed through the doorway into the stone fortress, and I was suddenly back in the bustle.

I wanted to go to Oliver first, but I was living under Marisol's rule now. She would expect the news immediately upon my return, and if anyone spotted me doing anything but heading straight to her, it wouldn't win me any points with the stone monarch. I was stuck in the fortress for the time being. I had to play along.

Curious eyes followed me as I made my way through the corridors to Marisol's office. Everyone in the Order knew of my errand to Melusine, and there was also still some buzz through the fortress and likely through all of Faerie over my victory in the battle of champions. The stares felt like strands of a spider's web, shooting out at me and falling delicately onto my limbs but clinging with stubborn stickiness as spider silk does. Each strand was only a barely-there filament, but together they seemed to be grasping me, softly anchoring me more and more firmly into Faerie affairs.

I kept my eyes straight ahead, avoiding the looks and pushing down a sudden pang of longing for my life across the hedge, where my bloodline didn't mean anything, and I was just another merc trying to catch my mark and make rent.

When I turned into the hallway leading to Marisol's lair of quarters and offices, Maxen was waiting. He fell into step beside me.

"You're back," he said, his face closed off.

Some of the chill between us had warmed after the servitor attack, but he seemed uncertain about where we stood. Or maybe there was no uncertainty on his part, and he knew exactly how he felt about my reluctance to throw myself whole-heartedly into the affairs of the Stone Order.

"Word travels fast in the fortress," I said, still glad to see him, in spite of the awkwardness between us.

"How did it go?" Some curiosity was cracking through his carefully controlled expression. I didn't blame him. Not many people tried to get audience with Melusine. Even fewer were granted it.

Hm, how did it go? Now there was a loaded question. Several things passed through my mind. The sprite attack. Getting swallowed by a giant koi. Sitting by the fire with the Fae witch. Learning my true blood father. Jasper's kiss. The unicorn that prevented that kiss from going any further.

I shrugged a shoulder. "Eh, you know. Over the river and through the woods, to Melusine's cottage we went." I said it in the sing-song of a nursery rhyme.

"She gave you audience?"

"I wouldn't have come back if she hadn't." I slid him a glance. "You know how I am about admitting defeat."

His lips twitched, and he nearly cracked a smile.

I gestured ahead at the open door to Marisol's main offices. "Is she going to let you hear my report?"

He nodded. "She summoned me when she heard you were back."

He let me go in ahead of him. The sitting room had a fire crackling in the fireplace, and the snooty page I'd dealt with before was posted at the small desk across from a pair of chairs.

"She's expecting me," I said to the page. He started to rise and protest, but I ignored him and continued into Marisol's office.

Maxen came in and closed the door behind us as his mother looked up from one of three tablets on her desk.

"My lady," I said, formally inclining my head. "I've returned from my errand with the information I was sent to obtain."

Her eyes widened only slightly, but I could sense her heightened attention. The air in the room seemed to still in her anticipation of what I would report. Maxen stood off to my right, just inside my peripheral vision.

"And?" was all she said. She folded her hands on her desk with her fingers interlaced.

"King Periclase is Nicole's blood father."

She blinked twice. "Jasper Glasgow witnessed the report of this?"

I nodded.

She drew a breath and pursed her lips for a second or two. "Very well. We know the truth. It doesn't change the fact that the changeling has New Gargoyle blood. She's already proven it by summoning stone armor."

She leaned back in her chair, her gaze roaming to one of the windows. Then she refocused, this time on her son.

"Where are her intentions leaning?" she asked.

I slid a glance at him. It was telling that she was asking him and not me, considering I was her roommate and had been formally assigned to be her buddy while she was in the fortress. Perhaps I was right after all in thinking that Maxen's attention on Nicole was partly out of duty. One might almost let Marisol off the hook for using her son that way. He was very handsome, charming, and practically Fae royalty.

He shifted his weight and clasped his hands in front of him, one hand covering the other. "She doesn't want to return to Periclase's kingdom. She fears him, and now that she knows more about the Unseelie, she's firm in her refusal to go back."

"How close is she to a decision about accepting her Fae heritage?" Marisol asked.

"She's still wavering," Maxen said. "But I think she's close to acceptance."

"We need to press her," Marisol said. "Make it very clear that if she rejects Faerie and returns to the Earthly realm, Periclase will simply take her again. If that happens, we probably won't be able to save her again. The safest route is for her to swear to me and the Stone Order. If she does that, Periclase can howl all he wants, but she's ours."

I had to check my surprise before it showed on my face. She sounded chillingly calculating, despite the truth in her words. Periclase would most likely kidnap her again, but letting Nicole think that we'd just let her waste away as a captive in the Duergar kingdom when she was also one of us bordered on cruel. I certainly wouldn't let that happen.

"I don't think we need to play that card quite yet," Maxen said carefully. "I think she may come around to it on her own."

"That would be nice, but we can't wait much longer for it to happen naturally," Marisol said. "You must make it clear that she can't simply swear to the Stone Order and leave to resume her life on the other side of the hedge. She'd be unprotected and completely vulnerable to Periclase. If she isn't ready to take the oath within the next two days and plan to remain here permanently, she'll need to be pressed."

I frowned. Why was Marisol so bent on keeping Nicole here? Sure, she was New Garg and the lady of the Order was constantly reminding us about how every one of our numbers counted. But Marisol's interest in the matter seemed overblown.

There was a sharp twang of sympathy in my heart for Nicole. Yes, in many ways all of this was business as usual in Faerie, but I knew the pain of being pressed under Marisol's thumb. I couldn't help wondering if it was something in our blood that fated me and my twin to being forced into undesired lives in Faerie.

"Understood," Maxen said. He inclined his head in an acquiescent gesture, but I caught the brief contraction of his face that indicated he wasn't happy about Marisol's orders.

I peered at him. Regardless of how much his mother was motivating him to spend time with Nicole, the idea of manipulating her seemed to bother him. Perhaps he had some genuine feelings for her after all. Rarely had I seen him show any objection to his mother's commands.

"My lady, I have more to report," I said. "Jasper asked Melusine about the rumors and rumblings regarding the Tuatha De Danann. She confirmed she's heard it from trusted sources. The Tuatha are preparing to return, and they're coming with the Bone Warriors. She's . . . concerned."

Marisol's brows drew together over her sapphire-blue eyes. She gave a slight shake of her head. "It's hard to imagine that it's real, isn't it," she said quietly.

I got the feeling she wasn't actually asking me, so I didn't respond.

"Have his Great Ravens discovered anything else about the return of the Tuatha?" she asked.

"Not that he shared with me," I said.

Her gaze sharpened on me. "The two of you are amicable, is that correct?"

I tried my best to avoid thinking about his mouth on mine. The way his hand had pressed into my lower back, drawing me against his chest and making me want to arch into him.

I tilted my head. "It depends on the moment, but considering all that's passed between the Duergar and the Stone Order, I guess you could say we are amicable," I said reluctantly.

I couldn't lie. But a sinking sensation filled my mid-section. I had a bad feeling I knew what was coming.

"That's good," she said. She leaned back in her chair, propping her elbows on the arm rests and steepling her fingers beneath her chin. "Periclase is refusing to deal with Maxen, and the Duergar king is not a particular fan of me, either. Not after the business with the changeling and your defeat of his brother in the battle of champions."

I forced down the groan that was trying to make its way up my throat.

"But if you and Periclase's son have a cordial connection, that could prove very useful," she said. "Very useful, indeed."

She was looking at me like I was a piece on her chess board she hadn't thought to move up to this point. It made me want to turn around and run straight out of the stone fortress.

Just as I was about to find an excuse to get the hell out of her office before she came up with some new assignment that would toss me even deeper into the mire of Faerie political affairs, there was an urgent knocking at her door.

"My lady," came the voice of the snotty page. "My lady, I'm sorry to interrupt, but I have a critical message."

"Come," she said sharply.

The page walked rapidly past me and handed her a note.

My eyes went wide. The paper was sealed with the stamp of Titania. It was a message from the High Court of the Seelie.

Marisol slipped her finger under the seal, and it gave as it magically identified her as the intended recipient. Her eyes darted back and forth over the words. She seemed to read it over twice.

When she looked up, her face had gone pale as a sheet.

Chapter 13

"CALL IN ALL of my advisors immediately," Marisol commanded.

The page turned and scurried away.

"What is it, my lady?" I asked, not really expecting her to tell me.

Her blue eyes focused on me. "Finvarra has returned. The Unseelie High King is trying to stage a takeover of the High Court in Oberon's absence."

"That . . . can't be good," I said lamely.

She'd turned to her tablet, and I started to back out of the office.

"Stay," she said sharply. "You're the champion of the Stone Order. You're an official member of the Stone Council, and it's time you started attending these meetings."

Well, shit. I hadn't realized that. I knew better than to feel honored. All this meant was that Marisol could pull me in more firmly to Order business.

My mind whirled with the news as people started to arrive. Oliver was one of the first, and seeing his face set off a cascade of little pinpricks of sadness in my heart. I hadn't even had the chance to tell him what I'd learned from Melusine. I hardened against my unexpected emotions. This wasn't the time.

As I tried to push thoughts of my bloodline away, Jasper's face cropped up in my mind's eye. Finvarra was his blood father. I wondered what Jasper thought about his blood father's possible coup.

I forced my attention to the present as Oliver came up to me. He leaned over to speak at my ear.

"I heard you'd returned, and I know you completed what you were assigned to do," he said. "Well done, Petra."

Praise from the stone man. I pulled in my lips and bit down. Why the hell did he have to say such a thing to me *now*?

The larger question loomed in his eyes, but I knew he wouldn't want me to speak of it here.

Maxen had returned. Jaquard, Marisol's personal guard and one of my old teachers, arrived. Several others came, most of whom I knew by face, but I could only recall about half the names. Amalie, a raven-haired and busty young woman, who was second cousin or some such to Maxen, was the youngest. Two years younger than me, if memory served. As I'd trained for a life of sword-wielding, Amalie had been equally focused on entering politics. I had no idea whether she was good or had gained her position by virtue of her blood ties to Marisol. The monarch of the Stone Order wasn't one to hand out positions based on nepotism, but if anyone in the fortress valued blood ties, it was Marisol. A strong family of royals was one of the things needed to gain the status of kingdom, and it was something the Stone Order lacked. Marisol's husband, Maxen's father, had died many years ago, and Marisol had no other children.

My eyes darted to the lady of the fortress as it suddenly occurred to me that Maxen might not be the only one who would be married off to strengthen the Stone Order's position in Faerie. Marisol was single, too. And I had no doubt she'd make almost any sacrifice, if it furthered her cause for the New Gargoyles.

Jaquard opened a side door in Marisol's office, revealing a room with a lectern at one end and diagrams on the walls. I followed everyone else, who was filing in. A closer look at the murals revealed that they depicted all the kingdoms of Faerie. There were illustrations of each kingdom's castle or stronghold, and of the king or queen of each realm. Seelie kingdoms on one wall and Unseelie on another. Under each leader's picture was some written information, such as kingdom population and notes about the royal family and kingdom alliances.

There were no chairs in the room, not even a table. It didn't entirely surprise me. New Gargoyles tended to be physical by nature, and sitting around a conference table really wasn't our style. Everyone gathered in a loose bunch. Marisol took to the podium, and Jaquard closed the door.

She repeated the news about Finvarra's attempt to take the High Court, which set off a burst of conversation. My sneak peek of the announcement allowed me a chance to observe the others' reactions. Oliver looked a bit more grim than usual. Maxen's blue eyes widened, and his head pulled back a bit. Jaquard just shook his head and looked briefly at the floor. Amalie's eyes, the deep purple of amethyst, sharpened. She looked neither shocked nor outraged, but intrigued.

Marisol waited for a moment for the initial reaction to die down.

"As you're already probably foreseeing, this will have an impact on our bid for an official court," she said. "With Oberon, the possibility of our independence was still on the table, and we had a chance. But Finvarra is Unseelie. He's much more likely to side with one of the Unseelie kingdoms that's trying to absorb the Stone Order. In particular, the Duergar."

She paused, and her gaze slipped over to me.

"I've also just learned that our changeling, Nicole, is indeed Periclase's daughter. This worsens our position and strengthens the Duergar's bid to officially bring us into their realm."

Several in the group shot looks my way, some of them charged with animosity, as if it were my fault that King Periclase had sired Nicole. I crossed my arms and glared back until every one of them averted their eyes.

"Now, let's hear your ideas," Marisol said.

"Any chance Titania might address the issue between us and the Duergar before Finvarra can muscle in on the High Court's business?" Amalie asked.

"We will certainly try that route," Marisol said. "But since Oberon left, she's seemed uninterested in the pending petitions in the High Court. And now she's going to be preoccupied with Finvarra's coup attempt."

Old Ones could be a childish and dramatic bunch. The rumor was that a quarrel between Titania and Oberon had become heated just prior to my battle of champions against Periclase's brother, and Oberon had disappeared before the battle. I'd nearly been forced to kill King Periclase's brother in the arena because Titania had refused to call a victor before the wounds grew too serious, as was Oberon's custom in recent generations. She'd slumped in the High Court box like a hormonal teenager who'd had a fight with her boyfriend.

The Seelie High Queen seemed to resent the expectation that she would do Oberon's job in his absence, and so far, she wasn't stepping up.

"Do we know anyone with a connection to Titania?" I blurted out. It was a question that most of the people in the room probably knew the answer to, but I didn't.

Marisol fixed her gaze on me. All heads swiveled my way.

"How did Melusine seem to receive you?"

"Uh, she was irritable, but I don't think she hated me," I said, not quite sure where Marisol was going with the question.

"Then you're our closest tie to Titania," Marisol said. "Via Melusine."

Ah, here it came.

I gave her a dubious look. "They're buddies?"

I seriously doubted Melusine considered any of the other Old Ones close friends. She and the Seelie High Queen shared a similar temperament, but Titania liked to be in the middle of things, whereas Melusine was the exact opposite.

"Legend says they were childhood friends," Marisol said.

My brows rose. I wouldn't have guessed that.

"I don't think Melusine would invite me back in her realm. In fact, she said she wouldn't receive us again," I said. Remembering how she'd tasted my blood and gained a view into my deepest self, I shifted uncomfortably. I had no desire to seek out the Fae witch. "I wouldn't even know how to locate her. It wasn't exactly straightforward."

"If things go poorly, you may have to try," Marisol said crisply.

Great. I just had to go and open my damn mouth. I resolved to keep my trap shut for the rest of the meeting.

There was more talk of using diplomatic channels to try to appeal to Titania and hold off any takeover of the Stone Order, but no one really had any bright ideas. Finvarra had been silent for so long, no one in the Stone Order had ties to him. I slanted my gaze off to the side, suddenly paranoid that Marisol would somehow guess that I had a connection to Finvarra. Well, not a connection exactly, but I knew someone who did.

In the end, the Council decided the best course of action was to go to Finvarra directly. And this time Marisol wouldn't be sending Maxen or some other representative. She'd be leading the visit.

She drilled me with a look. "And you will accompany us," she said.

I tried not to grimace.

"At the very least, we'll want to settle the matter of the changeling's fealty," Marisol said. She turned her attention to Maxen. "We need her to swear right away. Before we go to Finvarra."

Maxen's face tightened at the mention of Nicole.

"While I have all of you gathered, I'll update you on the servitor attacks as well," Marisol said.

She went on to describe the breaches in various kingdoms. There seemed to be no pattern. They attacked at random times and in nearly every Seelie and Unseelie kingdom and Order. The only things that stood out were that the servitors seemed to be able to appear wherever their unknown master pleased, and they were getting larger and stronger with each attack.

After that, the meeting began to break up. Maxen appeared at my side. "Will you help me convince Nicole?" he asked quietly.

His blue eyes were pleading.

"Yes, but only if you tell me one thing," I said. "How much of your interaction with Nicole is you, and how much of it is Marisol?"

His cheeks reddened slightly, and he looked off to the side. He could choose not to answer. But if he answered, he couldn't lie.

"I'm part of her homecoming, and my mother is keeping abreast of that process," he said. I could tell he was picking his words carefully, which put me on alert. "But I also enjoy my time with Nicole. It may be an assignment in part, but I do it willingly and happily."

"Are you trying to make her think you're romantically interested in her to persuade her to stay in Faerie and swear to the Stone Order?" I asked bluntly.

His eyes blazed, and his face reddened. "I'm not trying to *make* her think anything."

"Fair enough." I held up my hands in surrender.

I knew. There was something springing up between Maxen and Nicole. It might be subtle, and they probably hadn't acted on it, and maybe it was too understated for Marisol to even be aware of it. Or if she'd observed anything that seemed like more than friendly interest, she might have thought it was just Maxen being extra good at his job. But I knew Maxen. He wouldn't fake interest in a woman. He'd be polite and charming, but when it came to romantic matters, he wouldn't lead someone on.

If this—whatever was developing—didn't run its course or get cut off by Maxen, I'd have to tell Nicole. She deserved to know the truth, which was that Marisol would ultimately dictate who her son would end up with.

"When should we speak to Nicole about swearing to the Stone Order?" I asked.

"Later today," he said. "I'll let Emmaline know."

Holding back a groan as I escaped Marisol's lair, it struck me again just how entrenched I was becoming. Only weeks ago, I'd smugly observed how Maxen's every minute and movement were known and scheduled, thinking how awful it would be to live that way. But there I was, under Marisol's command and with my very own personal assistant to keep track of my agenda.

Oliver was waiting for me in the corridor, and regret slammed through me as I realized he'd just heard the news from Marisol. Not about Finvarra, but about Nicole's bloodline. *My* bloodline.

"I'm so sorry I wasn't able to tell you before," I said, my throat tightening around the words. "She got the memo about Finvarra while I was still in her office."

He bent over me, his eyes tensed and unblinking. "No matter what blood flows through your veins, you are my child," he said fiercely. "You have blood of stone, even if it's not mine. Don't ever forget that. Nothing between us has changed, Petra Maguire."

His voice had begun to crack, and once he finished speaking, he turned abruptly and strode down the hall away from me.

I could only stand there, trying to breathe through the thickness in my throat, feeling nothing but gratitude for having been taken in by Oliver with no hesitation on his part, even though, all those years, he hadn't known for sure that I was his.

I wanted space, a moment alone. But it wasn't to be.

Emmaline was hurrying toward me, her tablet in one hand and a tightly rolled piece of paper with a wax seal in the other.

She gave me the scroll. "This just arrived for you, by raven."

I broke the seal and a tiny curl of magic, like smoke, lifted into the air. My eyes went immediately to the bottom of the page to see who it was from. My heart bumped as I read Jasper's signature.

Chapter 14

THE NOTE DIDN'T say much, and I had to read it a couple of times to make sure I understood its meaning.

I have reason to believe the Unseelie High King may have a hand in the servitor attacks. I want to address him directly, and with a Seelie representative, but without any official fanfare or interference.

He named a meeting place, giving the sigils that would take me to that doorway. He also gave a time, and it was fast approaching.

Could he have possibly already gotten wind of Marisol's plans to take an envoy to Finvarra? She'd made the announcement less than an hour ago. It was almost as if he wanted to slip in before the official meetings could take place.

No, it had to be coincidence. There was no way he could know what had only just taken place in the private Stone Council meeting.

The idea that I was the best choice for a "Seelie representative" was a little ridiculous, but I figured this was another step in his bid to get my help repairing the rift between our leaders. I had no idea how he found out that Finvarra was behind the servitor attacks, but then Jasper did seem to have his unique ways of obtaining information. I didn't understand his desire to try to do all of this diplomatic work. He was a military man. He was no more a diplomat than I was.

"What's wrong?" Emmaline asked.

I could tell she was itching to get a peek at the scroll, but I crushed it in my hand. The magic it was imbued with responded, and the note shrank and then disappeared in a brief spark and a thin wisp of smoky magic.

I opened my mouth, ready to tell Emmaline to send a message back to Jasper saying that I declined his invitation. I had no idea why he expected me to accompany him to his audience with Finvarra, and he'd given no reason. But then I pressed my lips together, hesitating.

I *wanted* to see him again, but it had nothing to do with Faerie diplomacy or the threats we faced. It had everything to do with the way he'd kissed me in Melusine's barn.

No. I wouldn't go. If he wanted to force me, he could call in the binding promise I'd made him. Otherwise, I wasn't convinced I needed to be involved. I'd write a note back to him myself, though.

"Do I have any downtime this afternoon?" I asked.

She checked her tablet. "Let me update before I answer."

I followed her down the hallway a few feet, where there was an outlet set waist-high in the wall. She pulled a short cord from her page's vest pocket and plugged one end into the tablet and the other end into the wall. With no Wi-Fi in Faerie, the only way to keep up-to-date was to frequently plug into the fortress's network.

"Lord Lothlorien has requested you meet with him in your apartment at two," she said, frowning slightly.

That would be Maxen wanting my help with Nicole. "Accept it, and block out now until then," I said.

"What should I put in the appointment?"

"Whatever will keep people from expecting anything of me," I said.

I knew I should inform Marisol about what Jasper's note had said regarding Finvarra and the servitors, but I'd been in the belly of a fish and spent the night on a blanket in a barn spooning with a unicorn, and I had to smell ripe. I'd use the excuse of getting cleaned up to take a brief breather from official business and then go back to Marisol's office. I didn't see any harm in the small delay. She needed to know about the possible connection between the Unseelie High King and the servitors, but if it were urgent, then someone would have informed her directly already.

I'd let her know, and then she could decide what to do with the information. She was already planning to go to Finvarra, anyway. It was better to let Marisol handle it. This was her job. That was what I told myself, anyway.

I went back to my apartment to quickly shower and change. Nicole was away, probably working on her magic or some other aspect of her indoctrination into Faerie.

As I stripped off my clothes in the bathroom, tiny pieces of straw floated down to the floor. Yes, I'd spent the night in a barn with a fake unicorn and the unknown son of Unseelie High King Finvarra. My life was nothing if not bizarre lately. I jumped under the stream of steaming water, washed quickly, and got out.

Dressed in fresh jeans, a pale gray V-neck T, and a light leather jacket, I twisted my damp hair back into a loose bun and went to the kitchenette. I opened the fridge and grabbed the first container I saw. It held leftover steak and mashed potatoes, which I didn't bother to heat up.

Ten minutes later, I was out the door with Mort on my back, heading toward a courtyard with one of the less-popular doorways in the fortress. I wanted to step over to the other side of the hedge to touch base with Gus, my boss at the Mercenary Guild, to check on the status of my suspension from bounty work to see if my capture with Gretchen was going to get me reinstated.

I was just about to push the door open and step out into the midday Faerie sunshine when I heard shouts from down the corridor. Then there was a shrill scream.

I knew, even before I'd turned and started running toward the noise. It was another servitor attack.

I reached for Mort and drew magic, sending violet flames licking down the blade. Skidding to a stop at an intersection, I whipped my gaze left and right, trying to discern which way the sounds had come from. Hollers and crashes echoed down the hall from the left. I pivoted that way and took off at a sprint. Others were running toward the commotion, too, with swords drawn.

Another swell of magic washed over my skin as I summoned my rock armor. Fatigue hit me immediately, but I pushed it aside.

The noise was coming from a residential part of the fortress, an area of larger apartments where young New Garg families lived with their children.

"Get back inside!" I hollered as I ran past a teenage boy who'd poked his head out of a doorway.

I reached another intersection, this one a wide space where tricycles and other children's toys were lined up against one wall. There were sofas, and storybooks were piled on end tables. It was clearly a play area, and thank Oberon, I didn't see any children.

But it was full of ogres, like the ones I'd encountered with Gretchen, except these ones were larger. Their bodies were taller, and their battle axes heftier.

Anger exploded through me like spitfire. Had there been kids out here playing when the servitors appeared, it would have been a tragedy beyond comprehension.

The metallic clang of weapons rang through the air, cutting through shouts and panicked cries. I ran at the nearest servitor, whose broad, soft-armored back was turned toward me.

Fueled by my outrage, I gripped Mort with both hands and rammed the end of the blade down into the creature's upper back at an angle to pierce its heart. It screamed and arched, and I pulled Mort free before the ogre collapsed.

Whirling around, I attacked the next ogre, cutting off its head with a heavy swing. Then I was on to the next, and the next. I swung and drove Mort into flesh, my magic licking out to add razor slices to the damage of the blade. My anger became a cold burn in my muscles as my focus narrowed down to the enemies around me. In the trance of the fight, I mowed through horned, beady-eyed bodies until they were all still.

My chest heaving and my brow dripping sweat, I lowered Mort and turned a slow circle. The corpses began turning black and then shriveling like burning paper. They shrank and then winked out, disappearing one by one.

I happened to glance down at my clothes, and ogre blood streaked the fabric. It didn't seem to be dissolving away.

I released my magic, and the familiar ache rushed across my skin as my rock armor receded. The pain centered on the spot on my lower back where Darion had cracked my armor in the battle of champions. Other, lesser pains broke into my awareness. Upper arm, back of a knee, side of one hip. I'd taken axe blows that I hadn't even noticed.

I sheathed Mort and scanned the floor again, letting out a breath through pursed lips when I found that none of the bodies were our people, only those of the ogres who were quickly dissolving into thin air. The place was filling with soldiers.

Maxen arrived, and our eyes met briefly before I let myself get lost in the growing crowd. I had to get out before the fortress went into lockdown again. I'd changed my mind about going with Jasper to see Finvarra. If Finvarra really was behind these attacks, I wanted the chance to throttle his neck with my bare hands for sending servitors into our family quarters.

Everyone else was going toward the scene of the fight, and I got a few odd looks as I moved hastily in the other direction. My heart was still pounding with adrenaline from the battle and anger that the attack had put children at risk. When I reached the courtyard and found the doorway, my hand shook as I drew the sigils in the air and whispered the words that would take me to the place where Jasper wanted to meet.

The netherwhere spit me out in a meadow. I stood under a carved wooden arch. It was positioned in the middle of a clearing in the vaguely minty-smelling knee-high grass that waved in the slight breeze. I was in the Cait Sidhe kingdom, and it struck me that I had no idea why Jasper would have chosen this location to meet. It was the realm of the cats, a smaller Seelie kingdom whose leader was more into the social scene of Faerie than the politics.

It seemed an extremely unlikely place for the Unseelie High King to have landed. I shaded my eyes and squinted, looking at the Cait Sidhe fortress in the far distance and the village surrounding it. The nearest edge of the village was probably a couple of miles away. There wasn't much nearby. As I looked around at the peaceful surroundings, I suddenly realized something seemed off.

I frowned. And where was Jasper? There was no clock nearby, and my cell phone was useless in Faerie. I was probably early. I didn't like the idea of hanging out there for some unknown span of time until he showed up.

Just as I'd decided to return to the fortress and come back to check for Jasper later, the grass began to rustle.

As if on some unspoken cue, forms began to rise from the grass in unison. They were furry. Tall. Feline.

"Oh, *shit*."

I'd strayed about ten feet from the doorway as I'd been looking around. Wheeling around and drawing Mort, I sprinted for the arch. The grass rustled all around me as the man-sized cats pounced, clearing several feet in one leap. I sent magic over my skin to form rock armor.

I switched Mort to my left hand and began drawing the sigils and speaking the words as fast as I could. Knowing it would be stupid to turn my back on the cats, I stood sideways, brandishing my sword. The giant felines were stalking across the clearing at me, hissing with their heads slung low. One of them leapt at me a split second before I catapulted myself through the arch.

The teeth-grinding scrape of claws over stone was the last thing I heard before plunging into the void.

I emerged in the fortress courtyard. Twisting, I reached one hand over my other shoulder and pulled at my jacket. Yep, exactly what I'd expected. The back of my jacket, my shirt, and even the straps of my bra had been shredded by parallel claw tracks. The cat's claws hadn't sliced through my scabbard but had shoved it off-center.

Cursing Jasper's name, just because I needed someone to be pissed at, I sheathed my sword, righted my clothing as best I could, and stalked into the fortress.

I stopped the first blue-vested page I saw.

"What's the time?" I asked.

"Five 'til noon," he said.

I pressed my mouth into a grim line. Only five minutes before the meeting time Jasper had specified. I hadn't been very early after all. Was it a set-up? I suddenly wished I'd saved the note.

I took lesser-used hallways back to my quarters, where I quickly shed my torn clothing and dressed in a nearly-identical fresh set. Then I went to the picture of the San Francisco skyline that hung on a wall, swung it to the side, and opened the wall safe the artwork hid. Inside, there were several items—small vials of potions, my merc I.D., some jewelry that had belonged to my mother. I pulled out my little used wax and stamp, closed and hid the safe, and then rummaged around in drawers until I found a piece of paper and a pen.

I showed up a little early at the Cait Sidhe doorway you specified and nearly got torn to shreds by a bunch of huge cats. I'm not sure why you wanted me to go with you to Finvarra, but you need to come up with a different meeting place, or you're on your own.

I signed my name and folded the paper into a small rectangle. Then I broke off a piece of the soft wax and stuck it over the seam. As I held the metal stamp that was magically connected to me and me alone, I closed my eyes and pictured Jasper's face and whispered his name. A quick gesture to form the sigil that would keep the note invisible except to the intended recipient, and then I pressed the stamp into the wax. It heated under my fingers, sinking into the wax and leaving the imprint of a P that overlaid two crossed swords. A ring of stars enclosed the whole design.

I wrote Jasper's name and kingdom on the outside of the note and then returned the wax and stamp to the safe.

I could have dropped my message in the fortress lobby, where the mail handler would queue it to be taken by messenger raven, but I wanted it touching as few hands as possible. So instead, I left my quarters and made my way deeper into the fortress.

The fortress was once San Quentin prison, a structure that had been part of the Earthly realm before Marisol acquired it and had the interior transmuted into Faerie. Some of the structure had been altered significantly, but the large enclosed yard where prisoners used to be let out for fresh air and exercise remained. Now, it was our training and practice yard.

There were still guard towers overlooking the yard, two of which were used for messenger ravens—one for those arriving and the other for those departing.

Ravens had their own doorways through which they could go from location to location within Faerie as we did through our doorways. They were the only animals who could do so, which was one of the many reasons they were so ideally suited to carry mail between kingdoms.

I climbed the stairs to the north tower, where the birds departed with messages. On the way up, I passed a page with an empty message bag slung over his shoulder. At the top of the stairs, the door to the actual guard room was permanently locked, but there was a slot where messages were slipped inside. The outer windows of the guard room, inaccessible from the stairs or walkway, had been removed so ravens could freely move in and out.

There was a steady stream of birds flying from the south tower, where they'd just dropped messages, over to the north, where they would pick up those to be delivered to other kingdoms. It was a constantly running system that I'd always more or less taken for granted. But I watched the birds with new appreciation. Their efficiency and trustworthiness were remarkable. I'd often wondered how they knew where a message should be delivered, but apparently they had magic all their own that gave them that knowledge.

I slid my note to Jasper into the slot and watched through the glass in the guard room door as ravens alighted on a window sill, hopped to the floor, and plucked up notes in their beaks. I stayed there until I saw a raven take mine.

Then, remembering that I'd wanted to step out and check in with the Guild, I made my way to the fortress lobby. I expected to see soldiers from the battle ranks blocking the way, but by the look of things the most recent attack hadn't brought a full lockdown. Maybe Marisol had realized that locking the place up wasn't helping. From the accounts across kingdoms, the servitors were showing up at will, and no one had yet discovered how to keep them out.

I exited through the main doors. Crossing the invisible barrier between Faerie and the Earthly realm, I was met with a hazy San Francisco day that was about fifteen degrees cooler than the temperate perma-summer on the Faerie side of the hedge.

I powered up my phone, and instead of calling the Mercenary Guild, I tapped Lochlyn's number. She was part Cait Sidhe, and I was hoping she could shed some light on my cat attack.

She picked up on the third ring, accepting my request for a video link.

"Petra," she exclaimed, clearly glad I'd called. Her heart-shaped face suddenly scrunched in distress. "I'm sick of couch surfing! Did you get your job back yet, or what?"

I made a grumbling noise in my throat. "The disciplinary board hasn't even gotten to my case yet."

She echoed my groan. "That blows. How's life in the fortress?"

I pushed my fingers into my hair. "Restrictive," I said, my voice tight.

"I think I'm going to end up back in Faerie myself. I'm not having a lot of luck finding steady work. I really shouldn't have screwed up that gig I had."

Lochlyn was part Cait Sidhe and part banshee, and that combination had somehow gifted her with a shockingly soulful and beautiful singing voice. She'd had a well-paying job singing in a high-end chain of restaurants not long ago but had screwed it up when she decided to party around the world with some mogul. It wasn't particularly surprising. Cait Sidhe were known to be flighty, and although she was one of the most loyal people I knew, the flightiness aspect of her heritage seemed to crop up regularly in her work life.

"Question for you," I said. "Do you know anything about giant attack cats in the Cait Sidhe realm?"

Her eyes popped wide. "You were attacked in the kingdom of cats?"

"I went through a doorway before they could do major damage, but they seemed to want to rip me to shreds."

"Oh, that's awful," she said, truly dismayed. "Wait, they were unnaturally large?"

"Yeah, like seven feet."

"Those weren't Cait Sidhe," she said. "Someone has been impersonating the cat shifters."

Lochlyn didn't inherit the ability to shift into cat form, due to some quirk of her mixed blood, but many Cait Sidhe could shift. Usually they could only take the form of housecat-sized felines. A few very powerful

Cait Sidhe could take larger forms.

"Daoine Sidhe?" I asked, naming a race of Fae that could shift into many different animal forms.

"Yeah, must be. I don't know who else could turn into a giant cat," she said. "But I haven't been in touch with anyone in Faerie in a week or so. I'm not the best source of info."

We chatted for a minute more, mostly lamenting about our mutual fates and how we missed our old Boise apartment, dumpy as it was.

After we hung up, I tapped the end of my phone against my lower lip. The Daoine Sidhe rivaled the Duergar when it came to powerful Unseelie kingdoms. Fae with enough Daoine blood could shift into almost any mammal. And who just happened to be Daoine Sidhe?

Finvarra.

Not only was he the High King of the Unseelie, he was nearly pure-blooded Daoine Sidhe. He was behind the servitor attacks; I was almost sure of it.

I shouldn't have sent that damn message to Jasper because I'd changed my mind again. I *did* want an audience with the Unseelie High King, even if it meant fighting through a field of giant cats.

My hand was on the door, ready to jerk it open so I could stomp back in and write another note to send to Jasper, when someone called my name.

I turned, and through the San Francisco gloom strode just the man I'd wanted to talk to.

Chapter 15

"WHAT THE HELL?" I demanded, throwing my arms up in the air. "You sent me into a trap!"

He'd gotten my note quickly. Extremely quickly. Maybe he had some deal with the messenger ravens for express delivery.

"I sent another message warning you not to go," Jasper said, his tone annoyingly calm. He stopped a little farther away than was necessary, considering our history up to this point. Clearly, he was reluctant to get in the way of my sputtering wrath. "You must not have gotten it."

I huffed and dropped my hands to my sides. He moved a couple of steps closer.

"There was an attack on the fortress," I said. "That probably caused some delays."

I'd likely disappeared through the doorway to the Cait Sidhe kingdom before anyone could find me to deliver Jasper's second note.

"What happened in the kingdom of cats?" he asked.

I recounted how I'd nearly been attacked by giant felines. I also relayed what Lochlyn had told me about the unnaturally large beasts being imposters. I should have realized they weren't true Cait Sidhe. The cat Fae could be many things but weren't generally aggressive, especially not in packs like the one that had surrounded me.

"So, you heard Finvarra is behind the servitors?" I asked. I pressed a hand into the middle of my stomach.

"I've heard whispers, and it does make sense. Finvarra is very powerful, and he's Daoine Sidhe. Perhaps his magic combined with his shifter blood gives him the unique ability to control so many servitors."

I'd basically come to the same conclusion.

"That's means *you're* Daoine Sidhe," I said. There was an accusing tone to my voice that I couldn't hold back. I was still pissed. "You can't shift, can you?"

He laughed sharply. "No, not that I'm aware. My mother is mostly Duergar and New Garg. I obviously take after her."

I peered at him, suddenly more wary than angry. "How did you know that I shouldn't go? What tipped you off?"

"I had ravens watching the Cait Sidhe doorway," he said.

Okay. I should have thought of that on my own.

I crossed my arms. "And why would we go to the Seelie kingdom of cats to meet with the Unseelie High King?"

"He's not with the Cait Sidhe," Jasper said. "But we'd need to use one of their doorways to get to him."

"I don't understand," I said, shaking my head. "Where is he?"

"With the Undine."

One corner of my mouth pulled down. "Oh."

"Yeah."

The Undine were water elementals, Fae whose territories spanned oceans, rivers, lakes, marshes, and some of the shores that bordered waterways. The Undine kingdom was aligned with the Unseelie, but traditionally they weren't heavily involved in Faerie politics. That was primarily because they weren't like the rest of us. They were water people, with a culture and a language that made them foreign and strange to the land-dwelling Fae. They'd never cared much about the power struggles of other kingdoms because the affairs of the "land realms," as they called the rest of us, were irrelevant to them, except when the events on land affected their waterways.

To the rest of us, the Undine were one of the Unseelie shadow kingdoms, like the Baen Sidhe, Elves, and a handful of others. Realms that often didn't play by the same rules as the rest.

"So, we'd have to go through a few doorways to get into the Undine kingdom," I said. The shadow kingdoms didn't allow foreigners to come in directly in one jump. You always had to take a series of doorways to enter them, and you never knew exactly how many doorways you'd have to pass through to get to the final destination. It was suspected that through the series of doorway jumps, a warning was somehow sent that foreigners were approaching. It was a requirement only the shadow kingdoms knew how to impose, and a trick that the other kingdoms would love to get their hands on.

Jasper nodded, his golden eyes intent. "The Cait Sidhe doorway was just the first step."

"Okay, so what now?" I asked.

He cocked his head, and his lips twitched with mild amusement. "Does that mean you're coming with me? Your message strongly implied otherwise."

My face hardened. "That was before the Unseelie High Asshole sent servitors right into the middle of our family quarters," I said, my voice harsh. "They appeared in the kids' play area."

Jasper blinked, and his cheeks paled. "Damn it to Maeve," he breathed. "I'm so sorry. Was anyone . . .?"

I shook my head. "No fatalities. But that was pure luck. At a different time, the hallways would have been full of children much too young to defend themselves."

He lowered his eyelids for a moment and let out a breath. "Thank Oberon."

I snorted derisively. "Not really. Oberon has skipped town. I don't think he deserves our thanks for anything at this point."

Jasper lifted a palm. "Aye, but you know, figure of speech." His expression turned thoughtful. "Perhaps it wasn't luck?"

"What wasn't luck?"

"The timing of the attack," he said. "There have been a dozen servitor attacks by now, but almost no fatalities. Perhaps the attack was timed when there were no children about."

"We lost someone," I said. "Not this attack, but the one before."

"At the risk of sounding hard-hearted, could it have been an accident in the midst of the fighting? Friendly fire, so to speak?"

My brow furrowed. "Possible, I guess. I was looking elsewhere when it happened. But in the first attack, the one on King Sebastian at the nightclub, some of his men died by poisoned knife. Those little ninja guys were pretty deadly."

"Hm," he said. "True. But don't you think it odd that with so many attacks maybe only a dozen have perished?"

"Odd, perhaps, but that's not really my main concern," I said. "Why is Finvarra sending the servitors at all?"

"That's what I want to find out," he said. His gold eyes sparked. "Are you game?"

I spread my hands. "Why us? Seriously, it's not that I don't care about what's going on, but wouldn't this be best left to the people who normally handle this sort of thing?"

"I don't think so," he said mildly. "But that's just my opinion, of course."

"But *why*?" I pressed.

He sighed in a way that reminded me of Oliver, back when I was a teenager and I was pushing him on some point.

"Because I think the leaders you speak of, the ones who usually handle diplomacy, are the very problem," he said. "I think their ways are ineffective. The bureaucracy and infighting and power plays are *causing* our difficulties."

My brows lifted a little. Now Jasper was speaking my language. I was all for less bureaucratic nonsense.

"I don't believe Finvarra will receive them," Jasper continued. "Further, there is the small but notable fact that I'm his only son. I don't want to play that card, but if I have to do it to gain audience, I will."

"Or maybe he'll think you're coming for his seat on the High Throne," I said jokingly.

Jasper frowned, clearly not amused.

"Uh, I'm sure he won't think that," I said quickly.

"So? Are you in?"

I bit my bottom lip for a moment. "Yes. But I'm going to let Marisol know what I'm doing."

His face tightened. "I'd rather you didn't."

"I know, and I can't believe I'm saying this, but I think it's the right thing to do." I kind of hated myself as I said it. But going to the Unseelie High King was no small thing. I was the Stone Order's champion, and I had a responsibility in the way I represented my people. And as much as every fiber of my being railed against it on a daily basis, I had an obligation to my leader.

"Shall we meet back here later, then?"

I nodded. "An hour."

When I entered the fortress, Emmaline pounced.

"You have an appointment with Maxen and Nicole in twenty minutes," she said.

A different page trotted up to me and held out a scroll. "A message for you."

"Gee, thanks," I said wryly as I recognized Jasper's seal.

The page gave me a questioning look, but I didn't want to explain why the note was now pointless. I opened it and a quick glance showed it was indeed the second message from Jasper. I balled it up, and it disappeared with a wisp of smoky magic.

"Before I go to Maxen and Nicole, I need to tell Marisol something,"

I said to Emmaline. We started walking through the lobby toward one of the main arteries through the fortress.

"Let me check her agenda." Emmaline tapped at her tablet for a moment. "She's in a private meeting for the next three hours."

"It's really important," I said.

She shook her head. "This one is set to 'do not disturb.'"

I pulled a hand down my face and swallowed a grumble. Red tape, even when I was trying to do the right thing.

"Okay, what does that mean?" I asked. "Is there anyone at all who can give her a message?"

"You can pass it to her proxy, and he or she has the power to decide whether it's urgent enough to interrupt."

So. Much. Red. Tape.

"Let's do that," I said. At least Marisol would know I tried.

She pulled out a notecard and a pen from the pockets of her page's vest and took the pen's cap off with her teeth.

"What's the message?" she asked around the cap.

I gave her a side eye.

"Or you can write it yourself and then seal it with your stamp," she offered.

I flapped my hand. "Nah, it's not that sensitive. As long as you keep the contents to yourself."

"Of course," she said crisply.

"Jasper and I—" I started and then stopped. "No, scratch that."

She pulled a fresh card out of her pocket.

"Jasper Glasgow asked me to accompany him to question Finvarra about the servitor attacks. Finvarra is in the Undine kingdom."

Emmaline had paused when I said Finvarra's name. When I got to the part about the Undine, she looked over at me.

"You're . . . Finvarra . . ." she faltered. "The Undine kingdom?"

I nodded.

"I should get this to Marisol's proxy right away," she said.

I placed my hand on her arm. "Actually, I changed my mind. Wait until I've left before you deliver this."

She blinked. "But I shouldn't—"

"That's an order," I said. "Sorry, but I've gotta pull rank on this."

If I was going with Jasper, I wanted to do it without interference. Either I was doing this or Marisol was. If I gave her an opening to interfere, I'd likely end up trapped while the bureaucrats hemmed and hawed over who to send, what they should wear, how their hair should be done, and what drinks should be served while they talked. No. Just, no. I was going, and I was doing it my way.

Emmaline looked decidedly unhappy.

"I'll take the blame for it," I said. "In fact, here."

I held out my hand, flipping my fingers at the card she'd written out. She handed it to me reluctantly, and I folded it and stuffed it in my pocket.

"I'll find you before I leave and give it back," I said. "See? You can't give Marisol's proxy even if you wanted to."

She gave me a wry, lids-lowered look. "That's not exactly a solution to my moral dilemma."

I shrugged. "What can I say? I'm a huge pain in your ass, and we both know it."

She snorted wryly but didn't disagree.

We'd reached the hallway for my quarters.

"I'll be back for that," she said, giving my pocket a pointed look. Then she peeled away to continue on while I stopped at my door.

I let myself in, half-expecting Maxen and Nicole to already be curled up on the sofa next to each other. Nicole was there, but Maxen wasn't. I was a few minutes early for the meeting, and I was glad Maxen and I hadn't arrived together. It would look less like we were ambushing her.

Nicole looked up from her book.

Feeling like kind of an ass over what Maxen and I were about to do, I pasted on a smile. "They gave you a few minutes to yourself, huh?" I landed in the chair that was situated at a right angle to the sofa.

She kept a finger in the book to hold her spot. Her eyes, the same tawny colors and pattern of mine, looked tired.

"Yeah," she said. "It was a welcome break. They've been pushing me hard with all the Faerie homecoming stuff."

Poor sis. They weren't actually giving her a break. Not for her benefit, anyway. They'd just set her free so Maxen and I could corner her and, at Marisol's orders, try to get her to swear fealty to the Stone Order.

I leaned forward and propped my elbows on my knees. "So, how are you?" I asked, sincerely interested.

She shrugged one shoulder and looked at a spot on the floor. "I still have moments when I think I might wake up and find it was all a dream. Most of the time I wish it was." She looked up. "But not always."

I wondered if Maxen had anything to do with that.

"It's a lot," I said, leaning back. "And this business with King Periclase . . . I'm sorry that being kidnapped by the Duergar was your introduction to Faerie. I'm even sorrier that he's your father. Our father."

She let out a humorless laugh. "Yeah, that was a real kick in the stomach. How are you handling it?"

My brows rose. So few people knew the truth of my bloodline, so it wasn't a question I expected to encounter.

"Honestly, I haven't had much time to think about it," I said. I gave a small shake of my head. "But I'm not thrilled."

"Yeah, Dad seems like a real dick," Nicole said.

I let out an unexpected laugh. I'd never imagined I'd be sitting in my fortress quarters talking to my twin sister about our asshole Duergar father.

There was a soft rap at the door, and I got up to answer it. Maxen stood there. He nodded at me and then looked past my shoulder to give Nicole a slight smile.

"Lord Lothlorien," I said with exaggerated formality. "What a pleasant surprise. *Do* come in."

He shot me a warning look as he moved past me into the apartment. "How are your studies going?" he asked Nicole.

He sat down next to her on the sofa, moving in a familiar way that said he'd sat there several times before. He left a bit of distance between them but angled his body toward hers and rested his elbow on the sofa's back.

She set her book aside and smoothed a stray strand of hair behind her ear. "Progress is slow, but it's still progress, I guess." She sounded tired and gave a dismissive little shrug as she spoke, but her face had warmed the minute he'd walked in.

"By all accounts you're doing better than you let on," he said. He flipped a glance at me, his eyes widening slightly as if trying to send me a signal. "Why don't you sit down with us, Petra?"

I gave him my sweetest smile. "Oh, I'd love to," I said with inflated enthusiasm. I sashayed over and landed on the recliner.

Nicole's eyes narrowed slightly, and she looked back and forth between the two of us. I cleared my throat and sat up a little straighter. It wouldn't really do any good to try to sabotage the task Marisol assigned us. After all, she was right. It wasn't safe for Nicole to go back to the Earthly realm since Periclase knew he was her father.

I turned my gaze to my sister. I couldn't help what had happened to her, but I could at least be as straight as possible with her.

"Outing you as Periclase's daughter has changed things," I said.

She glanced at Maxen. "How so?"

"It's confirmed that you're a Duergar princess. And for whatever reason, even though you're not his, ah, legitimate daughter by his wife, he's latched onto the idea that he wants you in his kingdom. He's not going to let go of it."

She pushed her hands up and down across her jeans-covered thighs in an agitated little gesture. "I don't understand, though. He has that other daughter, Bryna. She's illegitimate, too, and actually lives there in the Duergar palace, but he won't officially acknowledge her as his. Why is he so hell-bent on bringing me into the fold?"

Nicole and I had talked about this before, but I understood why she still found it so bizarre. I didn't know the reasons behind Periclase's rejection of one daughter and obsession with the other, either. That was Faerie for you.

I glanced at Maxen. Tag.

"It could have to do with Bryna's mother," Maxen said. "Officially accepting Bryna as his could weaken Periclase's power in some way. That's my guess anyway."

"That's basically what Petra said before," Nicole mumbled. She'd crossed her arms and pulled up her feet, and seemed to be shrinking back into the corner of the sofa.

"Believe me, I'd like to know too," I said, giving Nicole a pointed look. Whatever I was saying about her bloodlines and her fate applied to me, too, though Maxen didn't know it.

The reminder that she had a relative in the room seemed to relax her by a small degree.

"What are you saying, then?" Nicole asked, looking at me this time. "That he's going to try to kidnap me again from now until forever?"

"If he has the opportunity, he probably will," I said carefully.

She frowned for a moment, and then her eyes widened and several emotions passed over her face in the span of a second or two.

"I can't go back," she whispered. "If I go back home, he'll come for me again. Is that what you're saying?"

Neither Maxen nor I responded right away, and by our silence she had her answer.

"I'm sorry, Nicole," I said. "But you'd never be completely safe. And if he takes you again . . ."

I couldn't bring myself to say that we wouldn't try to rescue her. It was too cruel.

I leaned back and looked at the floor, feeling like an absolute shit. I was done. If there was anything left to be said, Maxen would have to do it.

There was a tiny, helpless noise, and I looked up to see Nicole swiping tears away from her lower lids. Maxen moved closer to her and put his arm around her. He didn't pull her to him, and she didn't lean into him, but they somehow fit together and the gesture seemed to comfort her.

"We want you here," he said, his voice heating. "*I* want you here."

She gave him a watery smile of gratitude, and I saw it in her eyes: she was falling for Maxen.

I pulled my lips in and bit down hard. If he was playing her, I wasn't sure I could forgive him. If he wasn't playing her, Oberon help them both.

"What do I do?" she asked.

"Stay," he said. "You'll be safe with us. You'll have a life here. This won't be your jail. It will be your home. It already is because you're stone blood. You'll still be able to venture out to the Earthly side of the hedge. We'll find a way to make it safe for you to do so once in a while. But you'll live here."

She looked into his blue eyes, and I saw a wisp of relief in her face. She wanted resolution. She wanted to be safe.

"I should at least tell my father I'm alive," she said. "My mother has been gone a long time, and my father remarried and moved away, and he and I don't speak much anymore. But he should at least know."

"Of course," Maxen said.

"Okay," she said finally and then heaved a deep sigh. "I'll swear to the Order."

I stood quietly.

"I'm glad," I said. "I want you here, too."

It was true, I realized. I didn't know her. I had barely any sense of her personality. I wanted the chance to get to know my twin sister.

"Are you leaving?" Nicole asked.

I nodded. "I've got somewhere I need to be. But we'll talk soon."

My gaze met Maxen's, and in his eyes I saw a storm of emotions that took me aback. Trained as a diplomat practically since birth, he knew how to control his expressions. But right then, he was overwhelmed. I saw some guilt there, sympathy, and maybe a trace of sadness. He turned back to her, and I could see enough of his face in profile, read enough in his body language to know he was genuinely overjoyed that Nicole was staying, and it had absolutely nothing to do with his mother's strategies. I'd known Maxen since we were kids. He'd made plenty of overtures toward me. But this was different. He wasn't just smitten with Nicole. He was completely, head over heels, gone.

I turned, went for the door, and let myself out. In the corridor, I let out a soft chuckle. When Marisol caught wind of what was happening between Maxen and my sister, all hell was going to break loose. But maybe love would somehow find a way. I didn't see how, but stranger things had happened. Probably.

Blowing out a long breath and trying to shake off the emotions that had grown so thick in the room, I strode away from my quarters. Halfway down the hall, someone caught up to me.

"The message?" Emmaline said, slightly out of breath. She held out her hand.

Grumbling, I dug in my pocket and pulled out the card she'd written out for me.

"I'm off to deliver this to Marisol's proxy," she said in a sing-song voice.

That was my cue to get the hell out before anyone tried to stop me. She turned down a branching hallway, and as soon as she was out of sight, I broke into a jog, ignoring the curious looks of the people I encountered.

I made it to the lobby and out through the doors. Jasper wasn't there yet. Vincenzo was parked in a space off to the side. I went to my scooter and started it up. Just as the engine sputtered to life, a page burst out of the fortress.

He waved his arms at me, obviously trying to get me to come back inside. I ignored him, wheeling around and speeding off. Just as I was about to hit the gas and make my escape, I spotted Jasper sauntering up the road leading to the fortress. I pulled up to him, screeching to a stop, and moved forward on the seat.

"Hop on," I said.

He looked down at the scooter with a dubious expression. "I don't think . . ."

"They're going to drag me back into a giant wad of red tape if we don't leave now," I said hurriedly.

He shrugged and threw his leg over the back of the scooter. The shocks creaked as his weight landed on the seat behind me.

I tossed a look over my shoulder when I heard shouts. There were fortress soldiers running down the road toward us.

"Go, go," Jasper said in my ear, letting out a deep laugh.

I sped away, grinning like a demon.

Chapter 16

I DROVE US to the doorway in Golden Gate park, taking a circuitous route in case someone from the fortress got the bright idea to jump in a vehicle and pursue us. If anyone had, I'd apparently lost them. I was fully aware how juvenile it was to speed off as fortress officials tried to flag me down, but it was the right decision. I'd deal with the consequences later.

After I parked, Jasper slowly extracted himself from his position all snugged up behind me. He moved off to the side, and I caught a glimpse of the amused grin on his face. I couldn't help smiling back.

"Lady Lothlorien is so going to ground your ass later," he said, in a pretty good approximation of an American teenager. "She'll take your sword away for a week."

I chuckled and killed the engine. "We should probably get going before they catch up with us," I said.

We started side-by-side toward a stand of straggly trees. Some of the branches formed a subtle arch shape. Our doorway.

I looked beyond the point, taking in the sweeping view of the Golden Gate bridge and the bay, remembering that the last time Jasper and I had been here alone, he'd commented that it was a nice spot to watch a sunset. I'd brushed off the comment before, but a new thought suddenly occurred to me. Had he been here with someone else to watch the sunset?

I peered at him out of the corners of my eyes.

"What?" he said mildly, still gazing straight ahead.

"What?" I repeated, feeling a little dumb.

"There's a question on the tip of your tongue," he said, his barely-there brogue somehow deepening the word "tongue."

A little shiver spilled over me as I recalled our kiss in Melusine's barn. The shiver swirled around my insides and heated, settling low in my stomach.

I waved my hand. "Nah."

He flicked a smirking glance at me. "Okay, then."

Ugh. That left me wondering things I didn't want to be thinking about. Like whether King Periclase intended to marry Jasper off to some small kingdom princess or lord's daughter.

We reached the arch, and Jasper turned to me.

"Mind if we go through together?" he asked. "After what happened earlier, it seems wiser than passing through one at a time."

Without asking if I could take the lead, I stepped up to the arch and began tracing the sigils and whispering the words. We had to be in physical contact to pass through at the same time. The usual convention was to place a hand on the person's shoulder or grasp the upper arm. But just before I finished the ritual that would open the doorway, I felt the pressure of Jasper's fingers on my lower back. Heat zipped through me from the point of contact, but then it was immediately sucked away into the cold void of the netherwhere.

I drew Mort as soon as I felt my corporeal body return to me. Spinning around in the clearing, I eyed the waving grasses. Jasper was doing the same a couple of feet away.

"I think we're good," he said, sheathing his short sword.

I glanced at him, and he pointed up. When I tipped my head back, I spotted three dark-feathered birds tracing lazy circles high above. Ah. The ravens were giving the all-clear.

"Where to now?" I asked.

He nodded at the doorway. "Back through, this time to the Spriggan kingdom. After that, your guess is as good as mine. I'll just keep tracing the sigil for the Undine doorway until we finally arrive there."

"I wonder how many we'll have to go through," I muttered.

The shadow kingdoms had always seemed a world apart from the rest of the Faerie kingdoms in a social and symbolic sense, but then there was also this literal separation, this runaround you had to do to get into any of them. I tried to remember if I'd ever even known someone who'd spent time in one of the shadow realms. Lochlyn was part banshee, and the Baen Sidhe domain was shadowed, but she didn't grow up there. She'd been raised here, in the Cait Sidhe kingdom.

My stomach tightened slightly as I slowly sheathed Mort. Maybe I should have done a little more research before agreeing to this trip.

Jasper had gone to the doorway and was standing half-turned, waiting for me to join him.

"Have you been to the Undine kingdom before?" I asked.

He shook his head. "You're not going to back out, are you?" he said it with a casual tone, but one brow arched. In that, his challenge was clear.

"Hell no," I said.

He grabbed my hand with his left while he traced sigils with his right and uttered the words that would take us to the next doorway.

Just as we dropped into the void, I realized I had no idea where we would end up next. Too late, as the netherwhere claimed us and the ability to communicate.

When we emerged, I blinked at my surroundings, wondering if he'd made a mistake. We were standing in the Aberdeen, Morven's pub in the Duergar realm.

Morven was behind the bar, and he turned his Santa Clause gaze on us. His eyes brightened when he caught sight of me. I lifted my hand in a wave. I wasn't stupid, though—he probably liked me okay, but mostly he was interested in collecting more of my magic. New Gargoyles were rare, and few of us were strong enough to interest Morven. That made me a delicacy on the Faerie magic smorgasbord. I wasn't in need of his services.

Jasper was peering at Morven with a distrustful glint in his eye.

"Back in we go," Jasper said.

I grabbed his wrist before he could start tracing sigils. We passed into the netherwhere. So far, we'd gone through two doorways in Seelie territories, and I was at least somewhat familiar with both kingdoms. Not knowing where we would pop out set me on edge, even in the void.

The earthy, wet smell of a mud and stagnant water hit my nose as we came out into a wooded marsh.

"Where are we?" I asked, peering into the gloom.

We stood on a mounded semi-island surrounded by shallow water except for a muddy land bridge leading away like a forest path. Moss-covered dead wood formed the arch of the doorway. Off to the left I spotted stilted cottages with docks extending into the water.

"I'd say the Boggart realm," Jasper said.

I shivered. We'd crossed over into Unseelie lands. The Boggart realm wasn't a shadow kingdom, but it was a bit apart from some of the larger kingdoms. A shorter, beady-eyed race of Fae, Boggarts had brownish seal-like skin, though they weren't shifters. They frequented moors in the Old World and preferred to live near marshes and backwaters. Maybe our arrival in their territory meant we were getting closer to the watery kingdom of the Undine.

"How will we know when we're there? I have no idea what the Undine world looks like," I whispered. For some reason it felt unwise to speak too loudly.

"The ravens will tell me," Jasper said, his voice also low.

"So, they're traveling with us?"

"Aye, in parallel. They use their own doorway system, of course."

I was just about to ask how he told them where we were going if he didn't even know himself, but the words froze in my mouth when I spotted movement in the deeper water. Remembering our ill-fated trek through the pond bordering Melusine's territory, I tugged at Jasper's sleeve and pointed.

He grabbed my hand and pulled me back to the doorway. Just before we ducked into the netherwhere, I saw a head—bald and sleek, with two solid white eyes—rising from the water.

Then we stepped into a different realm. I started as salty sea air invaded my nose and mouth.

"We're there," Jasper said, his words echoing slightly over the soft sound of lapping water.

I blinked, peering into a gloom even darker than the one we'd just left.

I drew Mort and sent magic down my arm. The licking violet flames provided just enough light to show we were in a shallow cave on a beach. My boots sank slightly into the sand as I shifted my weight. I led the way out into the open, where a gray sea shrouded by thick fog greeted us.

Seeing no threat, I released my magic but kept Mort in my hand. "The Old World?" I asked.

The Faerie territories that were anchored to the Old World—mostly Scotland, Ireland, and England—had a certain feel to them that was hard to describe. It was like stepping into history. Even the air seemed to have a certain aged richness to it.

"I believe so."

He peered upward, and I followed his gaze. Ravens circled overhead. I tipped my head back farther and saw the cave was actually a shallow depression in a tall, nearly sheer cliff. Above, there were signs of humanity—houses with lights in their windows and curls of smoke trailing from their chimneys. The scent of cooking food wafted to us on the downdraft.

"So, we're here," I said. "Any idea where to find your pops?"

Jasper was scanning the water, his golden eyes intent. "Did you see that?"

"What?" I squinted out at the sea.

Was that a flash of fin?

I reached for my magic again just as several figures rose from the shallow water just beyond where the waves died on the sand. They walked like humanoids, but their bodies reflected the light in scaled patterns, and I caught a flash of a webbed hand. They were all male, naked except for a sort of seaweed loincloth, and each carried a spear.

I kept Mort at my side but gripped the hilt tightly, ready to swing if needed. The fish-men kept advancing.

Jasper stepped forward.

"We're here for an audience with King Finvarra," he called out. "We mean no harm. We just want to speak to him."

One of the fish men stepped ahead of the others.

"Who be you?" he asked in a voice that sounded as if he had wet sand stuck in his throat. I caught a flash of his teeth—wicked little points top and bottom.

He didn't make any threatening moves, but muscles rippled under his scaled skin, and the bicep of the arm holding the spear flexed in short pulses.

"I'm Jasper Glasgow, sworn to the Duergar King Periclase." Jasper gestured to me. "This is Petra Maguire, sworn to Lady Marisol Lothlorien of the Stone Order."

"Ahh," the fish man crooned. "Seelie and Unseelie. Victor and loser. Would-be enemies from the battle of champions." He cocked his head. "Curious that they travel together."

"We're progressive that way," Jasper muttered under his breath.

I covered a snort of laughter with a cough. The fish men all twitched in my direction, and I lifted Mort a few inches. They gripped their barbed spears more tightly.

Jasper gave me the side-eye and then faced the mean and held out his hands palms down. "We're no threat. We simply want an audience with King Finvarra."

The men moved forward and began to surround us. Jasper's hand nudged closer to the grip of his sword.

"We shall take you," said the leader. He turned to me. "As soon as she puts her spellblade away."

My jaw flexed as I locked gazes with him. I slowly sheathed Mort.

Jasper and I glanced at each other as the fish men circled us and began herding us parallel to the shoreline. I wasn't sure whether to feel encouraged or insulted that they hadn't demanded our weapons. It was a wise choice on their part. I didn't give Mort up easily, and things would have gotten ugly.

I peered ahead, trying to guess where they were taking us. There was a perilous-looking winding staircase carved into the cliff.

But instead of leading us to the stairs, the fish men turned into a cavern. It wasn't a shallow one like the cave housing the doorway through which Jasper and I had arrived. I squinted into the darkness but couldn't see the end of it.

"Go there," the lead fish man said, pointing deeper into the cave. "You will find King Finvarra."

He pronounced the name of the Unseelie High King as if it were foreign to him.

Jasper and I exchanged another look.

"Where does this lead to?" Jasper asked, doubt coloring his voice.

"The king's quarters."

"I have a bad feeling about this," I muttered, trying to make out anything in the gloom. The cave seemed to extend deep into the cliff.

I glanced back again, and the fish men had crowded into the entrance of the cave. When I took a couple of steps toward them, ready to demand they clear the way, they lifted their barbed spears.

I drew magic like a reflex, and between one blink and the next, Mort was in my hand.

Jasper had drawn his short sword beside me, and I felt a faint breeze of magic as he activated his rock armor. I did the same, acutely aware that I wouldn't be able to do it too many more times without a healing salt bath.

"Move," I commanded.

The fish men lifted their spears more menacingly. I hadn't noticed before the gills on the sides of their necks and over the tops of their shoulders. The flaps began to fan out, making the men look less humanoid and somehow more dangerous.

They took shuffling half-steps toward us, obviously trying to drive us back. I charged, swinging Mort and hoping to startle them backward. One of the fish men panicked and not having enough space to properly throw his spear, shoved it at me. I ducked, knocking it away with my arm. It glanced off my right forearm, seemed to stick there for a split second, and then fell to the ground. The sand it touched began to smoke. I glanced down and saw there was a new hole that went through my jacket and shirt, burned away by the sticky residue. It penetrated to my rock armor and began to sting.

I let out a yell, lunged, and whipped Mort in a tight arc at the nearest fish man, knocking the spear out of his hands.

The men were still shuffling forward, making glugging noises in their throats and pushing the spears at us in quick jabs.

"Stuff on the spears is burning my armor," I said to Jasper through gritted teeth. The slime hadn't dissolved my armor. That would have been much more agonizing. But it was painful enough to make my eyes water.

Jasper and I were both trying to hold our ground, but more fish men had appeared at the mouth of the cave. There were at least twice as many as before. They were all glugging and hissing at us, their gills flared.

They inched us back. I didn't want a massacre, but the fish men left us no choice.

"We're going to have to mow them down," I muttered at Jasper.

He didn't have a chance to reply. The ground beneath our feet gave way, and we fell. Sand rained down on us as we landed in shallow water about eight feet down. I scrambled to my feet and blinked sand from my eyes. Jasper and I both splashed as we tried to get our balance and our bearings all at once. The water wasn't deep—maybe eight inches—but the shock of landing in it disoriented me.

We'd fallen into a trap. Overhead, the fish men peered down at us and warbled a noise that sounded like victory. I stabbed Mort upward, and violet magic licked off the end of the sword, reaching out to slice one of the fish men across the face with razor cuts. He screamed and fell back.

A spear fell down at us, narrowly missing my upturned face. More spears rained down.

"Take cover!" Jasper shouted.

We pressed ourselves against the sandy walls of the pit. Not that it helped much, but at least we could see what was coming. The fish men were obviously trying to kill us. Maybe they were flesh eaters. At that point, I was pretty damn sure they had no idea where Finvarra was.

I held up an arm to protect my face as the fish men threw more spears. Burning streaks flared a couple of seconds after each spear contact.

My eyes met Jasper's in the semi-dark of the pit, and I could tell he was thinking the same thing I was: there was no way out.

Chapter 17

BURNS STREAKED MY body, and nausea reeled through me. Jasper squeezed his eyes closed for a moment, a look of pain on his face.

"Toxin," I said.

He nodded. "Aye."

My knees began to tremble, and about ten seconds later, I sagged, my ass sinking into the water. The cold sea immediately soaked through my jeans and began wicking up my shirt. Jasper was losing the battle against gravity, too. Somehow, the goo on the spears was penetrating through our armor and getting into our bloodstreams.

I lost my hold on my magic, and the violet flames sputtered out. The hand gripping Mort was spasming, and it took all my effort to keep my fingers wrapped around my broadsword. My rock armor began to dissipate.

The barrage from above had stopped, and the fish men were just watching us, making soft hisses that were almost soothing.

My muscles were succumbing to the effects of the toxic slime, and I slumped against the sandy wall. I was already listing to one side. If I faceplanted in the water, I wouldn't be able to lift my head. That really pissed me off. I didn't want to die in a watery pit, aware the whole time that it was happening and unable to do anything about it. What a dumb way to go.

I tried to push Mort into the ground to use the sword as a kickstand to keep me from falling in and drowning, but I didn't have the angle quite right. I was slowly sagging, and I didn't even have enough muscle control to move my head to see how Jasper was faring. But unless he'd been faking before, odds were he was just as badly off as I was.

My lids were getting heavy. Shit. Maybe I'd pass out before I drowned after all. I tipped another couple of inches toward the puddle that was going to kill me.

The world had become foggy, and my body almost pleasantly numb, when the noises above changed. The hissing became more agitated, and there was shuffling. Sand fell down from above, raining onto the water. Then there were angry hisses and a few cowering whimpers. More shuffling and sprinkles of sand.

An authoritative female voice spoke in a language I couldn't understand. My vision was gone. All I could do was listen.

Then I became aware of my body shifting. Grunts of effort. Air moving across my face. A slight temperature change.

I was being rescued. Or maybe carried off to get fileted into snacks for the fish men. Either way, there wasn't much I could do about it. At least I wasn't drowning.

There was the rock of motion and the shuffle of boots. More words in the language I didn't know. I wanted to call out to Jasper, to see if he was being carried away, too, but my vocal chords and lips refused to work. All that came out was a broken-sounding grunt.

The motion seemed to go on for a very long time. Eventually I felt the jostling and impact of being put down. The smell of dung hung in the air.

A sudden spray of water combined with a prickly wash of magic hit me in the face, and my sightless eyes reflexively squeezed closed. My face was tingling, but not with numbness—feeling was starting to return. I was pretty sure I was being hosed down, and it seemed to be helping with the toxin. The shower of water continued, and though it was freezing, I was grateful to have any sensation at all.

I tried to speak again, but it came out as incoherent mumbles.

But then I realized I was looking down at my own hand. Yay, sight!

The tingling spread, intensifying into a needling sensation that was on the edge of torturous. But I wasn't going to complain—my control of my body was returning. I jerked my head up and swung my still-spotted gaze around clumsily. Feeling as though my body had gone off and gotten drunk without me, I tipped my head back, taking in the figure standing about ten feet away with her arms at her sides and her chin lifted. She looked at me from under hooded lids.

I was outside, and the afternoon gloom was giving way to the dark of evening. But the weak light did nothing to dim the woman who stood before me. Her hair was pushed back from her forehead with a simple crown of gold that was studded with pearls. The strands of her aqua-streaked blond hair seemed to move slightly around her, as if floating gently on a current. Her skin had an effervescent quality by virtue of the fine scales that covered it. In spite of the cold, she wore a sleeveless dress of many shades of green that was belted at the waist with a simple rope. Her exposed arms were so muscled they almost looked manly. She wore no shoes. Dressed simply, but with a carriage that declared her royalty.

I gazed upon the Undine Queen Doineann. She was flanked by a dozen trident-carrying men who were bare-chested, dressed only in loose-fitting pants of the same green fabric that she wore. My eyes flicked to the one on her left. He was holding Mort.

Agitation snaked through me. I hated it when someone else touched my sword.

"State your name and sovereign," she said, her accent a combination of an Irish lilt and some other influence I couldn't place.

"Petwa Mageer," I slurred, tearing my eyes away from Mort. "Sworn to Leedy Mursel Lothlurn of th' Stone Erder."

Her gaze moved to my left. "And you?"

I managed to turn my head, and I found Jasper slouched and soaked about three feet away.

He gave a similarly mangled response, but Queen Doineann seemed to gain the information she needed. She gave a slight smile, but when her lips curled back to reveal pointed teeth like the fish men's, I tried not to cringe. It was a small thing—in most other respects she looked quite humanoid—but those teeth were nightmare-worthy. They spoke of the viciousness that lurked underneath her beauty. For Doineann wasn't just the queen of the Undine. Before she'd been crowned, she'd been the leader of the Mermaid Tribe, a crew of female shifters who were as brutal as they were beautiful. She'd retained both positions, which made her the most powerful Unseelie Fae of the sea realms.

"Why have you come unbidden into the kingdom of the Undine?" she demanded.

"We come to speak to King Finvarra, your majesty," Jasper said, his words a little crisper than a moment before.

Her eyes, the painfully beautiful aqua of a tropical sea, darkened to storm blue. She bared her pointed teeth.

"Who told you King Finvarra was here?" she demanded.

If I weren't already propped up against a wall, I would have drawn back. Her eyes somehow seemed inhuman—a bit too round and flat, like those of a fish. I'd heard stories of how, in a rage, she would attack and tear flesh in a frenzy like a shark who'd caught the scent of blood.

"I have ravens, your majesty," Jasper said.

"You dared send your feathered spies into my kingdom?" Her voice rose in pitch.

"Not to spy," he said, taking on his signature mild tone instead of letting her agitation escalate his response.

She cocked her head, peering at Jasper and seeming suddenly interested in him. "Is that so?" Her voice had softened to a purr.

"Yes, your majesty," he said. "I mean no harm. We simply need to speak to the High King about an important matter that concerns all of Faerie."

She moved closer to him with a slow, swaying stride, and then stopped and folded her arms.

"Which is?" She drew out the words with an unhurried drawl.

"The servitors that have been attacking the realms," Jasper said. "I believe they are originating from King Finvarra, and I want to ask him why."

"Hmm," she said, as if our quest were suddenly quite interesting indeed.

Her lips were closed, and the corners of her mouth widened in a smile that was nearly friendly. With her pointed teeth hidden, she looked almost like a humanoid, land-dwelling woman. And she was breathtaking. You didn't become the leader of the Mermaid Tribe without exceptional beauty, and as I stared up at her, I realized she rivaled even Titania.

I also suddenly remembered something other than violence that she was known for. She kept harems of both sexes, and her sexual appetite was as legendary as her viciousness.

And in that moment she was looking at Jasper as if she intended to make him her next conquest. One of her hands reached up to touch the spot on her neck just below her ear. Her fingers trailed down her neck, traced her collarbone, and then drew down between her breasts. She crossed her arms again. But now, her folded arms seemed to be accentuating her breasts. Same posture as before, but conveying something very different.

Unexpected jealousy spiked through me, slicing through my unease about being the Undine Queen's captive. I shifted, itching to jump to my feet, snatch Mort from the trident man who was holding my broadsword, and—what? Attack the Undine Queen because she was looking lasciviously at the man who'd kissed me? That would be an asinine move.

I blinked hard, pulling my focus back to the situation at hand. It wasn't easy, though, because Jasper was smiling up at Doineann. I knew that look. He was peering at her the way he'd looked at me a number of times. My right hand tightened into a fist. I forced it to loosen.

Queen Doineann tapped her lower lip with one white-painted nail. Her fingernails were filed into points reminiscent of her teeth, the tips of which showed just a bit when her lips parted.

"And tell me, Jasper of the Duergar, why would Finvarra want to see *you?*" Her aggressive demeanor had faded, the violence overshadowed by something much sultrier.

Jasper blinked. "This is vitally important to all realms, your majesty," he said.

"Not ours," she said. "No one dares attack the Undine."

Well, Finvarra was hiding out there, so it wasn't so surprising that he hadn't sent servitors into the realm. I was tempted to point that out but knew it would inflame her temper. My eyes flicked to my broadsword, and my fingers itched to clutch it.

"But you're no king," Doineann pressed. "Why you?"

"I'm the son of a king." Clever. It was the truth in more than once sense. He tipped his head at me. "And Petra is on the Stone Order's Council. She's the Order's champion. We both hold position in our respective realms."

His attempt to include me in the discussion was met with complete disinterest. She didn't even flick a glance my way.

"I can think of a few positions you can hold," she said with a slow smile.

He swallowed, and his expression faltered for a split second—slipping into something that was close to revulsion. I knew then that it was an act. Stupid relief floated through me. Damn, I felt like an idiot for it, but there it was. At least I could stop thinking about whether Jasper Glasgow liked Queen Doineann more than me. He didn't. Score one for me and my childish emotions.

"What do you want in exchange for taking us to Finvarra?" I asked a little louder than was probably necessary.

The Undine Queen looked at me, refocusing for a moment as if she'd literally forgotten I'd been there. Irritation flashed briefly in her eyes.

"I want him," she said, turning her attention back to Jasper. Her mouth widened into a pointy smile. "Tonight."

Jasper's jaw flexed, but he returned her smile. He inclined his head. "Anything you wish, your majesty," he said, his voice mild but his eyes intent when he raised his head and their gazes locked again.

I squinted at him. Well, I'd *thought* he was faking his interest in her for the sake of saving our asses. Maybe I'd been wrong. Whatever. It didn't matter. We needed to get on with this ill-conceived little trip and try not to die in this gods-forsaken watery realm.

"Yes," she said. "I do get anything I wish."

She flipped her fingers at her trident men, and four of them moved forward, two of them to me and two to Jasper. They pulled us to our feet and kept a hold of us. It was probably good because I wasn't sure I could have stood under my own power.

"But business before pleasure," Jasper said.

I made a soft gagging noise. He shot me a glare.

"We must speak with King Finvarra first," he said. "It's a matter of urgency. Then we can turn our attention to . . . other things." His voice grew heavy with implication.

She peered at him for a long moment. "Fine," she said finally.

Ugh. I'd find a way to escape after we met with the Unseelie High King. I sure as hell wasn't going to hang around while Jasper boinked the Undine Queen, if that's what he really intended.

I'd been unable to see much from where I sat in a puddle against a wall. But as we were escorted away, I discovered we'd been at the foot of the Undine castle, in a stall used for parking pack animals, by the snuffles and whinnies and aroma of dung. The castle was perched on a high cliff. I vaguely remembered from my Faerie history lessons that it was situated so that modern accommodations such as accessibility by car weren't possible because the paths leading up to the structure were much too steep and narrow.

The stronghold itself was like something out of a fairy tale. It literally looked like a full-scale elaborate sand castle from a human sand sculpture competition. It had turrets, walkways, battlements, and flags flying from the highest points. Legend said the sea god Lir formed the castle with his bare hands, using only materials from the ocean and beach. As we walked, I spotted shells embedded into the walls and walkways and even a couple of preserved starfish and seahorses.

It seemed odd that Doineann had descended clear to the animal stalls to interrogate us. But then, I wouldn't claim to know anything of the customs in the shadow kingdoms.

I shivered, and not just because my clothes were soaking wet. Jasper and I were in a foreign land, more so than any I'd ever been to before. My eyes kept slipping to Mort, still carried by one of the trident men. Another of the men held Jasper's short sword.

Jasper and I locked gazes for a moment, and then I looked ahead at the Undine Queen's back. Would she really allow us to see Finvarra, or had we been rescued from the fish men only to be tossed into some other trap?

We were approaching the castle's outer gatehouse, which was accessed by a bridge over a moat. I couldn't imagine how that volume of water didn't erode away the foundation of the structure and the cliff that supported it, but if the castle really was built by the sea god, maybe the usual logic didn't apply.

Queen Doineann stopped and turned, going to the trident man who carried Mort. She spoke to him in the language of the Undine and then continued through the gate alone while the men steered us around to the right.

I watched the Undine Queen disappear through the gate. It was strange to see a Faerie ruler walk around her castle without an entourage or any fanfare. Without shoes, even. That would never happen in any of the Seelie or even most of the Unseelie kingdoms I knew. Perhaps these details were evidence that the shadow kingdoms had not fully left behind their wild ways when Finvarra had united the Unseelie.

The trident men took us around to a side entrance, and servants stood aside to let us go in. Leading us through service corridors, we wound deeper into the castle. The sand-formed walls made me slightly claustrophobic. I knew the structure had stood for many hundreds of years. But in my imagination, they were insubstantial and might at any moment be crushed from above by a giant child's fist.

We were taken into what appeared to be a larger thoroughfare in the castle, where the usual servants and nobles moved about. None of the people we encountered looked like the fish men who'd trapped us. Here, they all appeared more human, with some showing signs of mixed blood. Perhaps the fish men were Doineann's early warning system on the beach.

The trident bearers stopped abruptly at a door. I heard the sounds of conversation and a high-pitched giggle from the room beyond. The man holding Mort knocked sharply twice and then opened the door.

Inside, there appeared to be a party in progress. At first glance, anyway. A closer look showed that some of the women were naked. Amorous noises drifted from behind a nearly-sheer curtain that revealed the silhouettes of two figures locked in an embrace.

And upon a wide sofa situated on a dais lounged a bare-chested man with white hair and eyes such a pale ice-blue they were almost colorless.

The Unseelie High King Finvarra.

Chapter 18

SEVERAL SCANTILY CLAD Undine women hovered nearby Finvarra, but he seemed to be a bit apart from the hedonism that surrounded him. Even though his posture appeared casual and relaxed, his gaze was sharp, and if he'd indulged in drink, it seemed it hadn't affected him. His pale eyes looked as ancient as glaciers. They locked on me and then Jasper as the trident men escorted us through the room toward the Unseelie High King.

King Finvarra didn't move as the trident bearers and Jasper all dropped to one knee. I sank into the deepest curtsy of my life—not an easy thing when you're wearing water-logged, skintight jeans. I waited until I saw the men rise before lifting my head.

The lead trident man stepped forward. "These are the travelers who are here to see you, your majesty. Lady Petra Maguire and Lord Jasper Glasgow." His accent matched his queen's.

The fish men must have informed Doineann and she had forewarned Finvarra that we'd come for audience with him. Her questioning had, perhaps, been partly just to play with us.

Jasper took a step. "Your majesty." He bowed at the waist.

Finvarra had been lounging on his side, propped on one elbow. His white hair and old eyes marked him ancient by mortal Fae standards, but his skin was exceptionally taut and his body firmly muscled for a man of his age. He slowly pushed up to a sitting position, swinging his boots to the floor and resting his hands atop his thighs.

"You've gone to some trouble to reach me," he said to Jasper.

"No trouble, your majesty," Jasper said. "We're honored that you would receive us."

Finvarra's eyes flicked to me. He wasn't an overly large man—not any taller than Jasper and a bit less broad in the shoulder—but the way he looked so coolly at me, Jasper, the trident bearers, and everyone else in the room left no doubt. He was the ruler of anyone and everything that existed in Faerie—at least in his own mind.

It was widely known that the Unseelie High King believed he was above even the Old Ones like Oberon. He saw the Old Ones as relics left from a time long gone. He saw himself the rightful ruler of the modern era in Faerie. Oberon's power and connections had been the only thing to keep Finvarra from attempting to seize the High Court the past several decades.

Only an idiot would think it coincidence that Finvarra had emerged from wherever he'd been for the past many years just after Oberon had disappeared.

I tried not to shift under Finvarra's gaze. "Uh, yes, your majesty, very honored," I said after a couple seconds of awkward silence while his eyes drilled into mine.

Then all at once, Finvarra's cold demeanor seemed to give way to something else. The corners of his eyes crinkled as his face relaxed into a smile. His expression softened. He propped one hand on the top of his thigh and beckoned to someone behind us with his other hand.

"Bring our new guests some refreshments," he said to a servant, his voice resonant and warm. He turned to me and Jasper and gestured at the dais. "Sit. Don't be shy. Come. We will talk."

My brows rose slightly as I tried to process the sudden change. Which was the real Finvarra? The chilly man with the glacial blue eyes? Or this smiling host waving us over to join him and calling for food and drink?

Maybe Jasper, being Unseelie, would know more than I did about the High King.

I couldn't help peering at Finvarra as I perched on the edge of the dais. He hadn't invited us up to his couch, and so Jasper and I were seated below him, forced to tip our heads back to look up at him. Probably deliberate on Finvarra's part. I watched Jasper watching the High King. Was Jasper wondering how the man would react if he knew his son sat before him? Perhaps Jasper was searching Finvarra's face for any family resemblance. Beyond similar statures, I didn't see any. As he'd said before, he seemed to take after his mother.

A servant brought me and Jasper crystal goblets of sweet-smelling wine and set a plate of fruit, nuts, and cheeses in between us.

Finvarra lifted his own goblet. "Cheers," he said and then took a pull of wine.

I raised my glass and then sipped from it, and Jasper did the same.

"Your hospitality is much appreciated, your majesty," Jasper said.

The High King shook his head deferentially and waved one hand. "It's nothing. Now, satisfy my curiosity. Tell me how two who might be considered enemies came to join together to seek me."

I nearly let out a little laugh. People sure seemed fixated on the fact that a Duergar and a New Gargoyle shouldn't be friendly with each other these days.

"We're trying to keep communication open between our two realms in a time of tension," Jasper said. "While it's true that Petra defeated my uncle in the battle of champions, she also fought alongside me to defend the Duergar palace against a servitor attack. I know she is trustworthy."

Damn, Jasper had gone straight to the heart of the matter, bringing up the servitors right away.

Finvarra's face sobered. "Yes, the servitors," he said thoughtfully. His tone was on the somber side of neutral. "This is why you've come."

Jasper nodded. "Aye, your majesty. Seelie and Unseelie alike have suffered. Some have died."

He didn't ask a question, but the feel of one hung in the air for several seconds while the Unseelie High King regarded Jasper with cool eyes.

Finvarra leaned back and crossed his arms, his face still thoughtful.

"When I united the Unseelie tribes, formalizing them into proper kingdoms under a single ruler and unifying their interests, it was not one smooth, bloodless transition," he said. "People died. Some tribes vanished completely, either killed or absorbed by others who were more powerful. Force, discomfort, violence—these are necessary components of transitioning to a higher state of existence. This is the price of our evolution."

My pulse seemed to stop for the briefest of moments. His tone was mild, but there was something so foreboding behind it.

"You sent the servitors as part of a grand plan, my lord?" I asked. I refused to call him "majesty." I wasn't Unseelie. He wasn't my High King. "Your aim is . . . a transition?"

He inclined his head.

I glanced at Jasper. His golden eyes shone with trepidation.

"Do you know what my nickname through the ages has been?" Finvarra asked.

"The Great Uniter," I said carefully. Some used the title derisively when speaking of Finvarra. I vaguely remembered from history lessons there was speculation he'd created the nickname for himself and had an entire propaganda campaign around it. I didn't know if it was true.

"Whatever else people may say about me, I managed to do what many thought could never be done," he said. He lifted a hand in a gesture that took in the entire room. "I took tribes such as the Undine, who were barely more than animals, and I civilized them. I took warring nations of near-beasts, and I untied them."

I kept my face studiously neutral, but I was taken aback at how he spoke of the Undine and the other Unseelie realms. He used subtle but significant terminology when he referred to them as tribes before his time and kingdoms since he'd become their High King. That could perhaps be overlooked. But if I were Unseelie, I would have bristled at his claim that they were "animals" before he'd come along to supposedly enlighten them.

"So you sent the servitors to punish us?" I ventured.

His mouth stretched into a smile, and he let out an amused laugh that reminded me exactly of Jasper's. A cool shiver ran down my back. It seemed wrong to hear that warm sound from the Unseelie High King.

"Not to punish," Finvarra said. "To infiltrate. To hasten the breakdown of weaknesses so that something stronger may be built up."

Anger lit in my chest, and I fought to tamp it down. Who the hell did he think he was?

"Oberon has had the upper hand for too long," Finvarra continued. "He's made Faerie weak, soft, and bloated with bureaucracy. The eternal summer has made the Fae kingdoms quarrelsome and self-indulgent. Why do you think the Tuatha are planning to ride against us?"

My eyes widened, and my gaze darted to Jasper. His lips had parted, but he couldn't seem to come up with a response.

Finvarra leaned forward, his former chill returning. "Oberon will not save you. He doesn't know how. I am Faerie's only hope. I'm the only one who can ease what's coming. That's why I'm aiding the gods."

Either the Unseelie High King was a deranged megalomaniac bent on usurping Oberon and thought he was helping the Tuatha De Danann or he really did have a connection to the Tuatha, and the servitors were part of their plan. Maybe both. Either way, he'd admitted to sending the attacks.

For one childish moment, all I wanted was to squeeze my eyes shut and then open them to magically find myself on the Earthly side of the hedge. Back in my mundane life as a Guild merc scraping together a living, where I didn't have to think about the gods, crazy kings, bloodlines, or coming battles. But no, there I was hearing things I really, really didn't want to hear. Fricking Faerie.

"You would break us before the Tuatha get the chance?" Jasper asked, his words heated with uncharacteristic force. "I don't understand your game."

"This is no game," Finvarra said, his voice low and harsh. "I'm Faerie's best hope at placating the Tuatha. I've seen the way forward, and I'm doing what must be done."

I narrowed my eyes, scrutinizing the Unseelie High King.

"Are you saying you have prophetic visions?" I asked. I set my goblet down abruptly, and wine splashed over the rim.

"I don't need prophecy," he snapped at me. I didn't flinch, and that seemed to irritate him. "Visions come only occasionally and randomly. What use is that?" He tapped his temple with his forefinger hard enough I almost winced. "I see it all with my own eyes."

Yep, megalomaniac. Great. How the hell did I keep getting myself into these insane situations? The memory of fighting ogres amidst children's toys rushed back, and with it my resentment.

"So you're just going to keep sending servitors who grow larger and more violent with each attack," I spat, not trying to rein in my anger.

He sat back, suddenly calmer. "You don't see it. You don't understand." There was no accusation in his statement. It was simply an observation.

"No, I *don't* understand why you're sending assassins into the middle of family residences, right where our children play," I said. Any respectful tone I'd managed up to that point was gone.

"The servitors aren't sent to kill, but sometimes they do develop a bit too much independence," Finvarra said, his brows lowering slightly. "The small ones with the poisoned knives were too much, I later realized."

It was all I could do to keep calm as he spoke so casually of his servitors, his creations who'd already killed several Fae. The fury I'd felt while battling his servitors while children of the Order hid in their quarters surged through me. I gripped the tops of my thighs, digging my nails in. I knew exactly where Mort was. If I were very quick, I might be able to snatch my broadsword. I was much faster and stronger than I looked. Maybe, with the element of surprise—

Jasper shifted, interrupting my thoughts.

"If you will not stop your attacks on our kingdoms, you are declaring yourself our enemy, your majesty," he said. He spread his hands. "In fact, you've already done so. How do you expect us, our people, and all the other kingdoms to react to this?"

"If you were people of vision, I would expect you to understand," Finvarra said. His tone was growing clipped. "But most aren't. You aren't. This is why the Tuatha are coming to raze Faerie."

"You?" Jasper echoed. "Not us? Do you not count yourself among us?"

"In theory, but in these days not in practice." Finvarra shifted his gaze to the trident bearers and raised his chin slightly.

Before I could get to my feet, four of the men had lunged, jabbing their tridents at us. The weapons lit up as if charged with electricity, and the magic crackled off the ends like lightning.

I stiffened as the magic ripped through me. It was like being stunned with a magi-zapper, but ten times worse, as the electric magic seemed to make every cell spasm and scream. I lasted maybe a couple of seconds before I fell over.

The last thing I saw was Jasper collapsing to the floor, smacking the side of his head hard on the edge of the dais.

Chapter 19

WHEN I CAME to, my first thought was that I was glad to be in one piece and able to move my limbs under my own command. Finvarra hadn't handed us over to the fish men. Not fish food, that was a good thing. Also good: I wasn't cuffed or tied up. I was in some kind of cell or holding room. The door looked substantial, and the only windows were small, open holes about ten feet up. And I wasn't alone.

"Jasper," I whispered, not wanting to alert any guards who might be nearby.

I crawled over to where he lay in a heap. Pain pierced my head and lightning seemed to streak up and down my spine. After-effects of the trident blasts.

I grasped his shoulder and jiggled it back and forth, trying to rouse him. He didn't respond at all. My pulse jumped in alarm when I took in how still he was. Just as I was leaning over to see if he was breathing, his eyes cracked open and he groaned.

"Morning, sunshine," I said as relief rushed through me.

He groaned again and then slowly sat up and passed his hand over his eyes.

"Where are we?" he asked, his voice hoarse and strained. The trident magic seemed to have affected him worse than it had me. Or maybe it was the crack to the head when he'd fallen against Finvarra's dais.

"Undine jail, if I had to guess," I said. "We need to get our damn weapons."

It was just about killing me to not know where Mort was. There was a small viewing slit in the door. I went to it and looked through. I couldn't see anything but the wall on the opposite side of the hallway, but I heard voices—sounded like men chatting casually. Our trident-bearing guards perhaps.

I drew magic and sent it through my right arm as if I held Mort. Then I let it flow off the end of my hand and outward, searching for the connection with my broadsword. Exhaustion thumped in my temples, but I tried to ignore it. There, to the left down the hallway, maybe twenty or thirty feet away. I let out a relieved breath. Much farther, and I probably wouldn't have been able to sense its location with any precision.

When I turned, Jasper had pushed to his feet, but he had one hand on the wall for support.

"My sword's out there," I whispered. "I bet yours is nearby, too."

I slipped my hand down into my boot, feeling for my spare karambit, a curved, claw-like knife. It was there. The guards had taken an identical knife from my scabbard, which I still wore, but hadn't done a great job with their search, as they'd missed the other karambit.

I went to the door. There was no interior handle. I stuck the point of the knife in between the door and the jamb, but the space was tight. I wouldn't be able to jimmy it open from the inside. I stuck the knife back in its sheath and tucked it into my boot.

"Any bright ideas?" I asked Jasper. I turned a slow circle, looking for any other possible way out.

"Once we're out, I can call a couple of Great Ravens to pick us up, but the birds aren't going to help us get free," he said.

"Shit," I muttered. I looked around one more time, but there wasn't even a vent to try to escape through. The windows were too small to fit through. I reached for my knife again. "Think I'm going to have to use the spellblade. I hope the sight of a lot of blood isn't going to bother you."

I started pushing up the sleeve of my jacket.

"Wait, what are you doing?" Jasper strode to me and tried to snatch the karambit away.

"Getting us out of here," I said. "Mort is a shadowsteel spellblade imbued with my blood and magic. If I bleed enough, it'll come to me through just about any barrier."

He covered my hand with his. "Don't do that."

"Believe me, it's not my first choice," I said. "But your pops is a fucking psycho, I'm sorry to say. And the Undine Queen isn't much better. We have to get the hell out of here."

His jaw tightened, but he finally pulled his hand back. "How much will you have to bleed, Petra?"

"Not enough to kill me," I said. "But I may lose consciousness. You're going to have to carry me out. Are you okay with that?"

"Of course," he said, his voice low and his gold eyes shimmering.

"Ready?" I said.

He nodded. I braced myself. This was going to be unpleasant for both of us.

I'd only invoked my blood connection with Mort this way a few times before. It was a dangerous thing to do on my own because it left me weak and powerless at best and half-dead at worst.

I took a couple of steps back, angled away from Jasper, and began peeling back the still-damp sleeve of my jacket and shirt. I'd never done this in front of anyone, and it felt strangely intimate. I didn't look to see if he'd turned away. If he had the stomach to watch, he was welcome to it.

I sucked in a breath, held it, and pressed the blade against my skin. Grinding my teeth, I sliced. It would take quite a bit of blood to call Mort to me. That was the really fun part—waiting to bleed enough to activate the spellblade's magic.

Letting my arm hang at my side, I tried not to focus on the warm wetness dripping down my hand and the faint splatting noises on the floor. Instead, I peered at Jasper.

"You might want to move to the side about five feet," I said, tipping my head to the left. "Mort will take a straight path to me and go through anything that's in between."

Jasper's eyes widened, and he quickly strode to the wall.

I glanced down once and shifted my feet so I wouldn't be standing in the puddle. From then on, I planned to keep my gaze lifted.

"So, what'd you think of your pops?" I asked with a forced conversational tone.

Jasper snorted at my attempt to sound casual, but then his face tensed. "Not much of an improvement over my first father," he said wryly.

I couldn't help a ghost of a wry grin. "Yeah, quite a shock." Then I sobered as I recalled what I'd learned about my own bloodline. It was still a blow, knowing that Oliver wasn't my blood father. The worse blow was finding out it was Periclase.

"Uniting the Unseelie *was* quite a feat," he said. "But I'm afraid only the madness of ego drives him. That's not good for Faerie. He's very dangerous."

"I'm not too proud to say he just about scares me shitless," I whispered. It wasn't the type of thing I'd usually say out loud. Or even think to myself. Maybe it was the lightheadedness from blood loss. "What magic gives him the power to call servitors?"

Jasper frowned. "Maybe it comes from his Daoine Sidhe blood. Or maybe not. Perhaps he has someone else doing it for him. He implied that he was doing it himself, but I honestly don't know if he's powerful enough on his own to do such a thing."

I swayed a little and braced my knees in response. Jasper took a step toward me.

"Don't," I said, and he stopped. "Seriously, you do not want to get between me and Mortimer. You'll end up with a sword-shaped hole through you."

I nearly giggled at the cartoonish idea of Jasper with a Mort cutout through his middle, as if someone had stamped his torso with a broadsword cookie cutter. I was definitely suffering from the blood loss.

There was a twinge at the base of my skull. Mort was waking up to the call of my blood.

"Almost," I grunted.

Damn, but this was unpleasant. I felt sick to my stomach, and the dizziness was growing more intense. I closed my eyes, turning my focus inward and concentrating on staying upright. I really didn't want to collapse in my own blood.

I couldn't say how long I stood there in silence. Maybe another minute. At one point I realized that Jasper had moved behind me. He wasn't touching me, but he was there, ready.

Then I felt a flash of pain at the base of my skull, and my vision went white. This was it.

There was an impact that shook the walls. Then an awful grinding noise that made me want to slam my hands over my ears. Mort had awakened. My sword was literally drilling through the walls toward me. I wasn't sure how the sand-castle walls would react. I hoped Mort didn't bring down the whole floor on top of us. The grinding rose in pitch. There were shouts. Jasper's hand on the small of my back. Then the sensation of him winding fabric around my sliced arm. Ah, a bandage. That was nice.

My legs must have given out because Jasper's hands were under my arms and my back rested against his chest. The walls shook again, and there was a boom like a boulder blasting apart.

With a movement that was more reflex than anything, my right arm shot up. A second later, the grip of my broadsword slammed into it.

This particular spellblade magic worked great for busting down walls, but it left me so weak I couldn't even swing the sword. Strong magic always had a steep price. If not for Jasper being there, the blood magic wouldn't have done me much good.

I was being swept up off my feet and into Jasper's arms. He was running. We both coughed as we inhaled the dust of Mort's destruction. My vision began to clear, but I could barely keep my eyelids open to make use of sight. I was too weak to do much of anything except hold onto Mort and try not to fall from Jasper's grasp.

Jasper's short sword. Would he go for it? It wasn't as valuable as Mort, but still. It sucked to lose one's prized weapon, even if it could be replaced. I didn't have the strength to ask him about it.

I knew he was carrying me through the giant holes that Mort had created. That was our only way out. There must have been enough confusion to mask our escape because it seemed we were moving unchallenged. Or perhaps Mort had killed the guards who'd been stationed in the hallway, and any new ones arriving hadn't figured out what was going on.

I had no idea how Jasper figured out how to get outside, but at some point I felt the soft, cool touch of the sea breeze on my face. My left arm, the sliced one, ached. My head pounded. I was so tired. I just wanted to let go and sleep, but I fought for consciousness. It would make things harder on Jasper if he had to carry a limp body. I focused on his breaths. He was breathing hard, and I could feel the pounding of his heart against my arm that was pinned against his chest.

I floated on the edge of consciousness, barely dipping down and then back. Once, I opened my eyes to find a giant black-feathered bird so close I saw my reflection in its beady eye. I was jostled, settled atop the bird's back on my stomach, riding it like a drunken cowboy on his way home from the saloon.

"Your sword is on your back," Jasper said in my ear. "Hold on tight."

Then feathers whipped my face, and powerful muscles pumped wings that took me aloft.

I managed a glance back and saw that Jasper had somehow gotten us to a large, open balcony that faced the sea. Trident men were running at him. Jasper was weaponless.

I saw him run to the balcony and hurl off the edge a split second before the Great Raven and I disappeared into the void of the netherwhere.

Chapter 20

MY HEART TRIED to jump in panic, but in the void there was no heartbeat. There was no body to feel. Still, the sense of alarm hung on me. And there was something else. This wasn't my netherwhere. I hadn't drawn the sigils or said the words. The Great Raven had taken me through. I didn't even know it was possible for a raven to take a person into their doorways.

We popped back into the world, and freezing wind laced with icy particles hit me like a slap. Inhaling sharply, I raised my head and saw nothing but white mountain peaks. Another blast of wind seemed to cut clear to my bones.

I didn't have a clue where the bird had brought me. We had to be still in Faerie, but I'd never seen a place on this side of the hedge where it was full-on winter. For generations, Oberon had kept the upper hand of power in Faerie, which had held the summer season. I'd never seen so much as an autumn-bare tree in Faerie in my lifetime, let alone a full snow storm.

Where in the name of the gods were we?

The raven seemed unconcerned, stepping carefully through the ice and shaking snow from its eyes. Then without warning it hopped a few times and took flight.

We blinked back into the nothingness of the netherwhere.

When we emerged, I began shivering. Getting hosed down, the

shock of blood loss, and spending a couple of minutes in a blizzard had completely sapped the heat from my body. I rolled off the raven and fell with a grunt onto soft grass. The sun was low, but the air was warm. I curled into a ball and tried to conserve my body heat.

Instead of taking off, the raven came close and extended one wing, forming a sort of tent over me. It settled next to me. We stayed like that, with the warmth of the bird keeping my body temperature from dropping too low, while I drifted in and out of consciousness.

Each time my mind surfaced to coherence, I thought to stand and try to figure out where we were, but I was too weak.

Eventually, someone was saying my name. There was a hand on my arm. I cracked my eyelids open to find a pair of concerned, golden eyes peering into my face.

I pushed up to one elbow.

"It was winter," I said, my voice a hoarse croak.

Jasper's concern deepened into a frown. "Petra? It's me. Is anything broken?"

"The Great Raven took me to winter," I said. Echoes of the confusion and dread I'd felt on the snowy mountain top pinged through me. "It was so cold."

"You were in shock," Jasper said gently. "You were probably hallucinating."

I shook my head vehemently. Bad idea. Nausea swirled through me.

"No." I sat up. I needed him to believe me. "It wasn't a dream. We were standing in the middle of a blizzard, and there were snow-covered peaks as far as the eye could see."

He reached for my arm—the one without the bloody bandage—and carefully helped me up.

"Maybe we could talk about that later," he said in an irritatingly soothing voice.

Frustration brought a small jolt of adrenaline. I clutched his forearm and clawed him closer until we were practically nose-to-nose.

"Jasper, listen to me. It wasn't a hallucination. It wasn't a dream. Full-on fricking winter has come to some part of Faerie. Do you understand what that means?"

He blinked and looked back and forth between my eyes. For a few seconds, he didn't respond. "Winter in Faerie would mean the Unseelie are gaining strength. It would mean the swing of power from the Summer Court to the Winter Court, from Oberon to Finvarra, has begun."

I let out a small breath of relief. At least he was listening to me.

"Yes," I said. "Is there any way to find out where I was?"

He looked over at the two Great Ravens who stood a few feet off. One of them was pecking at the ground. The other had its head turned nearly backward so it could preen at its feathers.

"I'll try." He turned back to me. "But first we need to get you home."

"Where the hell are we, anyway?" I asked, finally looking around.

We stood on a hilltop, one of many gently rolling hills. Streams wound through the ravines. The sun had sunk halfway below the horizon line.

"Spriggan land," he said. "I figured this would be an isolated but safe place to come."

My gaze sharpened on him as I remembered what I'd last seen before leaving the Undine castle. "How did you get away? I saw you jump off the balcony. It just about gave me a heart attack."

I pulled back and looked him up and down. He was dirty and bruised, his clothes stiff looking from our dunk in the pit and then getting sprayed down. But he didn't appear to be seriously injured.

A small smile quirked his lips as he took in my concern. "A bird caught me."

"Of course. Very useful creatures, those ravens," I said. "They've saved my ass, what, three times now?"

"Aye, they are magnificent," Jasper said. He lifted my bandaged arm.

"You need to get this properly cleaned and stitched."

"Nah, I'll be fine. I'm a very fast healer," I said.

My arm ached, and sharp pain pulsed in a line where I'd sliced through my skin. It hurt, but what I said was true. Fae with enough New Gargoyle blood tended to have exceptional healing capabilities. It would take a few days, but I wouldn't need stitches.

"In any case, you need to rest," he said.

He was right. I needed a strong salt soak and some time in the mineral sauna.

"Where's the nearest doorway?"

"We'll have to fly."

He whistled softly, and the two Great Ravens hopped over to us. Jasper helped me up onto the back of one, and he climbed on the other. A couple of hops and hard flaps of wings, and we were airborne.

As soft feathers brushed my face and hands, and the evening air washed over me, it struck me that I didn't even know where we were going. But I realized that was okay because so far Jasper had come through every time. It made no sense on the surface. He was Unseelie, a Duergar by oath, a subject of a kingdom on the brink of war with my own sworn Order, and the blood son of a truly evil man. But in spite of everything, he'd shown himself to be honorable. Good.

I turned my head to the left, where he rode his Raven about twenty feet away and slightly ahead of my bird.

Jasper and I had battled servitors, sought out the Fae witch, and discovered difficult truths about our own bloodlines. And then there was the night in Melusine's barn. The kiss. It was no wonder I felt some sense of familiarity and bonding with him.

The sharp feelings of jealousy that had surfaced as I'd watched Queen Doineann turn her seductive charms onto Jasper arose in my mind. So I was attracted to him. I didn't want someone else to have him. It didn't matter, though. After speaking with Finvarra and glimpsing winter in

Faerie, I understood that Jasper and I were irrelevant. We were all just tiny moving parts in what was coming. I couldn't forget that.

We touched down alongside a dirt road that led into a township. There was a cemetery with very old, crooked headstones. Burial sites were rare in Faerie because we generally did not bury our dead. Cemeteries were mostly for changelings who wanted to be laid to rest in Faerie and were more comfortable with that custom due to their time in the Earthly realm.

A path cut through the center of the cemetery, and there was a decorative arched brass sculpture marking the entrance. A literal doorway for the graveyard, and also a Faerie portal.

Jasper and I climbed off our birds and met near the arch.

"What are we going to do about Finvarra?" I asked.

I was achingly exhausted, but the things the Unseelie High King had said weighed heavily on me. Even more disturbing was the sense that there wasn't anything anyone could do to stop him. Not while Oberon was missing.

Jasper looked off into the distance and drew a slow deep breath before responding.

"Every kingdom and Order in Faerie needs to know that he's behind the servitors," he said. "Everyone must understand that he intends to break us down, supposedly at the behest of the Tuatha."

"I agree," I said. "But what actually needs to be *done*?"

He shook his head slowly. "We need Oberon. We need the Summer Court intact and strong. Oberon is an Old One. He's more powerful than Finvarra."

It was absolutely true, but it was odd to hear an Unseelie say such a thing. Oberon wasn't Jasper's High King. But as I was understanding more and more, Jasper had a sensibility that was able to ignore the partisanship within Faerie. He saw the larger picture. The real threats. He understood that it wasn't about Seelie and Unseelie.

My chest tightened as it really hit home: Jasper understood that we could only survive if we were united. Perhaps this was something he'd inherited from his father. Finvarra was, after all, the Great Uniter. But Finvarra was violent and ruthless and clearly wanted the darker and more chaotic Unseelie forces to prevail. Jasper seemed to take a higher-minded approach.

"So, we must appeal to our leaders to find Oberon," I said. "This has to be our uniting focus."

Our gazes locked.

"Yes," Jasper said. "Someone must bring Oberon back."

I nodded and then turned to the arch. My arm trembled with fatigue as I traced the sigils that would open the doorway and take me home. The chill of the netherwhere swept away my pain, but all too soon I was standing in the Golden Gate park. My aches and bone-deep exhaustion descended heavily. I trudged toward my Vespa, started it up, and shivered all the way to the stone fortress.

With a weary sigh, I went inside, squared my shoulders, and aimed toward Marisol's wing.

I made it about a quarter of the way there before Emmaline caught up with me. I'd been spotted along the way, and someone had reported my presence. This was one of the things that had changed since I'd been named champion of the Stone Order. I used to be able to move around the fortress almost unnoticed. Those days were long gone.

"Am I gonna catch hell?" I asked her, recalling how the fortress soldiers had run after me as I sped away with Jasper on my scooter.

"I would have said yes an hour ago," she said. She eyed my bloody bandage and my dirty, stiff clothes with a frown. "But something's changed. There's been news. Are you all right?"

My stomach tightened. Shit. I had a bad feeling I knew where the news had come from.

"News involving Finvarra?" I asked, ignoring her question.

"That's the rumor," she said. "But there hasn't been any announcement yet."

We walked in silence for a few seconds.

I peered at her. "You here to make sure I go straight to Marisol?"

She nodded and then gave me a head-to-toe sweep. "Are you sure you're okay? You look like someone tossed you in a clothes washer with a knife and then set the machine on high." Her eyes flicked down to the bandage again. "And you're really pale."

"There were a few rough moments, but I'm alive," I said drily. "That's what matters in the end. If you make it home, everything else is fixable."

"You need a salt soak after this." She peered at me, her lavender eyes intent. "Did you actually speak to the Unseelie High King?"

"Yeah." I shook my head slowly. "I thought King Periclase was an asshole. Finvarra takes the prize."

Suddenly a looming figure rounded the corner in front of us and stopped directly in my path.

Oliver.

Emmaline slowed. Oliver gave her a curt nod, and she turned and headed back the way we'd come. He waited for me and then fell in step beside me.

"Back in one piece," he said.

"Barely, but yes."

"You had to invoke your spellblade?"

I passed a hand over my eyes. "Yeah. But I'm fine."

"You shouldn't have left the fortress the way you did," he said.

"I had to. Jasper and I needed to speak to Finvarra without all the official interference."

Oliver's stride stuttered almost imperceptibly when I said the Unseelie High King's name.

"Petra," he said, his voice low with warning. "I know you can handle yourself, but there's protocol."

I sensed a lecture brewing like a storm on the horizon. I also knew I didn't have the energy for it.

"It was rash," I said before he could start to build up steam. "But I think it was worth it. Besides, he wouldn't have granted an audience to a diplomatic party. He's beyond all that. Come with me to Marisol, and I'll tell you everything that happened."

I slid a glance at him. His jaw was working.

"By the way, what's the news that has everyone freaking out?" I asked. "Emmaline said it was serious enough to distract Marisol from what I, you know, did . . ." I waved a hand in the air, not wanting to put a name to my little stunt earlier.

"Finvarra is starting to make his move in the High Court," Oliver said. His voice was soft, but his words fell like lead. "He intends to take Oberon's place as High King."

My heart plummeted. Had Jasper and I set Finvarra in motion? I knew it was coming but hated to think I might have had a hand in hastening it.

"Already?" I asked, sounding strangled.

He shook his head. "He'd begun before you had audience with him," he said, obviously reading my concern. "But your visit seemed to have prompted him to throw more energy behind his efforts."

I flinched but told myself I had no reason to feel guilty or responsible. Finvarra was going to forge ahead with whatever he'd planned, regardless of anything I'd done. Still, it didn't feel good to know I might have played a part in raising his ire.

Chapter 21

WE'D ARRIVED AT Marisol's door. Oliver pushed it open for me.

When Marisol caught sight of me, she rose swiftly from her desk and blinked a couple of times. I couldn't imagine how I looked. My clothes were stiff with salt water in some places, still slightly damp in others, and filthy all over from the dust of Mort exploding through the walls and carving up the sandy fortress of the Undine. I was limping and battered, probably deathly pale, and I had a blood-soaked makeshift bandage hanging off my arm. I couldn't imagine how I smelled—the competing scents of sea water, raven, sweat, and blood probably made for an eye-watering combination.

I could tell she wanted to be angry about how I'd rushed off to speak to Finvarra without consulting her, but I must have looked particularly pathetic, because pity and alarm seemed to be duking it out with anger, judging by the way her mouth was twitching.

"Petra—" she started, but her words cut off when I swayed unsteadily.

My head started to get fuzzy again. Oliver got me to a chair, and I sat down heavily. I closed my eyes for a moment, trying to get a grip on the dizziness.

"Blood loss," I heard Oliver mutter to Marisol. "She had to use her spellblade to escape."

I opened my eyes and drew a slow breath. "I'll be okay."

Marisol leaned against the edge of her desk, her arms crossed, while Oliver went to pour a glass of water from the pitcher on a little stand against the wall. He brought the glass to me. I had to hold it with both hands, I was shaking so badly. I took a few sips, handed the glass back to him, and cleared my throat.

"I know you're upset about how I left, and I admit it wasn't the most mature thing I've ever done," I said to Marisol. "But Jasper and I spoke to Finvarra. You and I both know that it could have taken days or weeks to get an audience with him through bureaucratic channels. And after speaking to the Unseelie High King, I can almost assure you that he wouldn't have granted you an audience at all. I hope you'll see that it was better we came by the information sooner rather than later."

Her eyes tightened, but I got the sense that she'd moved on from being pissed at me, and her focus had turned to anticipation of what I would reveal.

I proceeded to tell Oliver and Marisol everything that had happened, including my strange interlude in the wintery mountains somewhere in Faerie. Oliver stopped me at that part and made me repeat it.

He and Marisol exchanged a long look.

"You'd just nearly bled yourself to death," he said.

"I know what you're thinking," I said. "But it wasn't a dream. It was no hallucination. I felt the bitter cold and the snow against my skin."

I wasn't completely sure they believed me.

"Are you absolutely positive you weren't in the Earthly realm?" Marisol asked.

I nodded. "Great Ravens can't pass out of Faerie, and I was definitely still riding a Great Raven at that point."

For a few seconds, it was so silent I could hear a pop from the fire in the office's anteroom through the closed door.

"There had been whispers of autumn in the very remote regions," Marisol said quietly. "But none from reliable sources."

Oliver stared openly at her. "You never mentioned it."

She turned to him. "I didn't believe it," she said simply.

They shared a long look again, and the concern on both of their faces deepened.

"Oliver said Finvarra is moving on the High Court, trying to take King Oberon's place," I said. "Isn't Titania doing anything to try to stop him?"

I knew the Faerie High Queen was pissed at Oberon but couldn't imagine she'd be so stupid as to allow Finvarra to take over the High Court.

"She is," Marisol said. "But it may be too late."

I was ready to pass out with exhaustion, and they must have recognized I was out of juice. Marisol paged one of her errand runners, and not long after, Emmaline showed up to take me to my quarters. Oliver stayed behind with Marisol.

I walked painfully slowly, with Emmaline holding my elbow. Just putting one foot in front of the other required my full attention, so when someone came up behind me and scooped me up, I was so startled my knees buckled.

"Got you," a voice said in my ear.

I blinked into Maxen's blue eyes. He was carrying me.

"It was going to take about a week to get to your apartment at the rate you were going. It was too pathetic to watch," he said. His tone was bemused, but his face was drawn.

I didn't have the strength to protest.

"Being weak sucks," I murmured.

"You're not weak," Maxen said. "You just need some R and R."

He got me inside my place, where Nicole was sitting at the counter of the kitchenette writing in a notebook. Her eyes widened in alarm as she took me in.

As Emmaline ran a bath for me and helped me peel off my disgusting clothes, Maxen stayed in the living room. I could hear him and Nicole speaking in low tones. My assistant gave me some privacy while I soaked for about ten minutes, during which I kept dozing. Then she took me, wrapped in a towel, to the bedroom. She turned away while I put on clean underwear, a shirt, and old cutoff sweatpants.

She turned on the light to examine my sliced-up arm.

"It's deep, but it's already starting to knit back together," she said.

"I'll be good as new in no time," I mumbled. The bath had eased my pains, but I was exhausted.

She gently pushed me back on the bed. "Rest. I'll be back when you wake up."

I might have tried to mumble something resembling gratitude, but I was pretty sure I passed out before she even left the bedroom.

I awoke to a bright shaft of daylight slanting through the blinds and landing across my face. For a moment, I just stared at the slice of window I could see, watching the patch of blue sky at the top part of it and a swath of a juniper shrub poking up from below. My entire life and generations before, Faerie had been graced with summer—sunny, warm days and flowers that seemed to bloom forever. But winter had arrived in some part of Faerie, and according to Marisol, no one had seen it coming.

A glance at the clock on the bedside table showed it was past noon. I tossed back the covers and headed to the bathroom to brush my teeth. My mouth tasted like day-old beach scum. Still feeling weak, I decided another soak would do me good. I ran a bath and sat in it until the water cooled.

There was a knock at the door. Wrapped in a towel, I went to see who it was.

Emmaline stood there with a pile of fresh clothes in her hands and her tablet tucked under her arm.

I raised a brow at her and swung the door open so she could come in.

"I don't think your squire duties extend to tucking me in at night and making sure my laundry gets done," I said.

I was glad to see her and appreciated everything she did for me, but lately worried that her time might be better spent doing something more engaging or challenging.

"Actually, nearly everything I do falls within the job description," she said, passing me and going into the bedroom, where she left my clothes on the bed. She looked over her shoulder. "Besides, this is about a million times more fun and interesting than being a regular old page. Trust me, this is a big promotion over what I was doing before."

"If you say so. But I want you to be honest with me when the time comes that you want to move on. You have aspirations of your own, and I don't intend to be here in the fortress full-time forever, anyway."

She emerged from the bedroom and gave me a head tilt. "Where are you going?"

"Back to the Earthly realm and the Guild, eventually," I said.

She gave me a strange look, something between confusion and amusement. "If you say so," she said, echoing me.

Before I could respond, the apartment phone rang.

Emmaline picked it up. "You've reached the residence of Petra Maguire and Nicole, uh," she stuttered, clearly not sure what surname to give my twin. "This is the Champion's Squire speaking."

She listened for a moment and then glanced at me and said, "Certainly. We'll be there."

In the short span of the conversation, a knot had begun to form in the pit of my stomach.

"Something to do with King Finvarra?" I asked, already pulling the towel off my head and heading to the bedroom to get dressed. I left the door cracked so we could still talk.

"He didn't say," Emmaline said from the living room. "But the Stone Council is meeting in ten minutes."

Had to be Finvarra.

I quickly finished getting ready and grabbed my scabbard. Emmaline accompanied me to Marisol's office but stopped in the anteroom while I continued on to the Council chamber.

I went to stand near Oliver while the others filed in.

Marisol took the lectern, and Jaquard closed the door.

"Finvarra has breached the Summerlands with the aid of the Undine. His coup is underway," she said, not mincing words.

The Summerlands was the name for the Faerie territory where Titania, Oberon, and some of the other Old Ones resided. It didn't belong to any specific kingdom—it was its own realm within Faerie—and in the past many decades of Oberon's reign, it had become the seat of the High Court.

"Why aren't we sending forces to aid Titania?" Jaquard asked above the murmured reactions.

"That's the purpose of this meeting," Marisol said. "Oliver has proposed sending half our fighting legion to the Summerlands."

"Only half? This is dire, a disaster," Amalie, Maxen's young cousin called out. "We can't let Finvarra unseat Oberon and Titania. This should be our top priority."

"The Stone Order is our top priority," the lady of the fortress said, her voice carrying with authority. "That's true at all times."

I leaned over to my father. "You should just take half the legion and go," I whispered. "Otherwise the battle will be over, and we'll still be standing here arguing. If they decide more can be spared, additional forces can join you later."

"I'm tempted, trust me," Oliver said. "But I need to give the process a moment."

"I'm going with you, right?" I asked.

He shook his head. "I don't want to leave the fortress vulnerable. Neither does Marisol. We need leadership here, too."

"But I'm not part of the Order's battle ranks," I said. "I can't command them here. Let me go with you."

Just the thought of getting a shot at Finvarra gave me a nice jolt of adrenaline.

But Oliver's attention was on Marisol and the debate flying around the room. True to his word, he let the conversation continue for another minute or so and then strode up to stand beside our leader.

He raised both arms. "Enough. I've heard your arguments. The decision has been made. We can't leave the fortress defenseless. We'll leave thirty percent of our soldiers behind."

I quickly did the math. That was fewer than a hundred battle-trained New Gargs to remain in the fortress.

As the group began to break up, I found Maxen and snagged his sleeve.

"What's really going on in the Summerlands?" I asked.

"Finvarra's got several battalions of Queen Doineann's trident bearers," he said. "I don't know how he persuaded her, but it looks like he's borrowing the Undine army."

"And what does Titania have?"

"Her magic and the aid of most of the other Old Ones," he replied. Then he turned away as someone else caught his attention.

I hoped Melusine was going to help. If the Old Ones banded together, they might be able to hold off Finvarra and the Undine.

The next hour or so was a flurry of activity as Oliver and his soldiers prepared to leave. I found Shane, Maxen's frequent sparring partner and the man who'd be the second-ranking officer, after Jaquard, in charge of the soldiers left in the fortress once the others departed. He was younger than me and doubled as a weapons instructor for teenage New Gargs going through training.

"I know I'm not one of your soldiers, but don't hesitate to give me orders if there's anything I can do," I said.

He nodded, his yellow-flecked brown eyes intent under drawn brows.

"Just keep an eye out," he said. "Let me know if you see anything that seems off."

We were standing at the edge of the training yard, which also served as an area for the battle ranks to line up. As one of the older trainees, Emmaline had changed into a uniform that matched the legions' grays and blacks, and she wore an Order-issued short sword on her hip. Everyone who had any weapons training would be armed until Marisol gave the all-clear.

I beckoned to Emmaline, and she trotted over from the group of teenagers she'd been speaking to.

"You allowed to leave the yard?" I asked.

She nodded. I saw her eyes move over to Shane and linger there. When he looked up and they locked gazes, she bit her lower lip as if hiding a smile and looked away.

"Good," I said. "Let's stalk the hallways. I don't like so many fighters being clustered here like this."

Maxen and Marisol were still on site, but Oliver's absence left me edgy. Jaquard was the most experienced fighter who'd remained behind. The rest were fairly young, like Shane. Maxen was a skilled fighter, but his primary role was that of diplomat, so he didn't hold an official position as an officer in the battle ranks.

I started us in the lobby, intending to trace a circuit around the fortress that would take us past all the doorways. Pairs of soldiers from the battle ranks were already patrolling.

"Shane's your instructor?" I asked Emmaline.

She flicked a glance at me and then away. "Yeah. The past two years."

"He's quite a bit older than you are."

Her fingers moved to fiddle with the moto-style offset zipper on her jacket. "Um, yeah."

"He's pretty hot," I said. "Not that I'm interested. Just, you know, an observation."

"I guess . . . he's . . . yeah, not bad." She turned her head as if suddenly very interested in what was going on in the courtyard beyond the windows we were passing, but she couldn't hide the slight pinking of her cheeks.

I chuckled softly and decided not to torture her any further about her crush. For the moment, anyway.

Then her boots scuffed to a halt, and she went to the nearest window.

"What the . . . " she trailed off, tilting her head. "Does that look right to you?"

I went to peer through the window with her. We were looking out on a garden courtyard with some rose bushes, gravel paths, and a large cement fountain in the center. The water feature was about ten feet tall, with four cascading tiers and a pool to collect the water at the bottom.

But something odd was happening with the water. Instead of trickling down from one tier to the next, it was squirting out of the top with enough force to send the stream about five feet in the air. It was spurting wildly, as if the pump had gone haywire.

As we watched, the water gathered itself into an orb at the top of the fountain, as if collecting in an invisible globe-shaped vase. It grew larger and larger. Then the cement fountain began to fracture, cracks chasing each other up the structure.

"This is not good," I breathed.

A second later, the fountain exploded outward in a blast of cement chunks. The orb of water, temporarily disrupted, began to reform again, growing and stretching downward to the base of the ruined fountain in a sheet.

As the sheet of water began to part like curtains, I drew Mort and launched myself toward the nearest door leading out into the courtyard.

Chapter 22

"GET JAQUARD AND Shane!" I yelled at Emmaline.

She'd started to follow me, but at my command she wheeled around and sprinted off. I heard her yelling at a couple of Order soldiers who were patrolling down the hallway.

I burst out into the courtyard just as the curtains of water shaped themselves into an arch. I grasped my magic and then pushed it through my hand into Mort. Violet flames of power sprang from the blade. I sent more magic over my skin to form rock armor.

I stood there, poised and ready to fight, staring into the arch of water. I couldn't see anything through the arch—it was like looking at the shimmering sun-dappled surface of the ocean. Blinding and distorted.

Glancing back at the noise behind me, I saw the two Order soldiers, a man and a woman, pound out into the courtyard.

"What's going on?" the woman asked, coming to my right side with her broadsword grasped in her hands and her weight shifted forward, ready to attack.

"I don't know," I said in a low voice, my eyes glued to the shimmering area under the water arch. "But I think we're about to find out."

They flanked me.

"What the hell is that?" the man asked.

"I think it might be a doorway," I said. "I don't suppose either of you know magic that will close it."

"Unfortunately, no," the woman muttered.

There were shapes moving behind the shimmering curtain. I shuffled forward, gripping Mort tightly. Whoever came through first was going to wish they'd picked another spot in line.

As a man began to emerge from the mirage-like screen, I lunged and swung. I had just enough time to recognize the trident the man was holding before I sliced through the arm that held the weapon. He fell forward to his knees with an ear-splitting scream.

More figures loomed behind him, and another and then another came through. They were the Undine Queen Doineann's men. Did that mean Finvarra was coming here, too?

I managed to bat away one of the tridents, but Undine men were pouring through the other side of the arch, too, and the two soldiers and I couldn't fight them all.

Where the hell was Jaquard with the rest of the Stone Order's legion?

I took out a few more trident men, but they just kept coming. Three of them cornered me, took aim with their weapons, and let loose with an electric barrage. I braced myself and managed to deflect some of the zaps with Mort, but I couldn't keep my muscles fully under control as the crackling bolts hit me. My rock armor was almost useless against it. The electricity just seemed to pass right through.

My teeth clamped hard as one of the trident men attacked from the back, sending lightning magic into the vulnerable unarmored spot at the back of my neck.

Spots danced in my eyes as I whirled to defend myself. I caught a glimpse of a man—not an Undine—coming through the arch.

Oh, shit. It was dear old Dad. Not Oliver—Periclase.

Just as I was about to succumb to the trident attack, it suddenly stopped. I went down to all fours, gasping. My muscles were still twitching from the remnants of electricity flowing through me.

Order soldiers had begun storming into the courtyard, but there were trident men at every door ready to electrify them into submission. As I watched some of the best-trained fighters in Faerie fall to the ground under the influence of lightning magic, it struck home that rock armor was almost useless against some types of weapons. The Undine men were ruthlessly barraging the soldiers. I began to fear their hearts would shut down.

"Stop," I croaked at King Periclase. "Call them off."

He peered down at me, recognition flashing in his eyes.

"Hello, Princess," he said, drawing out the word. He crooked a partial smile at me, the stone-encased side of his face remaining frozen. "As you wish."

He raised a hand, and the tridents were withdrawn. The courtyard was suddenly eerily quiet in the absence of the crackling of electricity. Groans of pain rose from the Order soldiers.

I swallowed hard and glanced around. There were three trident men for every Order soldier in the courtyard. Our people were on the ground, all but incapacitated by the electric assault. Oliver and the rest of the legion was gone, off to aid Titania in the Summerlands. We were in deep shit.

I looked up at Periclase. "What do you want?"

He extended a hand to me, offering to help me up. I flicked a glance at it but didn't move.

"What do you want?" I asked again.

"Take my hand," he said. His eyes were challenging, his face hard.

I was in no position to resist. I could only hope that someone had reached Marisol in time and she'd sent word to Oliver to return to the fortress. The best I could do was stall Periclase.

I slowly reached up and grasped my blood father's hand. He pulled me to my feet and then let go. A handful of Undine men kept their tridents trained on me, primed with little bolts of electricity zapping between the forks.

"So you're in bed with the Undine, too," I said with unmasked disdain. "That must mean you're a pawn in Finvarra's game."

"Finvarra does what he wants," Periclase said. "I do what I want. One does not necessarily have to do with the other."

"Why are you here?" I demanded.

My strength was returning. I knew if I made a move the Undine men would fry me, but if I had an opening I was going to take it.

Periclase regarded me stonily. "I'm here to introduce myself as your new sovereign. The Stone Order is no longer. The New Gargoyles are now Duergar subjects."

I felt the blood drain from my face. Had Finvarra already taken the High Court and granted Periclase his petition to absorb the Stone Order? Or was Periclase acting on his own?

He raised one hand as if making a little wave. It was a casual gesture, but the Undine men responded almost as one, and every New Garg weapon in the courtyard received a bolt from the tridents. It wasn't a paralyzing shock, but it was startling enough that those of us holding our weapons fumbled or dropped them, myself included.

Mort clattered to the stone pavers, and I dove after my broadsword. When I touched the grip, sparks flew and white-hot pain lanced through my hand and up through my arm. The muscles spasmed, and against my will, I lost hold of my prized weapon.

I tried again with the same result. A hard magical vibration emanated from Mort, as if the sword was echoing my frustration. The trident men had somehow electrified it with their lightning magic, making it impossible for me to handle. Slowly I rose to my feet and watched the other New Gargs in the courtyard going through the same motions with their weapons, with the same fruitless results.

Our stone armor was all but useless against Undine lightning magic, and the trident men had turned our weapons against us.

It seemed we were a little bit fucked.

Under Periclase's direction, the Undine began rounding us up, prodding us with their tridents as if we were cattle. I tried to use the shuffle of movement to change my position and get closer to Shane, but I got zapped in the chest for my trouble. Once my pulse righted itself, my heart lifted a little when a scan of the courtyard revealed Emmaline wasn't there. Maybe she'd gotten to Marisol. Or maybe she'd made it out of the fortress and was going for help.

I twisted to look back at the courtyard as we were forced to the doors. Remnants of the fountain lay scattered around, and among the cement chunks, our weapons looked like a bunch of discarded toys. Lightning magic arced along the swords with soft crackles every so often. Magic emanated from Mort in a throbbing pulse, as if the sword were wounded and gasping for breath. My chest tightened as I lost sight of my spellblade.

Periclase and his borrowed army marched us through the fortress, taking us down to the basement. I managed to maneuver to a spot behind Shane.

"Where's Marisol?" I hissed at him.

He gave a slight shake of his head. "We thought it was a servitor attack at first. She made it into her lockdown room, I think. But she won't stay there once she learns what's going on."

"Emmaline's not here. Did she get out?"

"I hope so."

We were herded to the fortress jail, where Patrick, who must have been the jail attendant on duty, was being held by a couple of Undine.

All of us New Gargs were searched and relieved of our smaller weapons and then forced into the lockups, six or seven of us to a cell. I managed to keep close to Shane, so we ended up in the same one.

He pushed his fingers into his short dark hair and stared at nothing. He looked as stricken as I felt. We'd been jailed along with four other soldiers from the battle ranks—two men and two women. They were all pale and glassy eyed.

The Stone Order had been seized by another sovereign. Whether it had been by approval of the High Court or not, it hardly mattered.

"What the hell are we going to do?" one of the women asked. She was the same one who'd rushed into the courtyard right after me, one of the first on the scene when the Undine's doorway had begun to form in the fountain water.

I could invoke my spellblade. It might kill me to do it again so soon, and I wasn't sure it would do the others much good to bust out of the cell when there'd be a bunch of tridents waiting for them, but I couldn't stand just sitting around.

"Anybody manage to make it in here with something sharp?" I asked. "I can use spellblade magic."

We all searched our pockets and then scoured the cell, but the best we could come up with was zippers on our clothing. That wouldn't work. The magic required a large volume of blood quickly. It would do no good to try to bleed myself with shallow scrapes.

We took turns activating our rock armor and beating against the cell locking mechanism, but we only managed to bruise ourselves and leave some scrapes and shallow dents in the door.

With a strangled noise of frustration, I kicked at the door with my heel one last time and then released my magic. No use wasting more strength.

One of the men sank to the bed, dejected. He shook his head. "How did this happen?"

"Periclase couldn't have gotten in here without the Undine," I said. "Nothing in the Duergar bag of tricks could have breached the fortress, but somehow the Undine managed to form a spontaneous doorway using the water in the fountain."

"I didn't know that was even possible," he said.

"The Undine are a shadow kingdom. There's probably a lot we don't know about their magic. Obviously they can command water in ways we wouldn't have expected."

The woman who'd been beside me when the Undine started pouring through the water doorway peered at me. I didn't like the look on her face.

"What?" I asked irritably.

"King Periclase called you princess," she said. "What did he mean by that?"

The others had raised their heads to stare at me.

I couldn't lie, but I could evade. "You'd have to ask him."

I could tell she was unsatisfied with my answer, but I locked gazes with her and waited until she looked away. I wasn't in the mood to be questioned about Periclase's wayward comment. And I sure as hell wasn't going to reveal that I was his daughter.

But it turned out that I wouldn't have a choice in the matter of keeping that secret.

Maybe an hour later, there came the sounds of people moving in the corridor outside the cells. Our door released, revealing half a dozen trident men.

One of them stood in the doorway, his eyes roving over us and coming to rest on me.

"Petra Maguire. You're summoned to audience with your father and sovereign, King Periclase."

My lips parted, and for a split second, I couldn't move. Then the Undine man brandished his trident at me. I forced my feet into motion, having no choice but to comply with the summons.

Feeling like an unwitting traitor, I stepped out into the hallway. The trident men surrounded me, and the cell door slammed shut behind us, the sound of it echoing heavily.

Chapter 23

THE UNDINE MEN kept their tridents trained on me as they escorted me up from the basement and through the hallways of the fortress. It was eerily quiet with no New Gargs in sight. None of the Undines we passed uttered a word. After a few turns I gathered we were heading toward the administrative wing. When we arrived at Marisol's office, I saw for the first time that other Duergar had come.

Darion, Periclase's brother and the man I'd nearly killed in the battle of champions, stood with a group of Duergar officials in the anteroom of Marisol's inner office. Jasper wasn't there. Not that he would have been included in such a group, as he was a military man, but part of me kept expecting to see him. There were no Duergar soldiers in sight, though a few royal guards stood near the doors. It seemed that Periclase was solely relying on the Undine for muscle. Perhaps he'd sent his own army elsewhere, as we had with some of ours. Oliver could be clashing with the Duergar in the Summerlands at that moment.

When the trident men marched me past Darion, his eyes hardened. Across his neck was the purple-red line of a fresh scar. A souvenir from Mort. Even Darion's New Garg blood couldn't fully heal such a serious wound.

In Marisol's office, trident bearers stood guard over the lady of the fortress, Maxen, Marisol, and Raleigh, the non-military head of security for the Stone Order. Marisol was pale, but her eyes flashed and a red blotch of fury bloomed on each cheek. I couldn't fathom the outrage she was feeling. Losing the Order to another kingdom was her worst nightmare.

Maxen had a cut over one eyebrow that was still seeping blood down his temple. We exchanged a look, and he seemed relieved to see me, though his expression echoed some of his mother's anger.

King Periclase emerged from the adjoining room that was normally used for Stone Council meetings. Inside, I glimpsed several Duergar officials. He was wearing a floor-length cape over navy trousers tucked into brown studded-leather boots and a billowing white silk shirt. Atop his head perched a heavy-looking brass crown studded with green gemstones. Faerie rulers rarely wore actual crowns, except for ceremonies. He was obviously trying to make an impression.

He came to an abrupt stop when he saw me, and his cape swirled dramatically.

"You've arrived," he said. "Good."

"Did Finvarra grant your petition to absorb the Stone Court?" I demanded.

"What does that matter? This is happening regardless of the means," he said distractedly. His gaze shifted beyond me, his expression sharpening in a way that made me twist around to see what he was looking at.

It was my sister. Nicole was being prodded along by three Undine men. Her eyes were red as if she'd been crying. When she caught sight of Periclase, some of her fear flashed into anger.

The Duergar king beckoned to her. "Join us. We have important things to tell your former leader."

Nicole's eyes flicked to mine, and I tried to give her a reassuring look. Not that that I was really in a position to reassure anyone.

He crooked his index finger at us, indicating we should go to him. When I hesitated, I got a brief shock in the small of my back that was enough to make me jump forward. I glared over my shoulder at the Undine man who'd zapped me. Periclase waited until the trident men had prodded me and Nicole over to stand at his side.

"Now, face your former monarch," he commanded.

I'd been looking at Maxen, trying to judge how bad his head injury was, but I shifted my gaze to Marisol.

"I introduce to you my blood daughters," Periclase said. "Princesses of the Duergar royal line."

At his pronunciation, bile rose in my throat. I swallowed sourly.

Marisol's lips parted as she stared at me. Her face twisted up as if she were bracing for a slap across the face. "Petra?"

Many things passed through my mind, but I knew denial would do me no good. Somehow, Periclase had discovered that I was his. Melusine had given me proof. The truth of my blood father was out.

"It's true," I said, hating the sound of my own voice.

"You shouldn't have taken my changeling daughter," the Duergar king said to Marisol. Then he smiled darkly. "But in the end, it didn't matter because I've reclaimed her, and I've gained another. And now I have all of the Stone Order, too."

Maxen looked horrified. Shock still froze Marisol's face.

"Don't get me wrong," Periclase said. He gestured to me and Nicole. "This has nothing to do with fatherly feelings. I'm not a man of any such sentiment. It has everything to do with the usefulness of two more Duergar princesses. *That* is an enormous gift."

My hands clenched at my sides. "If you think you're marrying us off to some royal douchebag buddies of yours, you're out of your mind," I ground out through clamped teeth. "You're not our sovereign."

One of the Undine men raised his trident and let loose with a few quick bolts straight into my chest. I groaned and doubled over, barely managing to stay on my feet.

"But you understand this, don't you, Lady Lothlorien?" Periclase continued as if he hadn't heard me. "Your own son was to be used in advancing your cause. Your only child was to play a key role in your plans. Act as an important piece on the game board of your political career."

I stood with one hand braced on my knee, trying to regain my breath. I had to hand it to Periclase—he'd definitely called it right when it came to Marisol's plans for Maxen. But Periclase wasn't done. Oberon's balls, I'd had no idea the Duergar king was such a windbag.

He moved a few steps toward Marisol. "We're not so different, you and I. I'm simply playing the game much better than you are. I have a sizeable kingdom under my rule. I have powerful friends like the Undine. And, of course, I have several children to marry off to improve my relationships and position. You have none of those things. Did you really think you were going to succeed?" He tsked and shook his head. Then he leaned in. "Did you not sense the chill in the air? You should have at least had the foresight to align yourself with the Unseelie while you still had the choice. The season of Oberon and the Summer Court is coming to an end."

I could see Marisol's face from where I stood. As I took in the hatred that flashed in her sapphire blue eyes, it dawned on me that there had to be history between her and Periclase. The animosity between them went beyond Seelie-Unseelie rivalry, even beyond a small order trying to resist a large kingdom. I had no idea the exact nature of their past but felt slightly stupid for not realizing before that there was something more to all of this. I should have known. Grudges ran deep and lasted long in Faerie.

Marisol took half a step forward, drawing herself up to her full statuesque height. If she were only a bit taller, she'd be nose-to-nose with Periclase.

"You won't win," Marisol said, her voice cracking not with fear but with the passion of conviction. "Oberon will return, and when he does, you and Finvarra and the Undine and everyone else involved in this travesty will pay. Look outside. The trees are still green and birds still sing. Winter has not come to Faerie. You won't win."

My stomach twisted. Whatever had occurred between Periclase and Marisol, it had to date back to before I was born. But everything that had happened recently, including stealing Nicole from the Duergar and my defeat of Darion on the battle of champions, had fueled the animosity.

I glanced at Maxen. Did he know anything about Periclase and Marisol's history?

Nicole snapped me back into the moment when I realized she was trembling. I shifted closer to her, so our upper arms touched. She glanced at me. She looked terrified.

"It's okay," I mouthed at her. I squeezed her hand once and let it go.

It wasn't okay at all. Nothing was okay. But I sure as hell wasn't going to sit back and let all of this happen. I just had to figure out what to do next. I hoped to Oberon that Oliver and the rest of the Stone Order's legion hadn't been captured—or worse—but I had no way to contact him.

Periclase chuckled at Marisol. "Your High King is gone. He's abandoned you. And Titania won't hold the High Court alone. She's made too many enemies among the Old Ones over the generations. They'll soon see the writing on the wall and realize they should align themselves with Finvarra. She'll be lucky to last a day."

At least we knew the Summerlands hadn't fallen to Finvarra yet. Periclase turned away from Marisol to face me and Nicole.

"Now, my girls, it's time to go home," he said. He beckoned to the Undine men who'd brought in me and then Nicole.

Home?

My face twisted as I realized what he meant. He was taking us to the Duergar palace.

With a desperate, reflexive lashing out of my magic, I searched for Mort. The thought of leaving without my broadsword made my chest constrict. It was an irrational longing—the Duergar wouldn't allow me to be armed—but I couldn't help reaching out anyway.

My heart thumped with alarm. I couldn't even sense the vaguest twinge of the location of my spellblade. Maybe the Duergar or the Undine had encased it in some kind of magic shield, because I should have been able to feel *something*. Some sense of Mort's presence. But there was nothing. And the emptiness of it sent a swirl of vertigo through me, as if I were freefalling through space.

I felt sick as the Undine men forced me and my twin from Marisol's office. A tiny spark of hope lit in my chest when I thought we might pass the courtyard where Periclase and the trident men had breached the fortress. If I could just get a glimpse of Mort, at least I'd know whether they'd manipulated the spellblade to cut off the magic that bound us.

But the trident men took us a different way, to the training yard. I'd never seen it empty before. There were no bodies, but with no one in the sparring courts, no clang of weapons or calls from instructors, somehow it felt like a battlefield where we'd suffered a great defeat. Or maybe it was just the hollowness of it. All of that work. Years of honing skills. So many of us had dedicated our youths to training with our weapons. New Gargs were supposed to be the fiercest fighters in Faerie. But at the moment, it felt as if it had all been for nothing.

I looked up at the two towers, one where messenger ravens delivered notes to the fortress, and the other where the birds picked up outgoing mail. They were coming and going almost as if nothing was amiss. Amid the darting dark-feathered shapes there was one bird perched on the hand rail of one of the old guard tower walkways. I could have sworn its head was tipped down and it followed our movements, and I thought of Jasper. Was it one of his birds?

I wasn't sure why my mind kept going back to him. He was sworn to Periclase, and as far as most were concerned, he was still just the bastard son of the Duergar king. He'd come to my aid multiple times before, but I couldn't expect him to take such a risk again. He was just a soldier in the Duergar military. Neither of us could fix what had transpired between our two realms.

My heart felt like a stone as we were forced around a corner and then back inside to the fortress's lap pool. New Gargs didn't have a great affinity for water, and our dense bones made us ill-suited for swimming, but Marisol insisted that every young member of the Order learn to swim. She'd always wanted us to face our weaknesses so others couldn't use them against us. But it seemed she'd miscalculated.

I looked around, expecting to see a doorway similar to the one the Undine had formed in the courtyard fountain, but there was no watery arch. There was, however, something strange happening to the pool near the shallow end. It churned and stirred as if blowing in a storm.

The trident men took us up to the edge.

"What is that?" Nicole asked, her voice cracking with dread. She looked over at me with wide, terrified eyes.

One Undine man grabbed her upper arm, yanked her to the edge of the pool, and began whispering words in his language. He moved his trident, and I recognized the motions—he was drawing sigils in the air.

"A doorway," I said to my sister. "Just close your eyes, and it will be over in a few seconds."

He stepped off the edge, pulling Nicole with him. She screamed as they fell into the water, except there was no splash. They passed through the shimmering surface and disappeared.

I was treated to two Undine guards, with one of them repeating the same magic ritual to take the three of us through the doorway. I knew we weren't really jumping into the water, but just the same, I took a deep breath and held it. We fell into the void of the netherwhere.

Chapter 24

WHEN MY BODY and senses returned to me, I was standing outside the Duergar palace. We weren't at the grand front entrance, but in the back somewhere. The smell of smoked meat drifted by, which helped to orient me. We weren't far from where I'd come into this kingdom to save Nicole after Periclase had kidnapped her from the Earthly realm. Ironic, considering our current predicament.

Nicole and her Undine guard stood a few feet away, and relief crossed her face when she saw I'd arrived. I gave her a nod and what I hoped was a reassuring look. Ending up back here as the captive of Periclase once again probably felt like a living nightmare.

It was early evening, the sun out of sight behind the palace but probably not yet set, judging by the light remaining in the sky. I half-expected the trident bearers to take us to the bunkhouse where Periclase had kept Nicole but then thought better of it. He wouldn't want us to appear to be prisoners. No, we were objects of value, to be prettied up and auctioned off in return for whatever power and standing we might gain him.

Except that wasn't going to happen. No fucking *way*. I'd die first.

I curled my fingers, scraping my nails over my palms and wishing more than anything in the world that I had Mort. The need to physically fight back gnawed at my gut. But I'd have to bide my time. Wait until the Undine didn't have their damned lightning rods pointed at me.

We drew stares from the palace workers as the trident men moved us across the grounds. The Duergar gave us a wide berth, eyeing the Undine with a mix of curiosity and apprehension. The commoners, at least, didn't seem to give a crap about the two new princesses in the kingdom, and that was fine by me.

I tried to take in all the details of the things we passed inside the palace, filing everything away for later. You never knew what might prove useful. The Undine had escorted us into the belly of the palace, and we passed a few landmarks I recognized from my previous visits. We marched up eight floors and finally arrived at a door in a corridor that reminded me of a hotel. Sure enough, when I was prodded inside I found myself in a well-appointed suite. My Undine guards slammed the door, and when I rattled the knob, I found it locked, as expected.

I pressed my ear to the door and listened until I heard another door slam. It sounded like they'd taken Nicole to the suite next to mine. I went into the sitting room and banged my fist on the wall that was between two suites.

"Nicole?" I shouted. I banged and hollered again when there was no answer.

"Petra?" My name came out as a muffled wail of despair.

I cupped my hands against the wall, trying to project through it. "This place is full of secret passages," I said. "See if you can find any in your rooms."

"Okay." Her voice perked up a little.

I doubted Periclase would be stupid enough to put us in rooms with easy escapes, but it was worth checking. When I made it around the sitting room without finding a single loose panel or hollow-sounding section of wall, I suspected we weren't going to find a simple way out. I completed my check of the rest of the suite just to be sure and didn't find evidence of any secret passages.

The windows were barred on the outside with decorative bronze designs. Even if I could get through, it would be a death dive to drop eight floors to the ground. Well, probably not deadly for a New Garg, but two broken legs wouldn't exactly aid my escape.

I pushed my hands into my hair and swore, cursing Periclase and his bloodline three generations backward and forward. I stopped when I realized that technically I was cursing myself, too, and went back and tapped on the wall between my rooms and Nicole's.

"Any luck?" I asked.

"Nothing," she said. "You?"

"Same here."

I began going through the entire suite, looking in every drawer, under the mattress, on every shelf, searching for anything useful. There wasn't so much as a toothbrush or a spoon.

I went back to the window. Maybe I would have to go out that way after all. I drew magic and covered my arm with armor. Then I turned sideways and bashed my elbow into the glass. It shattered, but not too noisily, thank Oberon. I knocked the shards out of the pane. One layer of barrier gone. But the bronze scrolls were designed in tight curls, spaced so that I couldn't possibly squeeze through.

With a grip on one of the curlicues, I braced a boot against the wall and pulled back. It bent, but only under the force of my full strength. I kept at it, bending the metalwork until I was panting with effort. Pausing to wipe sweat from my temple, I surveyed my work. The opening wasn't yet big enough to shimmy through, but I could at least get a look around before the late evening gave way to total darkness.

Minding the jagged edges of glass, I stuck my head through the opening. This side of the palace faced an orchard. Swallows were swooping above and around the trees, hunting insects. Pleasant scene, if it weren't for the fact that I was a prisoner. It was a sheer drop straight down, with not a ledge, balcony, or drainpipe to help the descent. I twisted to peer upward.

My brows rose with interest. Directly above was some sort of cornice design protruding from the side of the palace. Above that, a window ledge. If I could make it up to the cornice and stand on it, I could probably get to the ninth-floor window. As long as it wasn't barred as thoroughly as mine, I'd be able to get inside and then find a way out.

I ducked back in, swiped my arm over my forehead, and gripped another bronze bar. A few more pulls and I'd be able to fit through. Just as I was positioning my foot against the edge of the molding for leverage, there was a noise from the hallway.

I left my little demolition project to check it out. I started to lean in to press my ear to the varnished wood when the lock mechanism clicked softly. I reflexively drew magic to my skin to form stone armor, even though it was useless against the Undine lightning magic.

But it wasn't the trident bearers at my door. It was a lithe young woman with long white-blond hair.

Bryna. Unclaimed bastard daughter of Periclase. Feisty little asshole who'd tried to kill me with a wraith.

I could do nothing but stare as she slipped inside and then closed the door.

Wait. Daughter of Periclase. Oh, damn. Bryna was my *half-sister.*

I closed my gaping mouth. "You're literally the last person I expected."

"Nice to see you, too," she said. She looked past me at the mess I'd made of the window. "Looks like I interrupted something."

"What are you doing here?"

"I'm breaking you out."

I blinked. "What? Why?"

She rolled her eyes. "Your bestie forced me into it. She knows how to play dirty." She huffed a soft laugh, and for a second, I thought I saw a glimmer of admiration in her eyes.

"Lochlyn sent you?"

"Yeah." She brushed past me and went to look at the destroyed window. "This is good cover, actually. Makes it look like you got out on your own."

"Is Lochlyn here?"

"She's nearby." Bryna faced me. "You wanna get out of here, or what?"

"Yes." Oberon's balls, *yes*. "But there's another prisoner next door. I can't leave without her."

Bryna crossed her arms and a look of irritation came over her face. "Oh, right. The other princess." She practically spat the word.

I cocked my head, peering at her. "Are you jealous? You are, aren't you, because dear old pops won't put you on the official Duergar registry of royals. Well, you're more than welcome to my spot."

Her lips twisted, and I could tell I'd hit a nerve. "I repeat, do you want out of here or not?" she demanded.

"I already said yes," I shot back. "But not without Nicole."

"Fine," she ground out. "Then, maybe the three of us can have a slumber party, talk about our secret crushes, and do each other's hair." Her words dripped with sarcasm.

I made a face at her back. It was immature, but I was having a hard time swallowing that I was actually related to this person. She was just so . . . unpleasant. Not to mention murderous.

Bryna went back to the door, and for the first time, I noticed she held a golf ball-sized glass orb in one hand. It gently pulsed with yellow-green light. She started moving the fingers of her free hand over the sphere.

"Trust me, I'm not any more excited about you than you are about me, *sis*," I said. "And I know you don't want to be here, so let's just get this over with and we can go our separate ways."

She paused what she was doing to shoot a glare in my direction and then went back to her glowing bauble.

"What is that thing?" I asked, stepping closer.

Ignoring me, she continued moving her fingers. The glass ball rose from her palm and hovered in between her hands.

I drew in a breath as I recognized the strands of green and yellow. "That's human magic."

Fae magic came from the blood of the Fae, originating in the heart of each one of us and pumping through our veins. Faerie itself nourished our power. Human magic was drawn from the elements—primarily earth, air, fire, and water. But I'd been sure that Bryna was Fae—more than one source had confirmed she was Duergar-Spriggan.

"That's an earth and air spell, isn't it?" I asked.

Bryna gave me a withering look that clearly expressed what she thought of my powers of deduction. I took it as a yes to my question.

She lifted her hands, the orb still floating between them, and flicked her fingers at the door. The object flashed brightly, and then in a blink it shrank and disappeared through the door's peephole. I frowned, trying to figure out how she was using a human-magicked object. Usually, human charms were useless to Fae.

"Okay, let's go," Bryna said. She opened the door with no hesitation, not even checking first to see if there was anyone out there.

I was still trying to figure out how the hell Bryna was using human magic when I followed her out into the hallway and right between two Undine men.

I whirled around, drawing power. Rock armor sprang over my skin.

"For the love of Oberon, relax," Bryna said with an exaggerated eyeroll. She gestured with one hand. "We're in the middle of an invisibility spell. They can't see or hear us."

I blinked, my heart thumping hard, and then noticed the glow surrounding us. We stood in the middle of what appeared to be a blob of greenish plasma.

Shaking my head, I followed her to Nicole's door. "How in the hell did you get this magic?" I whispered, still paranoid that the trident bearers would hear us.

First a wraith, then an extremely powerful piece of human magic that she was somehow able to command. Wraiths could be commanded by Fae, but human-magicked charms . . .

My eyes widened, and I stopped short as the realization hit me.

"Your mother is human," I said.

Bryna had pulled a small wallet from her pocket and opened it to reveal a lock-picking kit. "Ding, ding! She solved the mystery. Give the Faerie princess a prize," she said loudly.

She knelt down right between the Undine men who were standing guard at either side of Nicole's door. They didn't seem to have the slightest inkling we were there.

I shot a glance at the Undine men. Still no reaction from them.

"But Morven told me you were Duergar-Spriggan," I said.

"He's right," she said. "Mom's mother is full Spriggan. But my mother isn't. I'm a quarter human. Probably less, I don't know. I've never had my blood divined. I guess I have some New Garg blood from Periclase, too."

Things started to click into place in my mind. Human blood was considered inferior to Fae blood. Plenty of Fae cavorted with humans, but Fae rarely wanted to own up to producing a part-human child. It was an unattractive fact of Faerie culture. The prejudice against the children of such dalliances, called halflings, ran stronger in some Faerie kingdoms than others.

I grunted. "So that's why Periclase won't claim you as his daughter."

"Gee, thanks for rubbing it in," she said, working a couple of implements in the door's lock.

"Sorry," I muttered. I closed my trap and watched her work.

Many halflings preferred to keep their human blood secret. Halflings who were magically barren were barred from Faerie. For the halflings who had no magic and could pass for human, it usually wasn't too problematic for them to live out their lives in the Earthly realm. But for halflings with strong Fae features but no magic, it was a struggle to carve out a normal life. Most didn't fare well. Bryna was actually one of the lucky ones, as she could pass for full Fae.

Bryna muttered an expletive under her breath, but it wasn't directed at me. She was focused on her task. She exchanged one of her lock-picking tools for a different one and made a soft sound of triumph as the locking mechanism clicked with the *snick* of the bolt sliding back. Bryna stood, tucked her kit away, and reached for the handle. When she opened it, Nicole stood there wide-eyed and brandishing a chair with the legs pointed outward, as if ready to fend off a wild animal. When she saw Bryna, Nicole's forehead wrinkled in puzzlement, and then her attention shifted to me and her brows lifted.

"Bryna wanted to get together for a little family reunion," I said wryly. Nicole and I hadn't previously talked about the fact that we were related to Bryna, but I saw the realization dawn on my twin's face.

Nicole looked back and forth between the two of us for a second and then slowly lowered the chair to the floor.

She shrugged. "As long as Dad isn't invited, I'm good with whatever. He's turned out to be a world-class prick."

I let out a sharp laugh. Bryna even cracked a smile before she could pull it back into a scowl. Maybe there actually was one thing all three of us could agree on.

With admirable nonchalance, all things considered, Nicole set the chair down, straightened her shirt, and sauntered out to join us. She gasped when she saw the Undine men standing only inches away, guarding her door.

"They can't see us or hear us as long as we stay in the magic bubble," I said.

"Oh!" Nicole lifted her hand, sweeping it around in the yellow-green magic that surrounded us. "Wow. That's amazing."

"Just tell me when you're ready," Bryna said with annoyance, jutting out one hip and crossing her arms. She looked back and forth between me and Nicole.

"Sorry," Nicole said. "We're ready."

Bryna pointed to the right. "This way. Stay close and do me the favor of keeping quiet so I can concentrate."

She took off, and my twin and I stayed on our half-sister's heels as the three of us hurried down the corridor past the unsuspecting Undine men.

Chapter 25

"I CAN'T BELIEVE I'm wasting an invisibility charm on the two of you," Bryna muttered irritably as she led us at a swift pace through the hallways of the Duergar palace. "Do you have any idea what this thing costs? It's not even legal in the Earthly realm. I may never get my hands on another one."

"How much was it?" Nicole asked.

Bryna shot a murderous glare over her shoulder, as if the question were an affront to her very existence.

"Geez, you're the one who brought it up," Nicole mumbled. "I was just curious."

"You're not able to actually cast human magic, are you?" I asked.

"Um, no. If I could wield human magic, I wouldn't be running around rescuing *you*. I'd be much too busy leveraging the use of two magic systems into a fortune."

"And then what?" Nicole piped up, genuinely interested. I could see she wasn't trying to provoke Bryna but nevertheless seemed to fuel her bad mood. "What would you do with the money?"

"I'd carve out my own Faerie realm and make myself queen," Bryna said sarcastically. "Then, I'd renounce every blood relative I can name and start a new bloodline."

The answer was pointedly childish and an obvious insult directed at us.

Nicole made a face at Bryna's back. I snorted a laugh as I realized I'd made the exact same face only minutes earlier.

We reached the stairs, and Bryna paused. "Don't run into anyone, or you'll blow our cover," she warned.

Conversation ceased as we all focused on navigating down the many flights quickly but without bumping any of the other people using the stairs.

When we finally reached the ground floor, we were all a little out of breath. Bryna moved over to stand near a large column, seemingly to get her bearings, and Nicole and I followed. We faced a corridor that broke off into a T. We'd come down a different set of stairs than the ones the Undine men used to take us up to our quarters, and I didn't recognize this part of the palace.

Bryna seemed to have settled on taking the hallway that split off to our left and started in that direction. I took a step to follow her but stopped short when a familiar face caught my eye.

Jasper was descending the stairs with another Duergar soldier.

For some reason, I froze. Bryna didn't see that I wasn't keeping up, and too late I felt the soft touch of the edge of the invisibility charm's reach as it trailed over my skin. I was no longer hidden within the protective magical shield.

Jasper's golden eyes popped wide and he stumbled back, nearly falling. To him, I'd just popped into existence from thin air. His comrade was equally surprised but reacted faster, obviously recognizing me and knowing I shouldn't be roaming free in the palace. He drew his short sword in one hand and a magi-zapper in the other.

A disembodied hand reached out, clutched my forearm, and yanked me forward.

Bryna was hollering at me, the barrage of insults hitting me abruptly as I popped back into the bubble of the invisibility charm. She kept hold of my arm, her nails digging in painfully, as she dragged me down the hallway at a sprint. Nicole sprang after us, running hard to keep up.

"Seriously? How stupid are you?" Bryna screeched.

I looked back to see the soldier running after us. Jasper stood there blinking in confusion but then took off after his colleague.

We darted around corners, taking seemingly random turns, but the soldier with the magi-zapper stayed on our trail. Bryna was still yelling.

"How does he know which way we're going?" I panted, interrupting her tirade.

"Weren't you listening? I just told you! What you did weakened the charm," Bryna said, digging her nails in harder for emphasis. "They can't see us, but they can see the border of the charm's shield. All they have to do is chase after the magic."

Damn. I resisted the urge to smack my own forehead.

Bryna was really pissed. "What, did you think you were going to stop and flirt with Jasper or something? I've seen the way the two of you look at each other, and I heard about your romantic little journey to see Melusine. He's your half-brother, in case you hadn't realized, so you might want to rethink your crush. Maybe inbreeding is fine in the Stone Order, but here in the Duergar kingdom that sort of thing is frowned upon."

"Just shut up and run," I ground out. I jerked my arm out of her grasp, and her nails left tracks across my skin.

I knew Jasper and I weren't actually related, but for some reason Bryna's barb elicited a hot little flash of discomfort. I shouldn't have let my attraction to him reach the point it had.

More soldiers had joined the chase. We burst out through an exterior door and into the night. I watched over my shoulder as the men came out after us. Once outside, they paused in confusion. Apparently, the darkness was giving us some cover. But it only took a few seconds for one of them to realize our footprints were visible in the dirt. I scanned for Jasper's familiar silhouette but couldn't tell whether he was still part of our mob of pursuers or not. I couldn't help wondering what he would have done had he come upon us alone. He'd helped me escape before.

"How far?" I asked, breathing hard through my mouth. The three of us were running for all we were worth.

Bryna pointed ahead and slightly to the right. "There's an old temple with an arch in the garden. That's where Lochlyn is waiting."

We'd gotten a decent enough head start on the soldiers, giving us about a hundred yards of cushion. Still, we were going to have to get to the doorway and hustle through it right away to elude them.

There wasn't much light where we were headed, but Bryna seemed confident of the way. We sped around the side of an old stonework building and into a small courtyard enclosed by a low stone wall. A familiar figure stood near an arched portcullis that framed the temple's back door.

"Lochlyn!" I called, my voice thick with relief at the sight of my dear friend.

"She can't hear you," Bryna reminded me irritably.

"Oh, right," I muttered.

But then the ghostly yellow-green magic around us melted away.

Lochlyn jumped back and gasped.

"It's us," I said, rushing to her and throwing one arm around her neck in a quick embrace.

"No time for hugs and tears," Bryna snapped. "Hold on to her. She's taking us through."

I could hear the voices of the Duergar soldiers pursuing us. The ones at the head of the pack were already pounding around the side of the temple. The four of us crowded in front of the arch. Nicole, Bryna, and I each placed a hand on Lochlyn's shoulder, and she drew the sigils and whispered the magic words.

Together, we shuffled forward into the space under the arch, and the netherwhere claimed us.

We emerged into another night-dark place, this one with a gentle breeze and the faint fragrance of mint wafting on the air. As the chill of the void wore off, I blinked and spun around, my heart still racing from our escape. But we stood in a small grove of trees, the only sounds the calls of owls and night birds. The stars and moon were out, providing just enough light to see by.

"We're in the kingdom of cats," Lochlyn said to me. "I thought it safer to come here than try to go to any of the other doorways you usually use."

I threw my arms around her in an uncharacteristic display of affection. She returned my embrace, and then we stepped back from each other.

"I don't know how you managed it, but if not for you . . ." I trailed off.

With her trademark confidence, Lochlyn flipped a long lock of hair over one shoulder. "As if I'd let that nasty, stone-faced jerk hold you prisoner."

I laughed suddenly. Not long ago, Lochlyn had commented that Periclase was hot in a dark overlord kind of way. But since he was the enemy, he was a nasty jerk. That was Lochlyn—flighty on the surface, but with the people she loved, she was as loyal as they came.

"Well, it's been a real barrel of laughs, but I'm done here," Bryna said.

"Indeed, you've fulfilled your promise," Lochlyn said.

As if to punctuate that acknowledgement, there was a little electric shiver in the air that seemed to rise up from the ground and dissipate toward the sky. Oath magic.

Bryna stepped up to an arch formed by tree boughs, the doorway through which we'd just arrived, and without so much as a goodbye, she quickly drew sigils and disappeared into the netherwhere.

I turned to my best friend. "What in the name of Oberon did you have on her?" I asked.

Lochlyn shook her head. "It's part of our oath that I can't tell." Then she leaned in, and the moonlight glinted off her teeth as she gave me a conspiratorial little smile. "But let's just say that my youth spent in court among the children of courtiers is very good for the information trade."

Then she straightened as if started, and she spun around to Nicole.

"Where are my manners?" Lochlyn exclaimed. She took my twin's hand in both of hers. "You must be Nicole. I'm so pleased to finally meet you!"

Nicole was peering up at Lochlyn with wide eyes. I didn't blame her. Even in the dark, it was obvious how stunning my friend was. Her voice alone was smooth and sultry enough to hypnotize you.

"Nice to meet you, too," Nicole stammered.

Lochlyn put her hands on her slim hips and looked back and forth between me and Nicole. "Twins. Just remarkable." She shook her head.

"We don't look alike, though," Nicole said. "I mean—yeah. That was obvious."

"Still," Lochlyn said. "I don't think I've ever met Fae twins."

She was right. Twins were extremely rare in Faerie. But there was no time for such musings. My mind was turning to more serious matters.

"I've got to get back to the Stone Order," I said. The thrill of our escape from the Duergar palace was wearing off, and the earlier events of the day came crashing back. My pulse began to pump harder as the need to fight filled me. Anger infused my blood as I remembered the way the Duergar king had so flippantly talked about trading me and Nicole like property. "I've got to get Mort and take the fortress back from Periclase."

Lochlyn crossed her arms. "You're going to just march back there and do that all on your own?"

I pushed my fingers into my hair. "I have to."

She put a hand on my upper arm.

"No," she said gently. "Take a breath, Petra. You need to think clearly, or you're going to end up right back where you were—a prisoner."

I closed my eyes for a moment and nodded. "You're right. Have you heard any news from the Summerlands? Before Periclase stormed the fortress, Marisol sent Oliver and most of our forces there to try to help Titania fend off Finvarra. If they're in the middle of a fight, they might not even know what's happened with the Stone Order."

"I sent a message to Oliver in the Summerlands as soon as I heard that Periclase had taken the Order," Lochlyn said. "I'm sure I'm not the only one, though. Word spread fast. Periclase made sure of that."

My mouth twisted. The Duergar king really was a bragging windbag.

"Okay, so Oliver knows. Either he's trying to plan a counter-siege to reclaim the fortress, or he's caught up in fighting for the High Court. Or he's been taken prisoner." I shook my head, not willing to entertain the last option. "I don't even know how he'd choose between the Summerlands and the fortress. If the High Court falls to Finvarra, we're screwed. But if Periclase has legitimately claimed the Stone Order under his rule, we're also screwed."

"Do you have any other allies in Faerie you could call on?" Lochlyn asked.

I rubbed a hand across my eyes. "I honestly don't know. I'm not particularly up to date on the state of affairs between the New Gargs and other kingdoms. It's not the sort of thing Marisol talks about freely because many alliances are secret."

But Lochlyn was right. I needed help.

I sucked in a breath as something came to me. "Sebastian."

"The Spriggan king?" Lochlyn asked, clearly confused.

"Yeah," I said. "I saved his ass a couple of months back. There was an attack in one of his nightclubs, and a few of his men died. He even said that if Maxen and I hadn't been there, he might not have survived it. It wasn't an oath of debt to me, but still. It's something."

"That could work," Lochlyn said. "He's Seelie, so he's already aligned with the New Gargs. His kingdom is small, and given the way things are going, he'll be interested in preventing more hostile takeovers like the one Periclase is staging on the Stone Order. I'd think it would be in Sebastian's interest to take a stand against such bullying."

"Can we go to this Sebastian now?" Nicole asked.

"I'll go," I said. I turned to Lochlyn. "Can she stay with you?"

"Of course," she said. "We'll hide out at my aunt's place. It's only about a mile from here. No one will think to look for a runaway Duergar princess there."

"Thank you," I breathed.

"But I'd like to help," Nicole protested.

"Not this time," I said. "I don't want to put you in danger. Stay here, and I'll send for you when it's safe to come home."

She tried to protest further, but I went to the arch and quickly drew the sigils for a Spriggan doorway. I only knew a few that led into that kingdom, and I chose the one closest to Sebastian's castle.

The netherwhere spit me out at the edge of an open marketplace. The market was closed for the night, the stalls all dark. A few Fae roamed the area, probably hawking the types of things that were better sold under the cover of darkness. I turned to orient myself and spotted the silhouette of the Spriggan stronghold about a mile and a half away.

I aimed in that direction and set off at a quick jog. I could only hope that King Sebastian was home and would be in the mood to receive me.

Chapter 26

I FELT NAKED showing up at a foreign kingdom's stronghold without Mort. I tried to convince myself that going to Sebastian weaponless would help my case because it made me look less aggressive and more sympathetic. But really, it just pissed me off to no end that I'd been separated from my shadowsteel spellblade.

Fortunately for me, Sebastian was in the Spriggan castle, a great structure built of ironwood, an incredibly hard wood that grew only in this heavily wooded kingdom. The doors were plated, and many of the corners were also reinforced with metal.

The Spriggans themselves took after the characteristics of their realm—the men muscular and built like oak trees, and the women nearly as solid.

It took some time for my name to make itself up through the ranks of guards, from the watchers at the gate to Sebastian's personal detail. I'd expected the delay but still paced while I waited in the small sitting room I'd been escorted to.

Finally, Sebastian appeared. He was dressed in a very expensive-looking maroon track suit with white racing stripes, with a heavy gold chain around his neck and chunky rings on his fingers. The whole getup reminded me of a drug kingpin or mob boss. Not surprising. He tended to emulate stereotypes of Americans he considered powerful.

I curtsied—always fun and not at all awkward in skintight jeans.

"I hope you will excuse my casual dress," Sebastian said in a cultured voice. "At this hour, my business of the day is usually concluded."

"Of course, your majesty, don't give it another thought," I said.

In spite of how Sebastian liked to posture—I was almost sure the throaty voice with a slight but unidentifiable accent was phony—there was something about him I found almost likeable. Maybe it had to do with how he bucked the trend of most Faerie rulers, dressing in sleek business suits instead of old-fashioned courtly finery.

He gestured at the two loveseats that faced each other next to the dark hearth, indicating we should sit. I waited for him to be seated before I landed on the soft cushion.

"I've heard of the troubles at the fortress," he said, his forehead creasing with what appeared to be genuine displeasure. "I'm distressed to learn that the Duergar believe they have a right to the Stone Order."

I wasn't stupid. Sebastian's distress was probably over the fact that he believed Periclase had snatched the Stone Order out from under him. The Spriggan king had also been vying to absorb us into his kingdom, though by different means. He'd actually managed to persuade about a dozen New Gargs to break oath with Marisol and swear fealty to him.

I nodded. "That's why I'm here, your majesty. I frankly don't have time to mince words. I saved your life when the servitors attacked at your nightclub. No promise was made between us, but on the good faith of that gesture, I've come for your help, and I need it tonight."

His brows drew together. "What is your request?"

I took a breath. "I need someone to help me take back the fortress from the Duergar and the Undine. Rock armor, it turns out, isn't much defense against Undine weapons. But I suspect Spriggan shields will stand up to lightning magic."

Leaning back to rest one arm casually over the backrest of the sofa, his expression turned sly. He regarded me silently for a moment. I licked my dry lips. There would be a cost if he agreed to help, and it made me twitchy to be in the position of begging for him to come to my rescue.

"If you have other allies you could persuade to help, that would be even better," I said. "The Undine trident bearers are a uniquely difficult enemy for New Gargs to fight, which is, of course, why Periclase is using them."

His eyes widened the tiniest bit at the implication that his forces wouldn't be up to the task. He uncrossed his legs and leaned forward. "The situation must be desperate indeed."

"Yes. And extremely urgent."

"And what do you suppose I will want in return?" Sebastian asked.

We really didn't have time for this shit. I shook my head and tried hard to cling to my last shred of patience. "I wouldn't presume to know your mind, your majesty," I said.

"I want the Stone Order under my rule," he said. I began to protest, and he held up a hand, cutting me off. "I know the New Gargoyles have no desire to be Spriggan subjects. Here's what I'm proposing as a compromise. Everyone in the Order swears fealty to me, but you all remain in the fortress. You will have your own leader, who will stay in charge of most matters at the fortress, but instead of acting as an independent ruler, she'll be under me."

My jaw muscles worked. I didn't have the authority to make such a deal, but the Order was in a very bad situation. I had to do something.

"But Periclase has already claimed the Order for the Duergar," I said.

"The High Court never approved it. It's a coup, and he's trying to take you by overpowering the Order rather than through official channels, so strictly speaking you're not obligated to swear fealty to him. He will try to force Marisol's hand, but as long as she hasn't succumbed yet, the opportunity to swear to me still exists."

My mind whirled as I tried to calculate possible next moves.

"What's the name of your advisory council?" I asked.

"The Spriggan Leadership Assembly."

"Marisol and all of the current Stone Council members get seats on your Assembly," I said. "And, the New Gargs retain the right to continue to pursue kingdom status with the High Court."

I was pulling the strategy out of my ass but thought it might at least buy some time. The Order's bid for kingdom status would be a hundred times more difficult if we'd already subjugated ourselves to another ruler, but I had to try to keep that possibility alive.

"I must deny the last request," he said. "Why would I allow you to continue to pursue independence?"

I set my jaw and gave him an unwavering stare.

"You'd be dead if it weren't for me, your majesty," I said, my voice deadly calm. "You should have sworn a favor to me that night at Druid Circle, but you didn't, and I didn't ask. That doesn't change the fact that at least in principle you owe me a debt for your life. Beyond that, we both know the chances of kingdom approval will be virtually nonexistent once we've sworn to you. What does it really hurt to make that small allowance?"

We sat there, our gazes locked, for several seconds.

I knew he badly wanted the New Gargs under his rule. Without this deal, it was a victory that he could only dream about. His kingdom didn't have the size or the strength to take the Stone Order through official means, or by force as Periclase was attempting. I could see the greed gleaming in Sebastian's eyes as he weighed it all in his mind.

"Fine," he said finally.

My heart leapt.

"None of the New Gargoyles of the Stone Order will swear fealty to you unless you help us successfully force Periclase, the Duergar, and the Undine out of the fortress," I added quickly, while he was still distracted by the glow of imagining ruling the New Gargoyles. I shrugged a shoulder. "Obviously. But I just wanted to make that clear."

I knew he would ask for a binding oath to seal the agreement and wondered how it would work. I couldn't agree to something on someone else's behalf, so I couldn't promise that Marisol—or any of the other New Gargs, for that matter—would swear to Sebastian.

He opened his mouth to speak, and I jumped in again. "Oh, also, we have to move on the fortress tonight. As soon as possible."

He inclined his head. He was going to agree to all of the terms I'd laid out. My hands tensed into fists. Why wasn't he pushing back more? What had I missed? Shit. No time to work out every angle. We had to storm the fortress before Periclase forced Marisol to swear to him.

King Sebastian repeated my terms and magic shivered through the air between us as we set a binding promise in place.

After that, everything seemed to jump into fast-forward. Not an hour later, I stood with a borrowed broadsword at one of the doorways located in the Spriggan castle's military wing. I was going to take several brigades of soldiers into the fortress through a doorway that was located in a storage area. It was well away from the busy areas of the fortress, and little used. Only New Gargs sworn to the Order new the sigils to enter through it.

The first brigade of a dozen soldiers jostled awkwardly so they could all be in contact with me, enabling us to pass through the doorway at the same time. Once they were through, I went back for the next group.

I snuck all four brigades into the fortress undetected. With me in the lead, we crept through the dark hallways. It was impossible for that many armored people to stay silent, especially the large-statured Spriggans, but we managed to move closer to the heart of the fortress unnoticed.

In addition to a broadsword, Sebastian had given me a shield made of black, striated wood—ironwood. It was huge and heavy, about a foot and a half wide by nearly three feet tall. He claimed it would absorb the lightning magic strikes from the Undine's tridents. I sent out a prayer to Oberon that the Spriggan king was right. Otherwise, it was going to be a short and ugly fight.

I drew magic to form stone armor. It wouldn't protect me against Undine magic, but it would prevent injuries from other types of weapons if it came to that. It wasn't long before I got the chance to test the shield.

I led the Spriggan soldiers toward Marisol's wing. We had to go straight for Periclase and try to cut off the coup from the top. We got as far as the floor just above her office before we met our first Undine.

The four trident bearers took one look at our weapons and struck. Not having used a shield since training, I barely pulled it around quickly enough. Fortunately, the bulky shield was so large it gave me almost complete cover when I hunched behind it.

I used it to my advantage, charging under the lightning magic onslaught until I was close enough to reach out with my sword, knock away the tridents, and stab two of the Undine men through their stomachs in quick succession. The Spriggan soldiers had advanced right on my heels, and they quickly disposed of the other two trident bearers.

Breathing hard with the effort of hauling a heavy broadsword and the enormous shield, I turned to see how the brigades had fared. The shields weren't big enough to completely protect the tall, broad Spriggan, and few of them had fallen under the lightning magic strikes. But they were most likely just knocked out rather than dead. We didn't have time to check.

Suddenly, there was a flurry of shouted commands in an unfamiliar tongue, and the corridor was full of Undine. Bolts of lightning filled the air.

"We need to get to Marisol!" I shouted over the commotion. "Spriggan, follow me!"

And then I dove into the fight, quickly getting absorbed in advancing behind the shield and then stabbing and slashing with my sword. Thick smoke began to fill the corridor as the surfaces of the shields got fried by the Undine magic, but the Spriggan wood held.

I mowed through half a dozen Undine, with the Spriggan fighting right beside me. There were agonized screams every time one of them was hit with a trident strike.

But we were fending them off. Better yet, they weren't particularly skilled in close combat, and we were driving them back. After a few minutes, we finished them off. All of the Undine lay on the floor bleeding.

It was only a matter of seconds before more showed up. I was panting and soaked with sweat, but there was no time to pause.

"This way," I said over my shoulder to the Spriggan soldiers who were still standing. Then I took off.

Our footfalls pounded through the corridors as I led them down two flights of stairs to the ground floor that housed the administrative wing.

We were greeted by a crowd of Undine when we rounded the last corner. They must have known we were coming, and instead of attacking us, they'd decided to regroup. The air filled with crackling lightning magic so thick there was no avoiding it. The Spriggan around me were going down like felled trees. I managed to avoid the strikes only because I was small enough to hide completely behind my shield.

Ozone hung in the air like fog, a byproduct of the lightning magic. It mixed with smoke from the shields, stinging my eyes and burning my throat as I fought my way forward.

The Undine were crowded so tightly in the corridor, the ones in the front couldn't get out of the way of my sword. I mowed down three of them.

But my army was falling. In a matter of minutes, I would be the only one left.

The air turned into a choking, electric haze. Static plastered strands of hair to my face.

The Undine pushed forward, forcing me back.

And then the back side of my body lit up with pain. I screamed, my spine convulsively arching under the electrical barrage. Panic jolted through me as my shield began to slip. The lightning magic was paralyzing my muscles.

I lost control of my legs and fell to my knees. The top edge of the shield slammed into my forehead as it slipped from my grasp.

Damn it to Maeve, the Undine were going to fry me to death, and there wasn't a fricking thing I could do about it but lie there and take it.

But then the pain petered out. The lightning magic stopped. Bellows and hollers filled my ears.

With a shuddering breath, I opened my eyes.

I figured I must have been hallucinating or maybe even dead because it seemed I was having a wishful vision. My father Oliver was there, swinging his broadsword and relieving Undine heads from bodies.

When he bent and linked his elbow under my arm, dragging me backward, I knew it was real.

Oliver and the Stone Order legion had arrived.

Chapter 27

I TRIED TO struggle to my feet, but my muscles were still too fried from the trident strikes.

By the time I was able to shakily rise, the fight was all but over. I managed to stagger forward and run my sword through the ribs of an Undine. Oliver and his battle ranks took care of the rest.

When the air stopped crackling and the smoke began to clear, the corridor was littered with Undine bodies and blood. There were a few unmoving Spriggan soldiers, too.

"Marisol," I said shakily to Oliver. "We have to get to her. We can't let her swear fealty to Periclase."

He took off toward her office, and I tried my best to keep up. The door to her office's anteroom was closed, but it opened under his hand. We both rushed inside, brandishing our swords. The room was empty. Oliver went to the door leading to her office and kicked it in.

Half a dozen trident men hit us with lightning magic, but it hardly seemed to affect my father. He was so amped up with adrenaline from the battle, he charged forward, knocked away the tridents of four of them, and ran his sword through their hearts. I took care of the other two, thanks to the protection of my shield. There was no way I could have withstood more strikes.

Oliver's eyes were wild, and his chest heaved as he whipped around. He went to one knee beside one of the trident bearers who hadn't yet expired.

"Where is she?" Oliver bellowed.

But the Undine's eyes went vacant and his body still.

Movement through the window caught my eye.

I pointed. "There!"

Periclase had Marisol and Maxen in the courtyard outside.

Oliver went to one of the windows and stabbed at it with his sword, breaking out the panes of glass. Then he jumped through. I went out after him.

There was a small koi pond in the courtyard, and there was already an arch of water forming over it.

My father and I charged forward just as one of the Undine began moving his trident, drawing the sigils that would allow them to pass through a doorway. Periclase had a hold of Marisol's arm, and he hung onto the Undine with his free hand.

Oliver dropped his sword and launched himself through the air, tackling Marisol before Periclase could drag her into the netherwhere.

With a yell, I let go of my shield and gripped my sword with both hands, swinging and charging Periclase.

But he slipped through the doorway, disappearing. I nearly tumbled into the pond as the arch of water collapsed with a noisy splash.

I whirled around just as the Undine who'd been holding Maxen snarled and unleashed his lightning magic at me. Without my shield, I was defenseless against the onslaught. I toppled over, my head hitting the stone patio. I had a sideways view as Oliver sprang to his feet and tackled the trident bearer from behind. They went down, and my father lifted and smashed the Undine's head against a paver twice. The Undine didn't move again.

Maxen came to help me up. "Are you okay?"

I ran a shaky hand over my eyes. "I feel like I've been making out with a live wire for the past hour," I said, my voice wobbling. Then my gaze darted to Marisol. "She didn't swear to Periclase, did she?"

"No."

I sagged against him in relief.

"That's good," I said. "But oh, man, she's not going to like what I have to tell her."

The four of us limped back inside, this time using an actual door instead of going through the broken window.

Marisol immediately began barking orders at the fortress soldiers, mostly having to do with draining every pond, pool, and fountain on the property.

"I don't want to see so much as a glass of water sitting around!" she commanded.

Out in the corridor, she caught sight of Spriggan milling around and did a double-take.

"What in the name of Oberon are Sebastian's soldiers doing here?" she asked.

"Um, Lady Lothlorien? I can explain," I said. "But first, you should have the battle ranks take Spriggan with them to patrol through the fortress for any remaining Undine. The Spriggan shields are the only decent defense we have against lightning magic."

She gave the command, and then she whirled and pointed at her office. Oliver, Maxen, Marisol, and I went in. Oh, shit, she was going to hate this.

I told her the entire story, starting with me and Nicole getting taken to the Duergar palace. When I got to the part about Sebastian's payment, she first looked outraged, but then the inner corners of her brows drew down.

"You can't swear an oath on my behalf," she said.

"I know. But he agreed to it just the same."

Her frown deepened. "It must be some kind of entrapment."

"I didn't know where else to turn on short notice," I said. "I couldn't expect to reach Oliver in the middle of a war for the Summerlands, and I was desperate."

I knew she was angry, but she turned her attention to my father. "We need the Council in here, *now*."

He nodded. "I'll get someone to round up pages who can summon everyone."

The hallways of the fortress had been completely empty of New Gargoyles. I looked at Maxen. "Is everyone . . . ?"

"Periclase forced everyone back into their quarters," he said. "The Undine were guarding the residential wings."

I let out a breath of relief. As long as no one had tried to challenge the trident bearers, the regular residents of the fortress should have survived.

Maxen's sapphire-blue eyes were anxious. "We need to bring Nicole home."

"I'll get her as soon as I can," I said. I slid a glance over at Marisol. I had a feeling she wasn't going to let me go off on any adventures anytime soon.

"Maybe I should just go," Maxen said.

"No, you're not leaving, either of you," Marisol said. I wasn't even sure she'd heard our conversation, but apparently she had. "Nicole is safe where she is. We need to sort out what's going to happen next here. Not to mention get the full report about what's transpired in the Summerlands."

One of her assistants appeared, looking shaken but ready for his duties. Marisol sent him to collect the messages that had arrived by raven.

"Hurry, and come right back here," she told him.

He left at a run.

She went to her desk and pulled out a notecard and pen. She sat down and began quickly scribbling words.

"With the oath Petra has sworn to Sebastian, we can't avoid him forever," she said. "I'm sending him a proposal to meet on neutral grounds, and you're going to deliver it." She glanced up at me.

I blinked, surprised she was willing to allow me out of the fortress.

She finished writing, stuck the card into an envelope, and sealed it with her wax and stamp. The message would be visible only to the intended recipient. Then she pulled out another notecard and wrote a few symbols on it.

She handed both to me, with the notecard on top. "These are sigils that will get you through a doorway right outside the front of the Spriggan castle."

I glanced at it and then nodded. A shortcut, good. I didn't have the energy to run a couple of miles through the Spriggan kingdom.

"Find your spellblade, and then go," she said.

Mort. I was suddenly keenly aware of how light my empty scabbard felt.

It took nearly half an hour of roaming the corridors and asking every Order soldier I passed whether anyone had found the weapons that had been left on the ground in the courtyard where Periclase had made his entrance. Eventually, someone realized the weapons had all been locked up in a safe in the fortress jail. That was why I couldn't sense my spellblade—the safe was guarded against charms and other magic so prisoners couldn't call upon their confiscated items.

On my way to the lobby of the fortress, I spotted Oliver. I jogged up to him.

"What happened in the Summerlands?" I asked.

"Finvarra was winning when we left," he said. "Titania will likely never forgive us, but I couldn't stay when I learned what was happening here. I imagine the battle for the High Court is still waging."

"I'm sure Marisol will get word," I said. "She sent a page to pick up all the messages at the tower."

"You look like you're headed out," he said.

"She asked me to deliver her message to Sebastian."

A ghost of a frown passed over his usually-stoic face. "Her message?"

I grimaced. "She said, rightly so, that we can't avoid him. He and I have a binding agreement, and he's delivered on his part. I think she suspects there's a way out of the promise and wants to get on with it."

His eyes narrowed slightly. "Sebastian may be prone to posturing, but he isn't stupid."

"I agree. But hopefully he's left a loophole that we can exploit. And Lady Lothlorien ordered me to go, so . . ." I held up the envelope with Marisol's seal.

"There's no avoiding that." He hesitated. "Just . . . be careful, Petra."

I nodded. "You too."

I stepped out of the fortress and into the San Francisco night. It was blessedly quiet and still, the Earthly realm unaware of the war and drama transpiring just across the hedge. Standing before the doorway disguised in the side of the fortress, I pulled out Marisol's notecard with the sigils.

I traced the symbols in the air, whispered the magic words, and then stepped through the arch.

I emerged from the netherwhere into the flower-scented night air in Faerie. Turning in confusion, I realized I wasn't outside the Spriggan castle.

Just as I was reaching for Mort, someone jumped me from behind. A strong arm circled my neck and yanked me off balance. I started to struggle out of the grip and got kneed hard in the back for my trouble, right in the spot where Darion had cracked my stone armor in the battle of champions. My eyes watered as pain blasted outward from the injury.

"Petra, don't fight," a male voice said low in my ear.

I froze. I knew that voice. It was Jaquard, Marisol's personal bodyguard and the man who'd trained me in swordplay when I was a kid.

His arm around my neck slid down and switched to a hug grip, pinning my upper arms at my sides. The cold edge of a knife pressed against my throat.

Chapter 28

I FOUGHT THE urge to gasp as I felt the blade nick my skin.

My mind spun as I tried to come up with some explanation for what Jaquard was doing, and I quickly began to form the answer.

"Marisol," I choked out. I tried to twist so I could see his face. I needed to see his face. But the threat of the knife against my throat prevented me. "She sent you to kill me."

Even as I said it, cold shock gripped my body. I knew it was true, but some part of me didn't want to accept this turn of events. I went perfectly still.

"I can't defy a direct order from my sovereign," he said, sounding every bit as miserable as I felt. Like Oliver, the Order was Jaquard's life. He'd devoted himself to training young New Gargoyles and to upholding Marisol's quest for kingdomhood.

Then suddenly I was free.

I spun away from him and drew Mort, tensing into a crouch.

"But if you managed to knock me out and get away, I would have failed and you would be free," he said. "If that happened, you would need to get your sister and run. Get out of Faerie. It's your only hope."

"But why?" He was giving me a chance to escape with my life, but I had to know.

"Marisol believes Sebastian will oust her and put you in her place because you're the one who swore the promise to him. He can't control er, but by way of your binding agreement, he can control you."

"Marisol believes her son has become too attached to the changeling. She can't allow him to make such a mistake."

Betrayal and anger grew hot in the pit of my stomach. The sickening mix welled up through me and exploded.

With a strangled cry, I ran forward. I circled Mort over my head for momentum, and then struck Jaquard with the flat of the blade on the side of his head. He didn't raise his arms to try to defend himself. He barely even flinched.

Jaquard let out a grunt and crumpled to the ground.

Some part of me knew what he'd sacrificed to let me go. But the larger part of me was on fire with rage and hurt.

With a shaking hand, I traced sigils and then plunged through the doorway through which I'd come. I didn't even know what kingdom Marisol had sent me to. She'd obviously chosen a place that was remote. It didn't matter.

I arrived in the kingdom of cats and took off running toward the village where Lochlyn's aunt lived. I had no idea whether Jaquard or someone else was assigned to kill Nicole. Obviously, Oliver hadn't any clue about all of this. He was loyal to Marisol but, as I'd recently discovered, not blindly so. He'd distrusted her enough to try to keep hidden the fact that Nicole was my twin. He'd never stand by while Marisol murdered us.

As I ran, it struck me. This was the prophecy: Marisol's vision of achieving the Stone Court on the bloodied bodies of twin female New Gargs. It was playing out right then.

My heart gripped in my chest as my boots pounded the dirt. The full implication of what was happening began to dawn in earnest.

If Marisol's prophecy were true—and so far, her track record was perfect—then my and Nicole's survival meant the downfall of the Stone

Order. But our deaths meant the achievement of Marisol's dream. Maybe I shouldn't have been surprised that Marisol would kill so easily. She'd never pretended to be anything other than what she was: the single-minded champion of New Gargoyle independence.

But I was no sacrificial lamb, and I wouldn't let Nicole become one either.

I ran hard through the dark streets of the Cait Sidhe village where I'd left my twin. I'd only been to Lochlyn's aunt's house twice before. I took a couple of wrong turns but made it there. My chest heaved, ready to burst, as I pounded my fist on the door of the cottage.

"Lochlyn!" I called. "It's me, Petra."

My best friend threw the door open. She was barefoot and dressed in a t-shirt I recognized as one she liked to sleep in. A light flipped on behind her, and I saw her aunt and Nicole peering at me with bleary-eyed alarm.

"Oh, thank Oberon," I said, going inside and whipping around to lock the door behind me. "Who else knows that Nicole is here?"

Lochlyn blinked at me. "We didn't tell anyone."

"Good," I said. I looked at Nicole. "Get dressed. We have to leave immediately."

"What? Why?"

"Please," I begged. "Just go get dressed. Marisol tried to have me killed. You're next."

Her mouth dropped open, and then she whirled around and went back to one of the bedrooms. Lochlyn's aunt followed.

Lochlyn came to grasp my forearms, forcing me to face her. "What in the name of Maeve is going on?" she demanded.

I shook my head. "It's the fulfillment of Marisol's prophecy. She believes my bargain with Sebastian means she'll be ousted and he'll put me in her place because I have a binding agreement with him and he can control me by it." My words came out in a rush.

"But that doesn't put Nicole in any danger," Lochlyn said.

"Apparently Marisol's realized Maxen is in love with her."

Nicole emerged just as I said it. Her face paled, and then pink splotches bloomed on her cheeks.

She blinked at me. "He . . . what?"

I shook my head. "No time for that now. Are you ready?"

Her lips trembled, but she nodded.

"Wait, where are you going?" Lochlyn asked.

"We have to leave Faerie," I said.

"She'll find you."

"Probably. But for the moment it gives us a place to try to disappear, and Marisol doesn't know the Earthly realm as well as Nicole and I do. Same goes for most of those high up in the Stone Order."

Lochlyn's aunt—Anna, I now remembered—emerged with a bag in her hand. She thrust it at me. "Food and water."

I gave her shoulder a grateful squeeze. "Your generosity will not go unremembered. And I hate to repay you this way, but you and Lochlyn need to leave. It's not safe for you here. I'm so sorry."

She waved a hand. "We'll manage."

She put on a brave face, but I felt horrible. Their lives were at risk. I gave Lochlyn a pointed look, and she returned it with a slight nod. She understood. She'd make sure Anna was safe.

"I don't know when I'll see you again," I said to my best friend.

"Text me if there's anything I can do. I'll step out of Faerie periodically to check my phone."

"Where's the nearest doorway?"

Anna gave me directions. Thank Oberon, the doorway was only a couple of blocks away.

I hugged Lochlyn hard and then turned to my twin, who'd dressed in dark jeans, a gray hoodie, and athletic shoes. "Let's go."

"Wait, I'll kill the lights to give you more cover," Lochlyn said. "And you should go out the back."

We did as she suggested, stealing out through the cottage's mudroom and into the night. I took off at a sprint, heading for the public square where Anna said we'd find an arch to use for our escape. Nicole kept pace with me, running on her toes and managing to move much more quietly than I was in my boots.

We made it to the doorway, and I quickly drew the sigils and whispered the words as Nicole planted her hand firmly on my shoulder.

The netherwhere claimed us, and when we stepped out we were on the other side of the hedge, in the Earthly realm.

Nicole shivered and swallowed hard. "Where are we?"

"Boise," I said.

"I thought you didn't have a place here anymore."

"I don't. But I'm hoping there's someone here who can help us."

"Help us hide?"

"Yes," I said. "But only for a little bit. We can't run forever. That's no way to live."

In the time we'd sprinted from Anna's to the doorway, I'd begun to settle my anger into focus, and a plan had started to take shape.

I pulled out my phone as it vibrated and blipped, updating with the messages and calls I'd missed while in Faerie. I ignored them and scrolled through my contacts until I found Gretchen's name. I hit the call icon.

It rang a few times, and she picked up.

"Hi, Petra," she answered.

"Hey," I said. "I have a stack of cash for you if you're willing to help me out using your invisibility magic. Interested?"

"Just how high is this stack?"

I gave her a figure that was half the balance in my bank account.

"You must really be in trouble," she said, her voice wary.

"I'm in trouble in Faerie. I want to ensure the trouble can't find me out here." I had other things I wanted her to do with her magic, but that could wait until later.

"Does this mean you can never return to Faerie?"

"No," I said quickly. "This is just temporary."

"If that's true and you get things sorted out, I'll take half of what you offered," she said. "For the rest of the payment, I want you to be my escort into Faerie anytime I need to chase a mark through the hedge."

"What if things don't get sorted?" I asked.

"We'll figure that out when the time comes."

I barely knew Gretchen, but I already felt slightly less tense. She'd proven to be more than competent when I'd assisted on her assignment, and it didn't hurt that she was connected to the legendary Ella Grey. The fact that Gretchen wasn't trying to gouge me when I was in a desperate spot also spoke well of her.

"I know it's the middle of the night, but would it be possible to crash at your place?" I asked. I knew her house would be protected with human magic wards, and she was a powerful enough crafter she wouldn't take the risk of sheltering us if she didn't think she could handle a threat.

She sighed. "That wasn't part of the deal."

"I know. But I'm in a tight spot."

"Fine. But I want ten percent deposited in my account when you arrive."

I let out a small breath of relief. "You got it. I'll make the transfer now."

"I'll text you my address."

We hung up.

Nicole had been standing next to me, her eyes wide as she listened to my side of the conversation.

"I have a little money, too," she said. "If we need it."

I nodded. "Good. Hang onto it, and we'll consider it an emergency fund."

"Who was that?"

"Gretchen, a merc and human magic user. I worked with her not long ago."

"She can make us invisible? Like Bryna's charm?"

"Sort of," I said. I pulled up a taxi app on my phone and ordered a ride. "But she doesn't need a charm to do it."

"Whoa."

Our car arrived within a couple of minutes, and we were standing on Gretchen's doorstep ten minutes after that. On the way over, I transferred money from my account to hers. She lived in an apartment in Boise's North End, an area of historic and refurbished houses and buildings. Her place wasn't far from Crystal Ball Lane, a street where human magic users could buy supplies for their crafting and normals could go to get their palms read or buy magic-imbued trinkets.

Gretchen opened the door and narrowed her eyes at Nicole. "You didn't say there were two of you."

"She's my sister," I said. "They're after her, too. The deposit should have shown up in your account."

She huffed and pushed the door open wider, and Nicole and I went inside.

"You live alone?" I asked as I stepped inside. The place was small and dim, the only light from a low-watt bulb in a side table lamp.

"Yeah," Gretchen answered.

"Good. The fewer people who know we're here, the better."

"I've set wards that should trip if any Fae come poking around," she said. "But wards don't keep anyone from getting in. They're just magical alarm systems."

"Thank you," I said with sincerity. It was a relief to be able to say it, knowing that with a human the expression of gratitude wouldn't invoke a binding agreement as it would with Fae.

"Hey, this isn't charity," she said. "It's late, so let's all get some sleep. I don't have a spare room. You'll have to crash out here."

"Thank you for letting us stay," Nicole said.

Gretchen nodded and then went back into her bedroom and closed the door.

"Take the sofa," I said to my twin. I killed the table lamp, but there was still enough light from the street outside to help us get around without bumping into anything. "I'll take the recliner."

I didn't plan to sleep, so Nicole might as well have the more comfortable of the two options. She lay down and curled up with her back to me. Then she twisted around.

"I want to go back," she whispered.

"Back where?"

"To Faerie. I'd come around to life there, to living in the fortress and embracing my Fae roots and trying to learn everything I could about being Fae. Now that it's been taken away, I'm doubly sure that's what I want."

A small smile crept over my face, in spite of what we were facing. "Are you in love with Maxen?"

"Yes. But that's not the only reason I want to stay in Faerie. I know it's where I belong. I'm still adjusting, but I have this sense of . . . I don't know it's hard to explain. I have this confidence about who I truly am."

"It's good to feel sure, isn't it?"

"Yeah."

"Well, the good news is that we aren't just going to sit around and allow ourselves to be exiled. So if things go our way, you'll have the chance to live in Faerie."

"What if they don't go our way?" she asked.

"Then Marisol will have won."

The implication of it sat heavily in the room.

"But, I'm not ready to die, so there's that," I said in a cheerful tone.

"Me neither."

"Get some sleep, and we'll see what we'll figure out what's next in the morning."

"Okay. 'Night, Petra."

"Goodnight, Nicole."

I leaned my head back against the plush headrest of the recliner and stared at the ceiling. Only weeks ago, I would have given just about anything to be released from Marisol, to be free to go back to the Earthly side of the hedge. I'd made it back here, but I definitely wasn't free. I might be able to stay ahead of her assassins for a while. A long time. Maybe eventually she'd even stop chasing me. But that was no life.

My stomach tightened as if preparing for a punch. There was only one way out of this, and it was through Marisol. But I couldn't do it alone.

I pulled out my phone and began typing a text to Lochlyn, giving her messages to relay in Faerie. One would go to Oliver. Another to Maxen. And the last to my blood father, King Periclase.

Chapter 29

I REMAINED AWAKE the rest of the night, working out what to say in the various messages that Lochlyn would send for me, and thinking through our options and the possible outcomes of each thing I was considering.

I wanted Oliver to know that Marisol had tried to kill me and planned to kill Nicole, but that we were okay. I wouldn't tell him any of my plans, though. That would only endanger his life.

My message to Maxen contained the same information, but with a longer heartfelt plea. He needed to know just how far Marisol was willing to go to keep him under her control. And more than that, I hoped his feelings for Nicole were strong enough to finally drive him to stand up to his mother. If he were willing, he could be the essential element to what I needed to do to save myself and my twin.

The contents of my note to Periclase took the most crafting. I was requesting something that I never, ever would have expected to ask for: asylum in the Duergar kingdom. I needed protection not only from Marisol, but also from Sebastian. If Marisol's suspicion was correct, the Spriggan king intended to use me as his puppet to secure the Stone Order under his rule. That might take care of my Marisol problem, but because I wasn't sure of what Sebastian intended, I couldn't absolutely assume it would work out that way. I needed safety while I navigated the fallout of my binding agreement with him.

I needed protection, and I needed to be able to maneuver from within Faerie. Periclase had the strength and standing to give me a base from which to do it. But it would take careful bargaining on my part.

I couldn't help thinking of Jasper. He might be the one and only ally I'd have in the Duergar palace.

I looked over at my sister. She needed safe shelter, too. She deserved the chance to pursue the life she wanted. But all of this was going to come at a price.

By the time I finished crafting my messages and sent them all to Lochlyn, the pale light of morning had strengthened enough to shut off the streetlamps outside Gretchen's apartment. I got up and rummaged around in her kitchen until I found ground coffee and filters, and then I started a pot in the coffeemaker. When the percolator finished brewing, I poured two mugs and set one next to the sofa for Nicole. She turned and stretched a few minutes later.

While we waited for Gretchen to wake up, I got a text from Lochlyn that contained only a single word: *Done.*

I told Nicole about my plea to Periclase, as well as my message to Maxen.

Her face crumpled, and for a moment I thought she was going to burst into tears. But then she pressed her lips together, took a slow breath, and nodded.

"Under the circumstances, it's a good strategy," she said. "Plus, it'll give us the opportunity to bond more with Bryna."

I gave her a horrified look and then realized she was kidding about the Bryna part.

"Ha, good one," I said. We sipped our coffee for a moment, and I watched her out of the corners of my eyes. "What do you think Maxen will do?"

She lowered her mug to her lap, cradling it in both hands. "I know he's strong enough to stand up to Marisol. I think this threat to us will give him the resolve he needs to finally do it."

"Us?" I said. "I think the threat to *you* is the real motivation."

She shook her head. "He cares about you a lot."

Yeah, she was probably right, but his friendship with me alone wouldn't be enough. When it came to summoning courage and taking a real leap of faith, love was a damn powerful motivator. Even I knew that.

Gretchen joined us after pouring her own mug. "When and where will you need my magic?" she asked.

"Today, I hope." I held up my phone. "I'm waiting for a response from a Fae king, and if it's favorable, I'll need your invisibility magic to get us into Faerie without alerting anyone or running into any assassins."

One of her brows lifted at the mention of assassins. "Who's trying to kill you?"

"Marisol Lothlorien, leader of the Stone Order and our sworn sovereign," I said.

"Oh, damn," she said, drawing out the words in a low voice. "A Faerie queen trying to kill you."

"That's not even the half of it," I said. "Technically, she's not a queen yet, as the Order isn't a formal kingdom. A prophecy she had years ago said the Order would become a kingdom on the bloody bodies of female New Garg sisters."

I flipped my index finger back and forth between me and Nicole.

Gretchen's eyes widened. "A prophecy and a murderous sworn sovereign." She snorted a laugh. "You do realize you sound slightly insane right now, don't you?"

I echoed her laugh in spite of myself. "I can only imagine how it comes across. I wish it weren't true. I just want to go back to hunting vamps and crashing in some stupid apartment."

Gretchen's lips parted, and she gave me an offended glare.

I waved a hand. "Your apartment isn't stupid. You know what I mean."

"Just messing with you," she said.

I kept glancing down at my phone, though any responses might not come for hours. I'd asked both Maxen and Periclase to send their replies to Lochlyn in Faerie, who would relay them to me.

"Got anything in there for breakfast?" Nicole asked, rising. "I can whip up some eggs or something."

"Sure, you're welcome to whatever you find," Gretchen said. She stood too and disappeared into the bathroom. A moment later I heard the shower turn on.

I stared out the window for the next ten minutes, watching dawn brighten into morning. When my phone vibrated against my thigh, I looked down. A message from Lochlyn.

I snatched up the device and read the message.

From Periclase: I will give asylum to you and your sister. Expecting your arrival as soon as you're able to travel.

My heart skipped a beat. We were on. I pushed up from the chair and went into the kitchen to tell Nicole. She froze for a moment and then shoved a piece of buttered toast on a paper towel at me.

"Well, here goes nothing, I guess," she said and then bit into her own piece of toast and chewed mechanically, looking at me with wide eyes.

I nodded and stuffed a corner of toasted bread into my mouth, too.

Gretchen came in, her wet hair twisted up into a bun.

"It's time," I said.

"That was fast." She looked back and forth between the two of us. "I need the rest of the money, and then we can go."

I quickly used my phone to make the transfer.

Before we stepped outside, Gretchen drew magic and wove a spell that would keep us obscured from any observers as we made our way to her car. She stayed outside the boundary of the invisibility magic so it would look like she was going to her car and getting in alone. She drove us downtown so we could use the doorway in an abandoned parking garage.

I took the three of us into the Duergar kingdom, emerging through a doorway in a clearing at the end of a hard-packed road that led to Periclase's palace.

A rush of human magic filled the air as Gretchen pulled power and formed the shield that would keep us out of sight of any observers. The three of us trotted down the road.

"I'll need you again," I said to Gretchen. "But I'm not sure exactly when."

"Shoot me a text when the time comes," she said.

"Thank you."

At the front entrance of the palace, she had to drop the spell so I could identify myself to the guards at the gate. They were expecting us and ushered us in without hesitation.

Periclase appeared not a minute after we were inside.

"And so, you've returned," he said, his eyes sharp and his tone hard.

"Yes," I said. "You have our gratitude for your quick and positive response."

My insides tightened as what I'd done fully struck me. I'd given myself and my sister over to a powerful king who could exact almost any promise he wanted from me in return for providing us a safe place to stay in Faerie.

"Another small request," I said. "I need to ferry this woman back to the Earthly realm."

"I'll do it," said a familiar voice.

Jasper stepped forward from the contingent of soldiers grouped behind Periclase.

My shoulders lowered in relief when the Duergar king agreed. I trusted Jasper more than anyone else here to get Gretchen safely back across the hedge. I gave Jasper a slight nod just before he turned to leave, and he returned the gesture. After he returned, I'd have to find a way to speak to him alone.

A couple of women dressed in palace livery stood off to the side. Periclase flipped his fingers at them, and they came forward.

"These are your attendants. They'll show you to your quarters so you can freshen up. Then, we shall meet to discuss terms."

The women turned, and Nicole and I could do nothing but follow. For the time being, we were at Periclase's mercy. It was up to me to find a way to use the situation to my advantage and ensure that Marisol could never threaten us again.

**Look for *Rise of the Stone Court* by Jayne Faith,
the next book in the Stone Blood Series!**

About the Author

Jayne Faith writes fantasy set in the real world. She's a meditator, dog lover, TV addict, clean eater, homebody, sun baby, and Sagittarius. Her superpower is her laugh. She owns way too many colored pens and pairs of jeans. Visit her website at www.jaynefaith.com, where you can sign up for her VIP list and get free books.

Also by Jayne Faith

Ella Grey Series

Demon patrol officer Ella Grey beat death after an accident on the job, but something followed her back from the grave. Will it eat her soul or become her greatest ally?

Stone Cold Magic (#1)
Dark Harvest Magic (#2)
Demon Born Magic (#3)
Blood Storm Magic (#4)

Tara Knightley Series

Between paying off a debt to a Fae mob boss, working as a professional thief, and keeping up with her busy three-generation household, Tara Knightley barely has time to eat and sleep. But now she's going to have to choose: her family, love, or her freedom.

Oath of Blood (prequel)
Edge of Magic (#1)
Echo of Bone (#2)
Trace of Fate (#3)
more to come

Stone Blood Series

When vampire hunter Petra Maguire discovers she has a secret twin who's been kidnapped, she's determined to rescue her. But it could spark a magical war.

Blood of Stone (#1)
Stone Blood Legacy (#2)
Rise of the Stone Court (#3)
Reign of the Stone Queen (#4)
War of the Fae Gods (#5)
The Oldest Changeling in Faerie (#6)

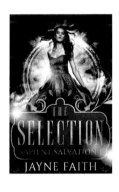

Sapient Salvation Series

An innocent young woman fighting to survive in a foreign land. A powerful overlord longing to leave his dark past behind. The moment they meet, worlds clash as forbidden love ignites.

The Selection (#1)
The Awakening (#2)
The Divining (#3)
The Claiming (#4)

Made in United States
North Haven, CT
12 May 2022

19127335R00159